DRIVES LIKE A DREAM

BOOKS BY PORTER SHREVE

The Obituary Writer

Drives Like a Dream

DRIVES LIKE A DREAM

Porter Shreve

Houghton Mifflin Company

BOSTON • NEW YORK • 2005

For information about permission to reproduce selections
from this book, write to Permissions, Houghton Mifflin Company,
215 Park Avenue South, New York, New York 10003.

Visit our Web site: www.houghtonmifflinbooks.com.

Library of Congress Cataloging-in-Publication Data
Shreve, Porter.
Drives like a dream / Porter Shreve.
p.   cm.
ISBN 0-618-14331-9
1. Parent and adult child — Fiction.   2. Automobile industry
and trade — Fiction.   3. Eccentrics and eccentricities — Fiction.
4. Detroit (Mich.) — Fiction.   5. Divorced women — Fiction.
6. Weddings — Fiction.   I. Title.

PS3569.H7395D75   2004
813'.54 — dc22   2004043658

Book design by Melissa Lotfy

Printed in the United States of America

QUM 10 9 8 7 6 5 4 3 2 1

For Bich

Acknowledgments

I would like to thank my editor and friend Wendy Holt for her tireless work, her faith in me, and her true understanding of character. Thanks also to Larry Cooper, Lori Glazer, Carla Gray, Jane Rosenman, Janet Silver, Megan Wilson, and everyone at Houghton Mifflin, near and far. I am indebted to Susan Shreve, Timothy Seldes, Elizabeth Shreve, Chad Holley, Claire Holley, Theju Prasad, Pavneet Singh, Glo DeAngelis, and Ching-chu Hu, great readers and friends.

I found a number of articles and books to be invaluable, especially "Making Sense of Detroit" by David M. Sheridan, from the *Michigan Quarterly Review* (Summer 1999); *The Detroit Almanac*, edited by Peter Gavrilovich and Bill McGraw; *Design and Destiny* by Philip S. Egan; *The Indomitable Tin Goose* by Charles T. Pearson; and *The Automobile and American Culture*, edited by Laurence Goldstein. Though parts of *Drives Like a Dream* draw on research, I have invented characters and, on occasion, altered the history to fit the narrative. So what seems like fact is sometimes fiction.

I am grateful always to have the love and support of my family — Dad, Carol, Sooz, Tim, Liz, Rusty, Theo, Caleb, and Kate. Most of all I want to thank Bich Minh Nguyen, who helped me tell this story and makes every story worth telling.

PART ONE

Henry Ford's inspiration for the assembly line began with a visit to a slaughterhouse in 1913. Noting the efficiency with which conveyor belts moved cattle and hogs down the line, the men at the Ford engine shop got an idea. Why not apply this same method of disassembly to the assembly of cars? A year later, production had doubled, and by 1923 Ford was building nearly two million Model Ts a year. As the shop foreman later quipped, those bones did not go to waste.

—From *Together on the Line: Henry Ford and the Rise of Mass Production* by Lydia Modine

1

ON THE MORNING of her ex-husband's wedding, Lydia Modine set the table for four. She had always made sure that her family ate breakfast together—orange juice, granola and milk, strawberry yogurt topped with wheat germ. "How many kids eat wheat germ?" the children used to complain.

"Only the ones who live forever," Lydia would say.

Now they were grown, and a year and a half had passed since Lydia had seen them together in the Detroit suburb she called home. Despite the circumstances, she planned to enjoy this time. She sliced a loaf of zucchini bread that she'd baked yesterday and laid out batik napkins and earthenware bowls on the kitchen table. It was almost eight, about an hour before she'd have to wake up the kids and hurry them downstairs.

She had once assumed, then later hoped they would all live in the same place, even the same neighborhood. But with Ivan in D.C., Jessica in Oregon, and Davy in Chicago, this had become more of a dream. *The Empire of Lydia*, Jessica had said on her last trip home—Jessica, who had moved so far away for reasons she had yet to explain—*Welcome to Historic Lydiaville*. But

Lydia wanted no such thing. Just the company of her family. Was that really so much to ask?

Waking before dawn this morning, she had pulled her knees to her chest, burrowed into the slide of pillows, tossed about on the king-size bed that Cy had bought for their twenty-fifth wedding anniversary. The bed had only put more room between them, and sleeping alone these days on this great raft, Lydia stayed close to the edge. When she couldn't keep her eyes shut any longer she got up and went downstairs, still in her nightgown. She had heard the kids come in late last night from the rehearsal dinner; they'd left cheese and cracker crumbs and an empty jar of olives on the kitchen island. Lydia rinsed the dirty plates and dropped the jar in the recycling bin, wondering if Cy and his bride-to-be had run out of food for their guests. She hoped there had not been enough food. She hoped the toasts had been embarrassing, that the whole evening had gone badly.

But she would not allow herself to think about that now. Her children had come home and here she was, up and about and for some reason excited, as if today were her day, too.

The morning sunlight filtered through the kitchen's sliding glass doors and spread over the table. Lydia unloaded the dishwasher and arranged the clean glasses in the cupboards, tall in the back, small up front. She wiped the countertop, swept the floor, ran a cloth over the tops of the picture frames that hung in the kitchen and along the hallway. She took a bottle of Windex to the mirror in the foyer and to the same glass doors that she'd already made sparkle yesterday. She cleaned the pictures in the living room—the fences and haystacks that her father had painted in high school, the architect's drawing of the Mackinac Bridge, which linked lower Michigan to the Upper Peninsula. She dusted the clock and the miniature pushcart on the mantel, and as a finishing touch straightened the cloth dolls that sat on the living room sofa. "One for me, one for Ivan, and one for Davy," Jessica liked to say. "What better way to keep an eye on us? Go on, Mom. Give my arm a twist."

Lydia went along with the joke, but it made her self-conscious about the dolls, these floppy-limbed harlequins in doublets and checkered skirts. To Lydia they were whimsical, with their orange, blue, and purple yarn hair, their bright expressions of knowing and surprise. When the children were young, people had marveled at the way Lydia could do so much at once—write books, help support a family, hold the household together, all with a seemingly absent-minded ease. She was more fluid then, with no time to worry over the details. But now she had too much time, and Jessica in particular no longer seemed awed by her mother. To Lydia the dolls brought a little life to the room; she thought they might cheer her back to the person she once was.

She did a final check of the downstairs, and, seeing that all was in order, she went out to the back patio. It was a beautiful day for a wedding, she realized with a mix of anticipation and regret. A clear sky, warmer than usual for mid-May. She breathed in the scent of lilacs. Last week solid rain had brought up the tulips in front of the house, and the magnolia bloomed magnificently beside the garage. She looked forward to getting on with the day, vaguely imagining the bride or groom panicking and calling off the whole thing. Such lovely weather seemed almost too auspicious for something not to go wrong.

Lydia remembered her own wedding day, in the height of summer 1965. The forecast had called for rain, and all morning the sky had threatened. As she got into her dress she kept looking out her bedroom window, her mother calling the wedding coordinator at the Book-Cadillac Hotel every fifteen minutes. In the afternoon it grew dark, the temperature dropping below 70. So the reception had been moved from the rooftop, with its view of the Detroit River and the lights of Belle Isle, to a ballroom on the first floor. Everyone seemed to have a good time, but Lydia couldn't help feeling disappointed, especially since, after so much trouble, it didn't rain after all.

Now she checked the patio chairs and table that she had spray-painted forest green earlier in the week. The chairs needed touching up, but no one would notice, certainly not today. She crossed the flagstones and admired her tidy patch of perennials and herbs, freshly weeded, bordering the patio. From the garage she got a pair of scissors and cut a bunch of day lilies. Licks of flame to brighten up the kitchen.

The sounds of animals from the Detroit Zoo drifted over the trees. It was the one exotic aspect of her quiet suburban neighborhood. As a social historian of the automobile, with four books to her name, she had always eyed the suburbs with suspicion, the way they leeched off cities, drawing all the benefits without paying the costs. And yet here she'd lived for more than twenty years, albeit just outside Detroit off the main thoroughfare of Woodward Avenue. Cy had won the battle over where to settle down, appealing to Lydia's sense of protectiveness. He had promised her that Huntington Woods had better schools, cleaner streets and parks than the ones in midtown Detroit, where they'd lived for the first years of their marriage. And while she'd felt compromised at the time, she had grown to love her house, this simple American foursquare with its roomy interiors and wide front porch.

Back in the kitchen she put the lilies in a vase, set them on the table, and went upstairs to shower and dress. The three doors at the top of the stairs remained closed. Lydia took a quick shower, careful to save hot water, then stood in front of the bathroom mirror in her towel and checked for gray hairs.

People always assumed that she dyed her hair, but at sixty-one she was still a glossy auburn. She pulled her hair back into a bun and pursed her lips, thinking they could use some color. She hadn't worn lipstick since before the divorce, three years ago, but searching the medicine cabinet she found a single abandoned tube. It smelled like a box of old crayons. The color was more orange than she'd remembered ever wearing, a matte persimmon hue that she blotted with a Kleenex. She added a touch of mascara, just enough to darken her eyes, then rifled through the bathroom drawers for the bottle of Eternity that Cy had given her for her fifty-sixth birthday. At the time she had resented him for not knowing that she didn't wear perfume, but today Lydia dabbed some on her neck and clavicle.

In her bedroom, she stared at the clothes in her closet. This morning, all of her suits and dresses looked pilly and worn, but she finally settled on a red tunic—Cy used to say that red flattered her—and a gray linen skirt. Standing at the bureau mirror, she put on her favorite silver bead necklace. She looked pulled together, even attractive, she thought, on a day when everyone would expect her to be a wreck.

Before heading downstairs she knocked on each of the bedroom doors. "Morning!" she called. She could hear a slight rustling on the other side.

In the kitchen, she poured herself a cup of coffee and listened to the sounds of her children as they gradually got out of bed. Ivan, always the first, walked in short, regimented strides. Not long after that, Davy's softer steps followed. Lydia could feel an energy returning to the house that seemed to move through every room, right into her own skin.

But she quickly checked herself. This energy was not intended for her. She had kept in constant motion for weeks preparing for her family's return. Now she realized she had nothing left to do but wait for the kids to get ready. Who was she kidding? *She* was not the story. All the preparation in the world couldn't change the reasons why her children were here.

She had to face the fact that this weekend would be a swindle.

Four winters ago her husband of thirty-three years had asked for a trial separation, citing the usual: they had drifted apart. Six months later, at his new job selling wireless accounts for Michitel, he fell for a woman he met at a trade show. Lydia had never seen Ellen, whose name was not easy to scorn, but she pictured the much younger woman with big trusting eyes, her head crowned with a hands-free phone set. This afternoon, at precisely one o'clock, Cy and Ellen were getting married. Till death do them part, they would be the hyphenated union of Mr. and Mrs. Spivey-Modine.

So the kids had returned to see the transition made official. They'd stopped what they were doing for their carefree, distractible dad. And today Lydia was expected to disappear. Jessica had said as much before leaving last night for the rehearsal dinner: Lydia's presence would be unnerving as they prepared for their father's second marriage. A groom at sixty. There was something unseemly about that.

She knew that Cy had always needed someone to take care of him. His mother had died when he was fifteen, and after high school he had drifted from one job to another. Lydia had spent years comforting him when he was out of work, encouraging his hobbies and meandering dreams. She had filled the role with an eagerness that only began to fade late in the marriage, when the house had finally emptied of all but the two of them.

After Davy left for college six years ago, Lydia poured herself into her research. She published a social history of the Interstate and began a new project, one she was still working on, about the General Motors design team that had put into practice on a grand scale the philosophy of "planned obsolescence." Out with the old, in with the new. Widen the fins, lower the chassis. Make this year's model just different enough so that last year's seems shabby and dull. Keep the wheels ever rolling.

Lydia had little patience for that old comparison between cars and women, and yet she couldn't help thinking, with increasing irritation, that her latest book mirrored her own life in uncanny ways. No wonder she was having trouble getting back to work.

She could hear the shower running and the heavy tread of Jessica walking down the hall above her. It was a familiar sound, something to take comfort in. How many times had Jess been the last to get up, late for school? She'd come downstairs unshowered, in sweatpants and a pullover, her hair in a ponytail. She knew this drove her mother a bit crazy. "Cut her some slack," Cy would say when Lydia couldn't resist making a comment. "She always looks great."

As a teenager, Jessica had been expert at playing her parents off each other. She and Lydia had always been close, even through the storm of adolescence. They shared a similar character, the same pragmatic point of view, and, as the two women in the house, they had been virtually inseparable. But when

Lydia and Cy had their occasional spats, Jessica would invariably take her father's position, assuming the role of daddy's little girl. She played both sides, almost as if to spark a charge into her parents' languishing marriage, forcing them to pay attention to her—and, by extension perhaps, to each other.

Lydia wondered sometimes if Cy would have left had she been more present, kept up with her personal ministry to him. Hadn't she buried herself in her work those last years, all the while ignoring the obvious signs that her marriage was coming apart? She took such pleasure in her research that living with an acquaintance who happened to be her husband had seemed not the worst circumstance. Men like Harley Earl, the legendary car designer who had been her father's boss at GM, had become more real, more attractive to her than Cy.

It was true that Cy *had* tried at times. Toward the end, he bought a 1957 Chevrolet Nomad, one of the classic GM family cars, and began a restoration project in the garage. It was a sentimental gesture. Lydia's workaholic father had helped design the original wagon. Inspired by the early Corvettes, it was one of the first cars of its kind to combine sportiness with the usual practical features. For a while Cy's devotion to the project gave Lydia hope that they could restore their marriage too, and she would join him in the garage to discuss the next phase for the car. But eventually, like the Nomad itself, the project failed. As with all of Cy's dreams, he grew frustrated and gave up.

Now Lydia filled the bowls with granola and took out grapefruit and English muffins from the refrigerator. She loosened the grapefruit sections with a paring knife, sliced the muffins, and stacked them on plates by the toaster. She filled a pitcher with cold milk, put glasses of orange juice at each setting, and took out the marionberry jam that Jessica had brought from Oregon. Then, checking her lipstick in the hallway mirror, she went upstairs, determined to appear, for her children's sake, as if this day were like any other.

Jessica sat on the edge of her canopy bed putting on a black choker. She wore a flowered dress and chunky-heeled shoes.

"Good morning," Lydia said, sitting down next to her. "Is that what you're wearing to the wedding?" Instantly she worried that she sounded too critical.

"Well, it's what I brought." Jessica got up from the bed and half twirled in front of the closet door mirror. "What do you think?"

"Nice," Lydia said, hearing the hesitation in her voice. In spite of herself, she still hoped to please Cy. She knew he would want the kids to look their best today.

"I wasn't about to buy an expensive dress. Even if I could afford it, what would be the point?" Jessica asked. "Maybe when you get remarried I'll go all out. Hoop skirt and crinolines. But I don't think Dad really cares."

Oh, he cared, Lydia knew. He didn't talk about Ellen per se, but he did call Lydia every couple of weeks, and once in a while they met for lunch to discuss the children. *How are their jobs? Any news on their love lives? Can you believe that Ivan turned thirty?* Cy would even talk about the upcoming wedding: *Will the kids arrive in time for the rehearsal? Can't they come in on Thursday instead? You're sure you don't mind all the trips to the airport?*

Which was why she had an impulse now to fetch a brush, sit Jessica down on the bed, and comb her mass of black hair until it fell long and straight. Jessica had always been a beauty, with her thick hair and wide-set brown eyes. At five foot nine, she was taller than Lydia, but she still had an adolescent slouch. From an early age, Jessica had never paid much attention to how she looked. A standout basketball player, sweats and running shoes had been her high school uniform.

"I think maybe your father cares more than you think he does."

Jessica pulled back her hair and turned to check her profile. She had shaved her underarms—a welcome development since yesterday, Lydia noted.

"If Dad has a problem with the dress I'm sure he'll let me know. We're going out for brunch before the wedding."

"But I've made breakfast downstairs." Lydia felt her perfectly planned morning slipping away. Cy had said nothing about brunch.

"Well, we're eating in less than an hour. But thanks, anyway."

Ivan, in a black suit and silver tie, came into the room and kissed his mother good morning. His hair had been clipper-cut so short that he looked like a Secret Service agent. Lydia wished he would grow it long and curly again, as it had been when he was young, to soften his strong features.

"You look nice, honey." She stood up and smoothed his lapel.

"I *am* the best man in my father's wedding. Tell me if that's not every boy's dream." Ivan stood behind his sister at the mirror and adjusted his tie.

"Where's Davy?" Jessica asked.

"Sewing a button on one of my old blazers. He didn't exactly come prepared."

"So, how was the rehearsal dinner?" Lydia tried to sound nonchalant, though she'd been waiting all morning for a full report. Last night she'd even offered to drive the kids to the restaurant, hoping to catch a glimpse of Ellen. Instead, Jessica had asked to borrow her car.

"My speech was brilliant. There were tears—" Ivan began, before Jessica clapped her hand over his mouth.

"It was fine," she said.

Lydia wondered how she could have such different children. From temperament to interests to where they had chosen to live, they had spun off in all directions. Out in Oregon, Jessica had discovered radical politics, and her phone calls home had become increasingly tense. She talked down to Lydia now, as if speaking to the unenlightened. Ivan, on the other hand, worked for the International Trade Administration; he was a government man, but Jessica never turned her hostility on him.

"Did Dad tell you he's shaving his beard?" Jessica asked her brother.

"For the wedding?"

"Yeah, this morning. It's probably headed down the drain as we speak."

Lydia realized that this news was meant for her. Cy had always worn a beard. For as long as they'd been married, he had groomed it every day with an electric razor that he kept at the same low setting. She hadn't seen him with a clean-shaven face since well before they were a couple. As he had aged—his hair and beard going from brown to grizzled to fully gray—he looked increasingly distinguished. People had often said they made a handsome couple. She favored long skirts and crisp blouses; he had worn his wire-rimmed glasses and the clothes that Lydia picked out for him. "The Mennonites step out on the town," Jessica used to joke. But during the separation Lydia realized how two people could put a lot of extra miles on a marriage if they looked as if they belonged together.

"Don't tell me he's going to dye his hair, too," Ivan said.

"No, he's been reading some men's movement book. It told him that the beard was a mask."

"Ah, yes. Of course." Ivan always responded badly to his father's soul-searching. Nothing infuriated him more than Cy's earnest talk about spontaneous healing, the God within, and random acts of kindness. And though Lydia would later laugh about this too—much later, after the tightly wound spring of her would at last uncoil—Cy's shaving his beard stood for something final.

"I should let you two finish getting ready. I'll be outside with the camera," she said quickly and headed back downstairs.

During one of his incarnations Cy had been an amateur photographer, and though he soon tired of lighthouses and freighters, he had continued to take pictures of the children. The result was a series hanging on the kitchen walls: of the kids on the front steps, a chronicle of their shifting hairstyles and demeanors, from the time Davy was five to just a few years ago. Lydia had decided this week to keep the tradition going. She'd bought film for the camera yesterday, and now she went outside to load it and wait on the porch swing.

She remembered when Jessica had sat here with her brooding friends or when the children had lined up with their duffel bags before leaving on trips: Davy to music camp at Interlochen, Ivan to college in D.C.—the only one in the family not to go to the University of Michigan.

All three kids came out at once, crisply dressed. Ivan sat on the third step down, Jessica in the middle, Davy on the top step.

Lydia knelt on the front walk and tilted the camera. "Look at these matinee idols!" she called out, and caught Jessica rolling her eyes.

After Lydia snapped a few frames Davy stood up. "Can we get you in here, Mom? Let me take over."

"That's okay." She waved him off.

He sat back down, cleaning his glasses with his teardrop-patterned tie.

"The groom will be here any second, you know," Jessica said impatiently.

"Just a couple more shots, then. How about some smiles?"

Jessica sighed.

"C'mon Jess," Davy said. "It's Mom's weekend too. She made us a nice breakfast and everything."

Thank you, Lydia wanted to say. It was about time someone noticed. Nobody had said so much as "The place looks great" or "Don't you look nice this morning." She did look nice, as a matter of fact. And it *was* her weekend, too.

She had clicked off half the roll, her hands shaking a little, by the time Cy pulled up in front of the house. The kids stood up, looking almost solemn as their father got out of his car.

Cy's cheeks were pink, his small chin newly revealed, a hint of the face Lydia remembered from long ago. She should have known that without the beard, behind the so-called mask, he would resemble an overgrown boy: bright-eyed like Davy, ruddy like Ivan.

"Sorry I'm late. Got caught up with the endless details. So you took some pictures?"

"I did," Lydia said emphatically, though she wasn't sure why.

He leaned forward to kiss her chastely on the cheek, and as

she felt for the first time, after more than thirty years of marriage, his shaven face touching her skin, flesh to flesh, a peculiar regret washed over her: she wished that she had been the one to shave him.

When Lydia was a girl, her father used to send her on errands to a tailor in Hamtramck. He was an ancient rheumy-eyed Polish immigrant, and often when she walked into the shop early, before school, the tailor would be sitting on a stool by the cash register with a towel around his neck. His face would be covered in shaving cream, and hovering over him, a bone-handled straight razor in her fist, would be his wife. She would shave him with quick, adept strokes, slapping the spent lather against a towel in her hand, lifting his skin and drawing the razor down. The tailor would sit there, waiting out the daily ritual until his face was smooth and clean. Then he would rise to his feet and gather Lydia's father's suits. His wife would put the razor away, neatly fold the towels. Then she would ring up the sale. And as Lydia turned to wave goodbye, the tailor would say, "Remember, young lady. Don't fall in love."

That was marriage, Lydia thought—every morning a straight razor shave, routine and precarious at the same time. The domestic trinity of care, trust, and repetition all contained in that simple tableau. How long had the tailor and his wife been married? Fifty years? A hundred and fifty? Lydia half believed that if she were to drive across town to Hamtramck right now, she would find the two of them still holding down the shop. "Don't fall in love," he would say. And Lydia would answer, "Maybe I never did." Or, "I never will again."

She stood on the front porch as the kids piled into their father's new Infiniti sedan.

"Well, bye," she yelled out. "Have a wonderful time." And, as the doors closed, "Congratulations."

But Cy must not have heard her because he didn't look back, just gave a quick wave. They drove off and Lydia stood staring down the street as the car turned the corner. "Well," she said, then realized that no one was around to hear her. "Well."

She went back into the house and looked at the uneaten

breakfast. Granola, grapefruit, zucchini bread, English muffins, even the jam that Jessica had brought—all of it went into the trash. Lydia poured the coffee, milk, and juice into the sink, put the dishes in the cupboard, wiped down the table, and turned off the light.

Then she climbed the stairs to her office and gathered her manuscript papers and laptop for the library. "Back when I am," she wrote on a white note card.

She put the note on the kitchen table, then locked the front door behind her.

2

TOO LATE FOR a sit-down brunch, Jessica, Ivan, Davy, and Cy decided to go to a coffee shop in Bloomfield Hills, land of the ladies' lunch. With their cappuccinos and scones they clustered in the window on high skinny chairs, looking out at the shoppers. Jessica was wondering if her father would quit his job at Michitel, since he seemed to be marrying into some family money. Or so he had hinted. The new Infiniti he was driving had been an early wedding gift from Ellen. He had always talked about retirement, even when the kids were young and he was making fairly modest sales commissions. But seeing him now, with his fresh face and newly whitened teeth, Jessica felt grateful—at least he was not on his own.

"So, let's talk about what everyone's going to wear today," he said, looking directly at Jessica.

She fingered her choker, surprised that her mother had been right. "This is all I brought, but I'm happy to get something else."

"Aren't we running late?" Ivan asked. "It's already after ten."

"We'll be okay if we hurry." Cy licked a spot of foam from his lip. "The bridesmaids will be in lavender, so we should find a nice complement. Maybe something celadon or sage green. I think it would mean a lot to Ellen."

Jessica glanced across the table at Ivan, who raised his hand to his mouth either to cover a smile or stop himself from saying something caustic.

"She'll only wear the dress once," Ivan said after a moment. "I don't see what the point is."

Davy ran his hand through his hair. He had let it grow long, so that it now flopped over his black-rimmed glasses. "I think a new outfit makes sense."

"Why?" Ivan asked.

"It's what Dad wants."

"Look, it's no problem," Jessica jumped in. "I'll get a new dress."

She was not in the wedding party, which relieved her considerably. She hated the idea of buying clothes that tomorrow would end up in a dark corner of her closet. But at the same time she didn't want to upset her father, who, without his beard, looked lost this morning. He kept rubbing his hand across his chin as if to see what was there—a fresh skin for his wedding day. He seemed nervous and fidgety, and once again Jessica understood why she forgave him, perhaps irrationally, for his considerable faults. While her mother, who despite her occasional dramas seemed the very picture of solidity, Jessica had always harbored a vague fear that she might lose her father. Invariably when she had nightmares about her family, they were about Cy slipping from view, disappearing off the edge of her screams. Not that he lived dangerously, but sometimes it seemed that he was more of a visitor, a ghostly figure in her life. She often had an impulse to reach out and grab hold of him.

She remembered the first time she had felt this way. She must have been ten or eleven, and up to that moment she had thought of Cy as an ordinary dad who left for work in the morning in his suit and tie and came home late—a successful businessman, perhaps. In truth, he had just switched jobs for the third time in as many years and was selling cars at

Bobby Szoradi's Ford dealership. Bobby and Cy had been college roommates, and since Bobby's marriage had recently broken up, Lydia invited him over for Thanksgiving dinner. Ivan had just brought a pumpkin pie to the table when Bobby asked Lydia how sales were coming for her latest book, a history of the assembly line.

"I don't care much about sales," Lydia said. "I'm just happy to see it reviewed."

"So sales don't matter?" Bobby asked. "They sure matter in my business. My business is all about sales."

"Don't I know it," Lydia said, and though her tone was probably more joking than critical, Bobby took it the wrong way.

"I don't read many books. I'm too busy for books." He shifted in his seat. "But I did read yours, Lydia. You're a fine cook, but you're not so hot at getting your facts right. You've got some nasty things to say about some good people."

Jessica had looked across the table at her father. He seemed to be biting the inside of his cheek.

Lydia cut into the pie. "Like who?" she asked.

"Henry Ford, for one." Bobby raised his voice. "I don't care what you write. He was a great man."

"Henry Ford was a terrible anti-Semite. And I'm by no means the first to say that." Lydia put a piece of pie on a plate and passed it to Cy, who immediately began eating. "He wrote a tract against Jews in the twenties that Hitler said was his greatest influence. The Führer had a picture of Ford hanging on his office wall."

Jessica had never seen her mother in a confrontation like this. Lydia spoke in calm, measured sentences, which only made Bobby more agitated.

"I'm not talking about the man's beliefs," he said. "The world is a better place because of the assembly line. That's my point."

Lydia picked up a plate. "How about some pie?"

Bobby took his piece of pie and began to have a bite, then put his fork down. His face glowed in the candlelight. "Ford did a lot of good for a lot of people, Lydia. My grandfather came to this country without a pot to piss in, and Ford gave him a job in tool and die with a decent salary and put him through language school, where he learned to speak English. He and my grandmother raised six great kids and my father was one of those, and by God *he* worked for Ford. You have a lot of nerve living in this city and writing the things you write."

"Look, I just tell what happened," Lydia said. "Some of the stories are nice, some not so nice. Do you know what Ford did at graduation from that language school? He put a replica of a melting pot onstage, a huge vat that he wheeled out for all the graduations back then. The immigrant workers would walk into it wearing their old-world clothes, the English instructors would stand above them stirring the pot with giant spoons, and a couple of minutes later the new graduates would emerge in American suits waving American flags. That actually happened, and it says a lot about Henry Ford's 'good' intentions. It didn't matter to him that these people were leaving a culture behind in order to become his worker bees. We live in a world where certain people seem to know what's best for the rest of us."

Bobby pushed his plate away. "Look, my grandfather had no regrets. He was a full-blooded American and proud of it. I don't know where I'd be without Ford—or where you'd be, either. Your husband is a Ford employee, need I remind you?"

"And you're his boss," Lydia said. "Which is why you feel entitled to launch into this speech at dinner at my house and insult me in front of my children. You might have chosen a different time to air your complaints. This is hardly my idea of a family Thanksgiving."

Jessica had watched Cy lower his head and finish the rest of his dessert without comment. He sat between his wife and the man who paid his salary, and Jessica saw that he would do nothing to stop their dispute. Cy took a large mouthful of coffee, ran his finger over his plate collecting what crumbs remained of his piecrust, then licked his finger. He had a sheepish look on his face. He couldn't defend his wife because she didn't need defending, nor did he have the ability to finesse the argument to a peaceful end. By the time it was over, Cy had retreated into his own secluded space. Jessica had wanted to reach across the table and pull her father back into the conversation. But Ivan cleared the dessert plates and asked their mother if he should make some more coffee. "None for me," Bobby said, and stood up to go.

Out on the front porch, Jessica heard her mother apologize, but Bobby told her not to worry. "I've been awfully irritable lately," he said. "The marriage and all."

"Well, see you at work," Cy called from the hallway, as cheerfully as he could. Later, Jessica overheard her father tell Lydia that his future at the dealership might never recover from this. And, in the end, he was right. Self-fulfilling prophecy or not, within the year he was back in the job market.

Today, hours before his second wedding, Jessica was looking across a different table at her father, but he was the same man. His cloudy green eyes, the way he retreated, the sight of him licking crumbs from his finger—all made Jessica realize why she couldn't be angry even on *this* weekend, when she had every reason to be. His life, she couldn't deny, was a series of clichés. He was marrying a woman who could have been her older sister. When the kids had needed him just to be around, he was forever chasing some new rainbow. And he'd run off with someone new within six months of separating from their mother, as if thirty-three years had meant nothing. And yet, amazingly, when she boiled over, Jessica turned her fury not on Cy but on Lydia. Perhaps for no better reason than that she knew her mother was strong enough to take it.

"So, where's Ellen?" Jessica asked.

"Getting ready. I'm not supposed to see her until we're in the church." Cy smiled, pink half-moons appearing in each cheek.

Though Ellen had never been married, Jessica and her brothers had expected a low-key wedding. But the rehearsal dinner had been a frilly affair, and this afternoon promised to be more of the same. Last night's crowd had looked like time travelers from the cocktail generation: chain-smoking, Scotchswilling veterans of the Big Band era. And Ellen, who had been a sorority secretary at Michigan State, fit the part: thirty-five going on sixty-five, a string-of-pearls and brass-buttons type with an inborn solicitous manner. Facing the American nightmare of a stepmother nearly as young as herself, Jessica had planned to despise the woman. But after meeting her at the rehearsal dinner and seeing her steer Cy from table to table, gently drawing him into the conversation, Jessica admitted this might be a suitable match after all.

"I like your bride-to-be," she said.

"That's sweet of you. We're very happy." Cy patted her hand. "She lets me be myself."

For a moment Jessica felt defensive on her mother's behalf, until Ivan asked, "And who is that?"

Cy missed the insult in Ivan's question. As with most unpleasant things, he ran it through an internal filter that turned it sweet. "There's so much I've never had a chance to do. Promise not to laugh at your old dad, but Ellen bought me a guitar for my birthday—and I've been practicing."

Ivan liked to call their father a serial hobbyist. One of the basement rooms in the house at 309 Franklin was a museum of Cy's abandoned projects. Half a dozen exercise machines shared space with dumbbells, fishing rods, camera equipment, a telescope, a radio-controlled biplane, a bread machine, a home brewery kit, woodworking tools and random pieces of a rocking chair that Cy had begun to build one summer. On the shelf above his workbench were books like *Plan B for a Better Life*, *So You Want to Be a Poet*, *How to Remember Everything That Ever Happened to You*, *1957 Chevrolet Parts & Accessories*, *All You Need to Know About Birds*, and *Fluent French in Five Easy Weeks*. Jessica wondered if her mother had cleaned out the room since the split. Not likely, since Lydia threw nothing away.

Ivan rolled his eyes and seemed ready to launch another insult. Jessica shot him a look and quickly changed the subject. "So what do you say we get going? I think I'm ready for my makeover."

Cy took a last bite of his scone and got up from the table.

"Does anyone else have the jitters?" He held out his shaky hand.

"Should we?" Davy asked.

Cy smiled, but did not respond.

Soon, Ivan and Davy were browsing in a nearby record store while Jessica stood before a mirror in the fitting room at Jacobson's, a place she hadn't been since her senior year in high school when her mother had dragged her to try on prom dresses. She had allowed Lydia to buy her a puffy, iridescent blue taffeta number. Her boyfriend at the time—a junk collector and bad boy—had looked stunned, and not in a good way, when he'd arrived to pick her up. Jessica didn't try to explain. Even she couldn't understand why her mother, so thrifty and practical in her own life, would have the random compulsion to turn her daughter into a princess.

Now she walked out of the fitting room in a pale green suit and beige shoes that her father had picked out for her, a getup that would have looked a lot better on a middle-aged junior executive. But not wanting to make a fuss, she said, "I love it."

Cy stepped back to admire the suit. "Me too. It's very retro."

"Haven't heard you use that word before, Dad."

"I try to keep up."

They bought the suit and collected Ivan and Davy, then drove to the nearby subdivision where the soon-to-be Spivey-Modines had been living for the past year. Cy and Ivan had some last minute details to deal with before their limo arrived. Cy asked Jessica and Davy if they'd take his car and pick up Ellen's parents, Casper and M.J., and deliver them to the wedding. "They could make it there themselves, but Casper's not the best driver," he explained. "I don't know what we'd do if they got into an accident today."

"What do you mean?" Jessica asked.

"Casper failed the vision test last time he tried to renew his license. But he's still on the road."

"So, why doesn't M.J. drive?"

"She gives him a hard time about it, believe me. Part of her is probably waiting to say, 'I told you so,' and another part must realize how hard it is for a Michigan driver to give up the wheel."

Jessica thought, That's an "I told you so" with some potentially awful consequences. She had met the Spiveys the night before. Casper had glasses that made his eyes look like beetles frozen in ice, but he seemed to get around fine and was almost graceful on his feet.

"And he hasn't been pulled over yet?" Ivan asked.

"Not as far as I know." Cy parked in front of a pearl-gray condo that looked like all the others on the block, save the wooden placard of a butterfly on the front door. "Anyway, it's Ellen's day. I want to make sure there are no unwelcome surprises."

Before carrying out their assignment, Jessica and Davy stopped by the house on Franklin so she could change into her new clothes. In the kitchen, she found a note her mother had left: "Back when I am." Whatever that meant. Jessica had begun to lose patience earlier that morning when Lydia had fished for details about the rehearsal dinner. She was relieved that her mother had left the house.

Jessica went upstairs and slipped back into the suit. The color looked even worse in her sunny room than it had under the fluorescent lights of the department store. It was more of a mint than a sage green. With a bob cut and a shellacking of Aqua Net she could have passed for Lady Bird Johnson, circa 1965. She pulled back her hair in a barrette and went looking in her mother's bathroom for some makeup. To her surprise, a tube of lipstick sat on the sink. Maybe Lydia had taken it out and forgotten to give it to her. It was a bit orange for the green suit, but better than nothing. As Jessica leaned into the mirror to put on the lipstick she tried to remember her mother's face from this morning. Had Lydia actually been wearing lipstick?

People often told her how alike she and her mother were. Both were tall and dark-haired, and they shared a strong-mindedness that sometimes put strangers on edge. As a girl she had loved hearing that she was her mother's daughter, and she used to tell everyone that she would be a historian someday, too. In spite of their arguments, they'd been close through Jessica's high school years. But college in Ann Arbor was too nearby. Lydia would drop in for unannounced visits and call every day, often in the evening when Jessica had work or was on her way out with friends. Her mother would complain about Cy or money, subjects frequently entangled, and ask a thousand questions about Jessica's life. Unable to resist, almost wincing as she spoke, Jessica would answer. Lydia had a way of getting her to spill the details.

Her mother's presence had become especially overwhelming when Jessica lived back home after college, hoping to save a little money. Lydia seemed to be everywhere, and the more Jessica tried to get away—working longer hours at Clean Water Action, taking a second job at a bookstore just to stay out of the house—the more her mother pushed to be included. She wanted Jessica's friends to talk to her too, and at times she invited them to dinner without saying she'd done so. They'd appear at the front door, and Jessica would fume—feeling, increasingly, that she had no choice but to remove herself physically from her mother's sphere. Now she worked at an organic grocery in Eugene, Oregon, stocking shelves, scanning herbal extracts, weighing bok choy, bulk grains, and broccoli. Perhaps she and Lydia were too much alike—a problem, Jessica had to admit as she switched off the bathroom light, that she had gone clear across the country to avoid.

Downstairs in the kitchen she turned over Lydia's note and considered what to write in reply. It was just like her mother to turn on the melodrama at a time like this.

Davy came into the room, with that same distracted, bleary-eyed expression he'd worn since yesterday. "What are you writing?" He looked over her shoulder to catch a glimpse.

"Oh, nothing," Jessica said. "But try to tell me Mom's note isn't a plea for attention."

"Come on, Jess. This isn't easy for her. Just because we're all pissed at Dad doesn't mean we should take it out on Mom."

Jessica was about to say, "I'm not pissed at Dad," then stopped herself. She knew there was more to the note than

Davy was willing to admit. Often enough when Lydia grew frustrated with Jessica she'd say, "I've reached the end of my rope," then get into the car and drive off, just long enough for the kids to worry. After a while the phone would ring. "Where are you?" they'd ask. "Does it matter?" Lydia would say. Then Ivan and Davy would talk Jessica into apologizing, and the kids would follow the old ritual of coaxing their mother home. "Back when I am" was another version of "I've reached the end of my rope." The message was equally clear: *I've gone for a drive, if you care. Your father may be getting married today but who knows where I might be or when, if ever, I might return.*

Jessica crumpled the note and threw it in the trash. Better not to respond, she decided.

Sometime after she and Davy left the house and drove in silence to Royal Oak to pick up Ellen's parents, Jessica had a shiver of guilt for being angry with her mother.

"So they take us for a couple of invalids, can't drive ourselves," Casper barked when they arrived. He answered the door in a blue dress shirt and pink boxer shorts. "Listen to this, M.J.," he called toward the back of their spacious condo. "Ellen sent these nice young people to be our chauffeurs." He was a tall, broad-shouldered man with a certain elegance despite his big glasses and pale skinny legs. "My wife complains about my eyesight. Don't listen to her. I'm telling you, I see fine." He gestured toward Jessica. "You, for example. You are very beautiful."

M.J. came into the foyer in a lacy black dress. Long, pearly beads hung around her neck. "He's right about that," she said in a slight accent that Jessica hadn't been able to place the night before. "You are great-looking children." Since she stood no taller than Davy's chest, she had to pull him down by the lapels when she kissed him on each cheek.

Casper sat on the back of a fleur-de-lis-patterned sofa. "Don't mind my wife," he said, as M.J. gave Jessica a kiss. "In the last couple of years she's turned European."

"I did grow up in Montreal."

"That's Canada," Casper said.

"Quebec," she corrected him. "My name is Marie Jeanette. I go by M.J. to accommodate my husband's limited memory."

"So she likes French cookery." Casper buttoned his shirt to the top. "I'll give her that. She's always enjoyed those sauces."

M.J. invited them to sit for a minute, and Jessica noticed that Mrs. Spivey also liked French furniture, toile fabrics, Louis XIV clocks, reproduction Manets and Rouaults, and period portraits of French girls with miniature dogs.

"Your place is lovely," Jessica said.

"She's an interior decorator," Casper put in. "She's on a one-woman mission to turn every room in Royal Oak into a Parisian salon."

"For God's sake, put your trousers on," M.J. said, and her husband, who did not seem at all embarrassed to have answered the door in his boxer shorts, retreated obediently to the back rooms. "He's lived in Detroit his whole life," M.J. added. "Forty-two years putting out the good word for Ford." Her face was plump, her mascara brushed on thick. Her ankles swelled over her stylish T-strap shoes. "Two summers ago I took him to Europe for the first time. I'd been there several times with Ellen, but Casper could never pull himself away from the boardroom." She played with the beads of her necklace. "Wouldn't you know he'd start losing his vision before he saw Europe? It's a tragedy when an American stops seeing clearly, since sight is the only sense that Americans ever use."

M.J. was still talking about Europe when Casper returned in a red tie and tailored charcoal suit.

Jessica saw Davy glancing at the antique clock over the mantel. A little past noon. She wondered if her father was already at the church, sweating bullets.

"Don't forget the flowers Ellen had delivered," M.J. said.

Casper went to the kitchen and came back with a rose corsage and boutonniere.

M.J. pinned the flower to her husband's lapel. "You know he's going to have to drive," she said, as if this had been assumed all along.

Jessica looked over at Davy. "I think we should drive," she offered meekly.

"I know you do, sweetheart. But you heard what I said about forty-two years. What's he supposed to do? Just hand over the keys?"

Soon Casper and M.J. were pulling their black Lincoln Town Car out of the condominium complex and onto the street. Jessica and Davy followed in their father's Infiniti.

"We should have gone with them," Jessica said.

"Relax." Davy seemed unconcerned.

"We shouldn't let them do this."

"We don't even know these people."

"You should drive up beside them. Make them pull over or something."

"He's doing fine," Davy said.

It was true. So far, so good. Casper's car stayed straight in its narrow lane. M.J. leaned into the driver's side, as if she were giving directions.

"His back lights are blinking. He's pumping the brakes." Jessica put her hands on the dashboard.

"He can't help it, Jess. We're in stop-and-go traffic."

They were headed into the heart of Royal Oak. Both lanes were bumper to bumper. Lunchtime shoppers were out in droves. It was a perfect spring afternoon, warm with a gentle breeze—a lovely day for a wedding, Jessica thought for the first time.

But it didn't matter how well Casper was managing. Jessica was letting her father down. He had given her a simple assignment: make sure that Ellen's parents arrive safely at the wedding. But here was Casper driving illegally. The cops could pull him over at any moment.

At an intersection just ahead, Casper stopped at a yellow light. "That's it." Jessica ripped off her seatbelt.

"What are you doing?" Davy yelled as his sister jumped out of the car. She ran to the passenger side of the Spiveys' Lincoln and tapped on the window.

M.J. rolled down the glass. The light turned green.

"May I please get in the back? I'd like to ride with you." The drivers behind Davy began leaning on their horns. M.J. hit the unlock button, and as Jessica climbed into the back seat of a car driven by a man with failing eyesight and no driver's license, she felt the most profound sense of relief.

"Beautiful day for a wedding, wouldn't you say?" Casper turned his head.

"Perfect," she said, and fastened herself in.

3

FTER LEAVING her note for the kids, Lydia sat on the front steps, car keys in her hand, trying not to wallow in self-pity. A couple of months ago Cy had asked her if she'd like to go to the wedding, but she never received a formal invitation, and she knew that his offer was nothing more than a gesture. Lately when he called her it was always on his cell phone at odd hours, as if Ellen didn't approve of their keeping in touch. As curious as Lydia was about the wedding—she wondered what kind of dress Ellen would wear, wondered how it would feel to see some other woman walking down the aisle toward Cy—she knew she had no place there.

It was odd, she thought now, that she spoke to her ex-husband nearly as often as she talked to her kids. Jessica called the most, but seemed to know when Lydia was not around and would leave messages on the machine that sometimes sounded obligatory. Ivan called every Sunday evening. "So, what's for dinner?" he liked to say, which made Lydia feel as if he were nearby. Davy called sporadically, depending on how his relationships were going. When lovey-dovey he could disappear for a month; when frustrated, as he was recently, he called all the time.

But the phone wasn't enough. She hadn't seen the children together since her sixtieth birthday in Chicago, well over a year ago. Davy had reserved a table at the Mashed Potato Club, a restaurant that served comfort foods like carved roast beef and chicken pot pie. After finishing off their chocolate cake and ice cream they walked to Davy's apartment, broke out a bottle of champagne, and Lydia opened her gift. The kids had pooled together to buy her a laptop to replace her old computer. Ivan raised a toast. "To finishing your new book."

Lydia had been overcome. "It's too much," she exclaimed, knowing that the laptop had cost far more than the kids could afford.

"This'll get you out of the house," Jessica added. "You can plug in at a coffee shop. You'll have divorced men eating out of your hand."

"Just what I need." Lydia laughed.

Then Davy handed her another gift—a carrying case for the laptop with a large patch sewn onto the middle. Stenciled on the patch in red block letters was the word "Mamarama."

"I saw that in a vintage store—had your name all over it," Davy said.

Lydia loved the Mamarama bag because it reminded her of the Motorama, the old car convention her father used to prepare for every year. It made her think of her mother, too, and she imagined a huge convention hall strung with bright ribbons and filled with mothers of all kinds. *Welcome to the Mamarama.*

Her '84 Ford Escort had a hundred and eighty thousand miles on it. Jessica had theorized that Lydia drove the car for attention, as a way to keep her children worried about her. She wanted them to picture her broken down on the shoulder on a winter night or stuck on a darkened street after staying too late at the library. The car did rattle a little, but as far as Lydia was concerned, it ran just fine.

She was driving down Woodward Avenue, the great thoroughfare running through the heart of Detroit, from the boarded-up buildings downtown all the way north to the wealthy suburbs of Birmingham, Bloomfield Hills, and beyond. She loved to take this street, the world's first paved highway, where Charles King drove Detroit's first car a whole three blocks before the engine gave out. The length of Woodward, from Cadillac Square to the edge of Pontiac, covered an entire spectrum of magnificence and ruin, gentrification and blight—a miniature history of the automobile and its effect on the landscape.

Crossing Eight Mile Road from Ferndale, Lydia entered Detroit. *Better bring your guns,* read the graffiti on a bridge south of Palmer Park. She drove past auto body shops, adult video stores, empty lots overrun by weeds, an employment office with knocked-out windows, then the long-abandoned Highland Park Plant where Henry Ford had pioneered the assembly line. Beyond billboards offering "Free Pregnancy Tests" and "Cash in a Flash" came Renaissance Liquors, La Renaissance Motel, and the Renaissance Beauty Supply shop. Then Northern High School and a stretch of renovated housing, the Hecker Mansion, divided now into lawyers' offices, and the blue and gold banners hanging from streetlights around the cultural district.

She pulled up in front of the library, then decided she was too restless to work. She thought of crossing the street to the Detroit Institute of Arts or driving out to St. Clair Shores or down to Hart Plaza to watch the freighters—anything to stay in motion, to keep her mind off of Cy's wedding.

Had she been a different person, she supposed, she might have invited someone to lunch. But her friendships tended to work in one direction: she safeguarded people's secrets but rarely shared her own. When she and Cy had first separated, her friends called or stopped by, but to Lydia the attention seemed peculiar, a kind of care that she did not believe she needed. They stood in her foyer with faces of concern, trying to make sure she was all right. When they asked "What happened?" she didn't know how to respond. She shrugged, tried to smile. Her sentences began and ended with, "Oh, I'll be fine." At first she had turned to Jessica for support, but she was stunned to discover that her daughter blamed *her* for breaking up the family. "You gave up on him, Mother. Of course he left," she said after Cy moved out. "What choice did he have?" Now, more than four years later, Jessica still seemed to hold her accountable, though in a low-radiation kind of way.

So, like her ex-husband, she too had retreated—not to the big box suburbs, but further into herself. She began screening calls with the answering machine. Her long daily walks— through Huntington Woods, around the zoo, or across Woodward to the busy sidewalks of Royal Oak, which was a denser, more eclectic suburb that she sometimes thought would be a nice place to live—had become shorter and much less frequent. Mostly, when she was not at the library, she would leave the house only to go to the Kroger, the post office, or sometimes the art museum. There, in the skylit garden court surrounded on all sides by the Detroit Industry murals, Diego Rivera's sweeping tribute to the automobile assembly line, Lydia would sit and read or take notes. It was her private sanctuary, a room full of color and energy in the heart of dreary Detroit.

But today demanded something different. Enough of hiding away indoors. Instead, she drove farther into the city, past the Resurrection Promise Church and the corner of Woodward and Forest, where her parents had lived briefly after they were married. Their apartment building, once one of the finest in the city, had been demolished years ago, replaced now by a Church's Chicken. Lydia passed more vacant lots, then the optimistic one-block stretch of condominiums that had gone up near the new Tiger Stadium.

She figured Cy and Ellen would be getting ready for their wedding now. Ellen's hair would be done up, the veil secured in place. She'd be wearing a voluminous dress, surrounded by her bridesmaids. Lydia was glad that Jessica was not a bridesmaid, but she still pictured her floating nearby, bending down to straighten Ellen's train. Ellen wasn't just marrying Cy, after all; she was becoming the children's *stepmother.*

Turning from Woodward onto the Fisher Freeway, then

west on I-94, Lydia imagined a funnel cloud blowing out the windows of the church, snuffing out the candles on the altar. The tornado would sweep through the reception, where the tables were set up so beautifully, and blast the back doors open. Tablecloths, plates, glasses, and silverware would catapult into the air—chairs, gifts, and garlands trailing each other in a bright arc. The thought came on so suddenly that Lydia almost had to pull over to the side of the road. She breathed deeply, slowly recovering as if from an involuntary reaction. All the sadness, even the betrayal that she'd kept to herself, was hitting her at once. She had protected Cy from his angry bosses, even from his own kids, screening them from his disappointments so they would grow up proud of their father. She'd devoted years to her family while Cy had disappeared offstage to put on some new costume for his next performance. She'd listened to his stories, even advised him as he prepared for his wedding. So why, today, was Lydia the one being banished?

Beyond the airport and across the pale, flat landscape of southeast Michigan, she took the first exit into Ann Arbor. As she headed down Washtenaw toward the University of Michigan campus, she passed the ramshackle house where Davy had lived for three years, red paint peeling off its squat façade. A plaid loveseat sat in the driveway that might have been the same ratty one from Davy's old room. On Hill Street she drove past the co-op where Jessica had lived during her senior year and where Lydia had stayed over when it got too late to drive back home. Nearby was Angell Hall, where she had taken her core assignments as an undergraduate, and the Michigan Union where she and Cy had watched President Kennedy announce the formation of the Peace Corps. She drove by the library stacks, which had been her retreat while Cy had worked nights for building services. Everything Lydia passed on these familiar streets contained a memory.

Up ahead was the Brown Jug, a greasy spoon where she and her girlfriends often met for breakfast. In 1961, her sophomore year at the university's architecture and design school, she had been sitting in a booth at the Brown Jug when someone walked by, stopped suddenly, and stared at her. He was lithe, with a bristly beard and eyes that looked at her and beyond her at the same time. "You seem familiar," he had said after a moment. "You wouldn't happen to be from Detroit?"

"Detroit's a big city." Lydia was concentrating on cutting up her French toast. She would always remember that detail because the friend she was having breakfast with, a fellow honors student named Tess, kept signaling her to wipe powdered sugar from her cheek.

"What part of the city are you from?" he persisted.

"What part are you from?"

"East side. I went to Southeastern. How about you?"

Lydia turned to Tess, whose gestures, compounded by the rare event of a stranger coming up and talking to her, had put Lydia in a flustered state. "What? What's the problem?" she snapped.

"You've got a spot." Tess pointed to her own face.

Blushing, Lydia wiped her cheek.

But the guy with the beard kept talking. "I know I'm going to figure this out. I swear I know you from somewhere."

Lydia's plain style and scholarly good looks had changed little since ninth grade, when she grew four inches over one snowy winter. She did not like feeling assessed.

"Oh, I'm Cy, by the way." He offered his hand, seemingly embarrassed at forgetting to introduce himself. He had long, gentle fingers.

"Lydia." She shook his hand. Her voice sounded more imperious than she'd intended.

"That's it! Of course! Lydia Warren!" He clapped. "Don't you remember? We were supposed to have an affair!"

"Excuse me?"

"Yes. We took a class in seventh grade: Marriage and Family. You got paired with that overdeveloped kid the football coach at Southeastern had been eyeing since grade school. I was matched with Angie Bynum. Remember her? She wore the tightest sweaters in class—not that I noticed—and used to tell the non-Catholics they were going to hell. We made a secret agreement. To get out of our bad marriages, we promised to run off together."

Lydia looked closely at him. She could hardly believe that it was Cyrus Modine—Cy, as he was calling himself now. She had not forgotten this boy who liked to inform his classmates at Townsend Middle School that he'd been named after the founder of the Persian Empire. He was popular and outgoing and Lydia had been drawn to his confidence, which seemed to spring from a sense of safety in the world.

It was true. They had made a pact to run off together, leave their unhappy classroom-arranged marriages. Lydia's husband, the monosyllabic Newt McArdle, was, at thirteen, well on his way to a life of slumping at bar rails and complaining about the tyranny of women. Their teacher, Mrs. Friendly, who did not live up to her name, had assigned the couple to imaginary jobs—Lydia was a part-time dental assistant; Newt, a factory worker. But the ill-matched pair always argued about their budget. When Mrs. Friendly told them that their make-believe five-year-old daughter had fallen off a slide and broken her arm, Newt objected to Lydia's offer to pay half of the medical expenses. He'd had it up to his neck with his wife earning a salary and told Mrs. Friendly that Lydia was too bossy to be a dental assistant—any dentist in his right mind would fire her without severance. Mrs. Friendly did not much care for Lydia, whose reticence came off as judgmental, so she took this opportunity to reduce Lydia's hours at the dental office from three days a week to one, then announced to the class that any recalcitrance would result in a poor grade. "In marriage and family, life is not always fair," she advised. "We should be wise to brace ourselves for the frequent storms of disappointment."

Word had gotten around that all was not well with the union of Lydia and Newt. And perhaps because Cyrus was having his own marital difficulties with the proselytizing Angie Bynum, he raised his hand in class one day and said that as regional manager at Parke-Davis he was looking for an assistant, preferably someone in pharmaceuticals. "My ideal candidate," he said, "would be Lydia Warren. I'd like to offer a part-time position, with benefits to cover her daughter's injury."

Mrs. Friendly, like most women, had a soft spot for Cyrus, but she squashed the hire outright. "That's a generous offer," she said. "But I make the rules."

Over the next weeks and months this bright, outrageous boy would talk about his proposition: "If you had come to work with me, we would have been more than co-workers." She couldn't tell if he was joking. The slight turn at his mouth could have gone either way. "That's what happens to people who aren't happy at home. They have affairs. Maybe we should have an affair." But the school year ended too quickly. Lydia received a B in the class, her lowest grade before or since. Not that it weighed on her mind. She knew that she'd gained her first admirer, and all summer long she thought of little else but Cyrus Modine.

Then, in August, out of the blue, her father announced that the family was moving, and not just from Indian Village and the Townsend school district but clear out of east Detroit to a far north suburb. She and Cyrus lost touch completely—no letters, no phone calls. Lydia did not have the nerve to tell him she had left, let alone how she felt, and chose instead to mope around their spacious new house, her memory of Cy expanding into myth.

She hadn't seen him since 1954. The following year James Dean crashed his Porsche Spyder on a winding Southern California road, colliding with a college kid named Donald Turnupseed. In Lydia's mind, James Dean and Cyrus Modine had developed a similar radiance: the treasured ideal, the eternal boy. In high school Lydia had dated a couple of feeble-eyed strivers who could have easily been Donald Turnupseed. And at the diner she wondered if Cy could bring back the figure in the Porsche, his racing number 31 painted on the hood—if he could still be the person that she had romanticized. Or would he be like Donald Turnupseed, an ordinary student who drives on while the hero swerves into the firmament?

In the booth at the Brown Jug she said, "Yes, I remember you." And though she hadn't meant to sound insulting, added, "You certainly look different."

She had not expected to see him ever again. He had been an image in her mind for so long, and even now as she watched him pull at his beard, saying, "Oh, this thing; I only just started growing it"—she had a sinking feeling that between Cyrus and Cy, between her memory of that boy and what she saw of this man standing before her, between then and now, a light had gone out.

"You look terrific," he said.

Lydia could only smile.

"Last I heard, you had moved to Bloomfield Hills."

"Farmington Hills, actually. It wasn't my choice, believe me. My parents were tired of the city. But here we are, both at Michigan."

"Off the waitlist for me."

"What's your major?"

"Haven't decided that yet."

Tess took a few dollars from her purse, placed the money on the table and excused herself. "I should be getting back to the library," she said.

Cy quickly replaced her in the booth, as if by tacit arrangement, and so began more than thirty years of Cy and Lydia sitting across a table from each other.

Their shared history had gone beyond the youthful flirtation that Lydia had sanctified. Her father had worked for the great automobile designer Harley Earl and had scorned the unions. Cy's dad was a line foreman at Chrysler and an active member of the United Auto Workers. Lydia grew up in a five-bedroom Victorian on the nicest street in Indian Village. Cy lived alone with his father in a bungalow two blocks from the Jefferson assembly plant, where Kurt Modine worked his entire career. Still, the conversation in both households, particularly in the 1950s—the age of the dream machines—had always centered on cars. The look of them, their parts, wheelbase, and horsepower. How to improve on last year's model or keep workers on the line happy and efficient.

And though Cy seemed to have lost his sureness, his luminescence somewhere along the way, he did still share those memories. Lydia believed in the past so strongly that later when she realized he wasn't really the same person that she had remembered, she convinced herself that the myth could sustain her. For Cy's part, he seemed only too happy to settle down, to ground himself in this one certainty. Lydia's mother had resisted the match. She didn't want her only child to commit to a man straight out of college, as she had done, tying herself down and giving up her own future. But Ginny Warren's resistance only added urgency to Lydia's desire to get married, and right away. It wasn't long before Ginny conceded; as soon as she got to know Cy, she fell for him, too. He and Lydia joked that at last they could make good on their long-standing promise of an extramarital affair. When Cy asked Lydia to marry him, in front of an abandoned lighthouse on St. Clair Flats, he said, "It's time to take the 'extra' out of our extramarital affair, don't you think?"

She recalled how throughout their engagement they had lived apart at their parents' houses in metro Detroit. Lydia got a research job in the city's development office and Cy delivered sports cars for a custom builder whom his father knew. At their wedding, downtown in the ballroom of the old Book-Cadillac Hotel, she wore white gloves and a gown with a fifteen-foot train. Of the two hundred and fifty guests, only fifty were from the groom's side, a fact that did not bother Lydia until after the honeymoon when she was writing thank-you cards and the imbalance finally became clear. Cy shrugged it off, said it hardly mattered.

Now, driving down South University in Ann Arbor, she decided on this day of Cy's second wedding that she might as well have a ceremonial meal—French toast, of course—at their old rendezvous, the Brown Jug.

On a certain level, Lydia wondered if she had ever given Cy a chance. In her mind she had married her adolescent sweetheart, not the person he had become. He had worked his way through college as an errand runner and a handyman, and in Evanston, while Lydia took a degree at Northwestern in Urban and Regional Planning, they lived rent-free in the building where Cy was superintendent. He knew how to field a complaint, smooth things over, keep the engines running for a while. It seemed he could learn to do anything, and though Lydia admired his flexibility, his openness, his willingness to adapt, these same characteristics confounded her. For him a job was a job, and a passion was something else entirely. Try as he might, he could never bring the two together. So he pursued his shifting passions with a fervor that left Lydia feeling isolated. And somewhere in those many years, she stopped believing that Cy's protean nature and her own desire for permanence could ever make an ideal complement.

Funny, how in the Marriage and Family scenario that had started her infatuation at school, she would have been the other woman. The idea of Lydia in such an arrangement was ridiculous, of course. But what did it matter? Lydia had been playing make-believe, when Cy, even now, was marrying a real-life other woman.

She parked in front of the Brown Jug, dug into her purse, and fed the meter two quarters.

The restaurant's door was locked. Taped to it was a message:

The Brown Jug, family-owned and operated since 1938, is closed for renovations. Please accept our apologies and check back with us in the fall.

—The Management

Lydia peered into the darkened space. The booths were piled up like firewood, the checkered floor covered in dust. All of the pictures had been removed from the walls, exposing the bright yellow paint that lay beneath the layers of bacon grease and cigarette smoke.

She got back into the car and sat there, her hands on the

wheel, not knowing what to make of this. Was she on the wrong end of some elaborate joke?

She started up the car, the engine sputtering for a moment before it settled into a steady whir. She turned around on South University and drove back in the direction she'd come from — past the stacks and the Union, the co-op on Hill Street, and Davy's old house.

Just beyond a garden store on the road out of Ann Arbor, the steering wheel of the Ford Escort began to tighten up. She pressed the gas pedal, but the car wouldn't accelerate. Coasting through a yellow light, she put on her hazards, and wrenched the car into the nearby Uncle Ed's Oil Shoppe, where it came to a stop a few feet short of the garage.

Lydia watched as the needle on the battery gauge went from normal to dead in a matter of seconds. She turned the ignition. Nothing. She pumped the gas and tried again. Still, the engine would not turn over.

She pounded the steering wheel. "Goddammit!" she yelled.

She cursed the car, the restaurant, everything that seemed to be closing down on her today. Jessica had always said that something like this would happen: her mother abandoned in the old car, far from home.

4

JESSICA FELT responsible for the Spiveys, but Casper hardly needed another backseat driver. He couldn't go a block without M.J.'s scolding him for driving too fast, too slow, too carelessly, too cautiously. "Keep your eyes on the road" was her refrain now echoing in Jessica's head as Casper parked the car. But the trip had gone without incident, and now the three of them stepped out of the Lincoln in the back lot of the Kirk in the Hills, a Scottish Presbyterian church. Davy parked his father's Infiniti and came over to lend a hand. Casper leaned on the side of the car. "Gotta stretch the legs. Ellen warned me it's going to be a long service."

"I wouldn't worry too much," Davy assured him. "My dad's not big on religion."

"Neither are we." Casper stretched his right leg behind him, then the left, bouncing slightly. "So what are we doing at this church, I'd like to ask?"

"My husband is spectacularly out of it," M.J. said. "We are at this church because your father and our daughter have had a recent rebirth. This is something couples like to do to erase any evidence of a former life. Ellen is celebrating her Scottish heritage—Casper is, after all, about an eighth Scottish." She turned toward Jessica and Davy. "As for your dad, I don't know. But God bless them both, I say. Live and let live—that's the Spivey credo."

Davy gave Jessica a quick glance. "Well, it's quite a place," he said, as they made their way toward the imposing Gothic church. It had spires and gabled arches, elaborate traceries and stained glass windows, with gargoyles looking down along the parapets. "I'd say it was built in the thirteenth century if it weren't so new and set beside a man-made lake in Bloomfield Hills."

"Kinda freaky," Jessica said. She'd decided to put a good face on the day, but she did wonder about her father's recent turn toward organized religion. When they were young he'd made a few overtures, insisting on a Sunday service or two beyond the usual obligations of Easter and Christmas, but his devotion never lasted long. She couldn't help feeling it was a shame on such a cloudless day to celebrate a marriage inside this old-fashioned, somber-looking place.

"I know where we are." M.J. stopped at a plaque on the outside wall. "This is Colonel George's house of worship. Edwin George. He's the lawnmower man."

"Where would we be without him?" Casper ran his hand along the limestone façade as they approached the partly opened red doors that led to the sanctuary.

"Up to our ears in grass," M.J. said. "Covered in crickets and beetles, that's where. Pay your respects, my dears. The man who invented the lawnmower also bankrolled this church."

Ivan appeared at the sanctuary doors and stepped into the sunshine. "So what connection can we make between this wedding and lawnmowers? I think it means that the grass is always greener on the other side of the highway."

"Ivan," Jessica scolded.

He turned to the Spiveys. "May I take you in?"

"With pleasure." M.J. grabbed his arm and they walked into the entryway.

When he returned from escorting them to the room where Ellen waited with her bridesmaids, Jessica pinched his arm. "Try not to be an ass today," she whispered.

"Yeah, go easy on those two," Davy said. "Looks like they don't want to be here any more than we do."

Ivan fiddled with a pocket watch. "See my best man's gift?" He held it out. "Pretty useful, huh?"

"Let's try to get through this without a scene," Jessica said. "As for me, I'm taking a deep breath." She inhaled the scent of roses on the trellis around the church door. "Breathe in, breathe out. Repeat after me. All dharmas are contained in this mantra: *Om Mani Padme Hum.*"

"Oh, lordy," Ivan said.

"The mantra of the Beloved Chenresig radiates the whole Universe!" She raised her hands to the sky, drawing the gaze of a pack of widowers who were making their way up from the parking lot.

Her mantra was a private mockery of her ex-boyfriend, Blane, known in the family as the ersatz Buddhist. Jessica had gone to Oregon in the first place because of him. How else to explain getting picked up by a stranger at the Royal Oak Starbucks, then two weeks later following him clear across the country? "It's not like you to hitch up with a spiritualist playboy," Lydia had said, in one of their touchier phone calls. "We're not in the sixties anymore. You shouldn't put a lot of faith in someone who lives out of his van." Jessica had slammed down the phone that time, but eight months later, she found herself stuck with a lease and a rowdy German shepherd/collie mix when Blane was called away to a monastery in southern New Mexico: *The water is all wrong, baby. I need to go to the desert for a while.*

"So, how is the ersatz Buddhist?" Davy leaned against the railing outside the church door.

"I wouldn't know." Jessica sighed.

"You don't hear from him?"

"Every once in a while. Sometimes the dog will look out the

window wondering where his daddy is. I think Bedlam wants him back more than I do," she said, though part of her wished that Blane had joined her here today, with his amulets and ponytail. That would give the old folks something to talk about — Blane gazing soulfully into their eyes.

As the widowers arrived at the door, Ivan asked if they'd like an escort.

"Ah, we'll have our escort soon enough," one of them replied and the others laughed.

"Jesus," Jessica said as the widowers went inside. She turned to Davy. "So, what time is it getting to be? I guess we should go in, too."

He checked his watch. "We've got a few minutes."

"What's going on with you? You've been quiet since yesterday."

"You don't want to know," he said. "Talk about the brink of death. We thought we had a big investor at work, but he just bailed on us. What can I say? We're barely hanging on." After finishing college in Ann Arbor two years ago, Davy had moved to Chicago to work for an old housemate, Sanjay Patel. The company, Lowball.com, was a regional variation of *Consumer Reports* that relied on a subscription service. At this point, Davy explained, Lowball could collapse or be bought at any moment. Sanjay said that if a buyer turned up, the investors would make a nice windfall, but if the venture tanked, much more than their months of nonstop work would be sacrificed. When the business had just started, Davy persuaded his girlfriend, Teresa, to invest in the company half of the eighty thousand dollars she'd inherited from her mother's estate.

"Now," Davy said, "not a day goes by when I'm not thinking of some way to give it back." In two whirlwind years the startup had become their entire lives, the bond that could strangle them or hold them together for good.

No wonder Teresa had stayed in Chicago this weekend, Jessica thought. Davy claimed that her allergies were acting up, but she probably just needed a break from the drama.

"So what about you?" he asked. "I hear you've found a new, edgier Blane."

"Yeah," Ivan added. "Mom's nervous about this one, Jess. He's some kind of anarchist, right?"

Ivan's blind support of their mother's every opinion irritated her. "Mom thinks he's an anarchist. He's just wiry and a little mean-looking, that's all." Jessica smoothed the sleeve of her suit jacket. "Do you really think Lady Bird Johnson would be dating an anarchist?"

"Lady Bird Johnson?"

"My suit. It's mint green. It's very, I don't know, First Lady-ish." She was about to say that she wasn't dating an anarchist at all, that she was only casually seeing an androgynously handsome melancholic who had come into the store one day to buy tofu and ginger candies. He had returned wearing revolutionist T-shirts: one with Che Guevara holding a machine gun, another with a Nike swoosh that looked like a dagger dripping blood. She told her mother that she'd met an anarchist, and Lydia grew alarmed. Later, when Jessica started seeing him— "Void," he called himself—he turned out to be a pussycat. But she hadn't bothered to clarify this with her mother, having recently made a pact with herself to keep some semblance of a private life.

"So your boyfriend doesn't trust the government?" Ivan pressed.

"Did I say that?" She didn't need to get into this, and she certainly wasn't going to debate politics with Ivan in the middle of her father's wedding. He had always been a quivering Jell-O of sentimentality when it came to baseball, apple pie, Chevrolet, and the U.S. government. Like their grandfather, Ivan's hero and paragon who had been a car designer at GM, Jessica's older brother had no time for people who held what he considered to be extreme beliefs.

"I don't know if it's healthy to choose men according to how much Mom will disapprove of them." Ivan twisted his cuff links. "Isn't that a little juvenile?"

"Listen—" Jessica began. She wasn't about to suffer collateral damage from Ivan's fury at their father.

Davy stepped in. "Come on, people." He cupped the back of his brother's neck with his hand, a playful half nelson. "It's time to go in anyway."

As they walked inside another group of guests appeared. Davy and Jessica made nice for the new arrivals, and Ivan offered to help them to their seats. When he left Davy whispered, "You must be looking for some real fireworks today. Why are you stirring him up?"

"He's stirring himself up. I was just talking about this guy who I'm not even dating, and for no good reason he got his knickers in a twist."

"Still, your timing could be better. You're not worried about the best man's toast?"

"What about it?"

"Ivan's not good when he gets all riled up. You know that, Jess."

A few latecomers gathered in the entryway. Ivan came back up the aisle. "Five minutes until the service. Whatever's available, folks," he said to the guests filing in. "And you guys—" He turned to his siblings. "We're about to get started. You should find a seat." He disappeared to look for the minister.

Davy took Jessica's hand as they walked toward the front of the sanctuary. Scanning the room, she noticed that her father's side was badly outnumbered. Apparently, he kept in no better touch with his friends than he did with his children.

Soon after they were seated, the organist began the processional. Jessica and Davy watched from the front row as M.J. walked in alone, followed by Ellen's bridesmaids—a college friend and a coworker from the phone company. They were not in lavender, as Cy had promised, but in dresses a shade of green similar to Jessica's suit. She wondered whether to feel flattered or annoyed.

Ivan and Gisele, the maid of honor who had flown in from Phoenix for the occasion, were next down the aisle. Ivan took

46

his place at the front of the church, and Gisele joined the bridesmaids.

As they waited for the bride and groom to appear, Jessica watched Ivan. At the rehearsal dinner, he had commented on Gisele's good looks—blond, willowy, small-featured, very much his type—and Davy had teased him for showing an interest in Ellen's best friend. Ivan grew defensive, saying it would be too trashy-talk-show to go after a friend of his father's wife. Now, however, Jessica caught him smiling at Gisele, who seemed to reciprocate, glancing down shyly at her bouquet, then up again. Maybe, Jessica hoped, this would be just the distraction her brother needed to calm down and behave for the rest of the afternoon.

Cy appeared suddenly at the sanctuary door, looking a bit florid and pinched in his tuxedo. It occurred to Jessica now that this wedding marked a pivotal moment in their family history. After this, they would go in one of two directions: together, or each alone.

Unlike the rest of her family, Jessica was almost happy to see her father gaining a new life apart from them. She knew that feeling of wanting her own life, knew also the frustration of not yet having a defining purpose. Her mother had always had a purpose—her work, her family. In Lydia's perfect world, the Modines would be one contiguous group, like a prairie township or an island monarchy. Not that Jessica opposed the idea of a big noisy family, but when she thought about having children she pictured an open door through which they could come and go as they pleased—without the emotional whipcord attached. She refused to engage her mother on this subject, because Lydia's way invariably won. How could she not win, when every conversation took place in her domain, always with the door closed? Her mother liked to talk about her front-porch policy, but in fact she wasn't nearly as open as she let on. Her place, her way prevailed.

Just once, Jessica wanted to hear her mother say: "Pick a weekend. I'd love to come out and see you in Oregon." But such a gesture was out of the question. Like the secluded queen who rarely ventures beyond her territory because off the palace grounds she's merely a traveler, Lydia could never concede her authority. It was no wonder she refused to fly. Out of sheer terror at the prospect (*of crashing*, she would say; *of giving up control*, Jessica would reply), Lydia had not stepped on an airplane in fifteen years. So, *together as a family* could only mean here, in Detroit, same as it ever was.

Everyone in the church now turned to watch Ellen and Casper walk arm in arm down the aisle. She wore a simple white A-line dress with cap sleeves and pearl beading around the neckline. With her fingertip-length veil she looked like another showcase for the relentless bridal juggernaut. At the end of the aisle, Casper kissed his daughter lightly on the cheek and, grabbing the side of the front pew, made his way toward his seat. Cy stepped forward, his clean-shaven face a bloom of scarlet, to claim his bride.

By high school, when most of Jessica's friends' parents were divorced, she would feel a thrill whenever she saw Cy and Lydia sitting together in the stands at her basketball games. Her family did not live in a large house. She and her brothers did not have their own cars. And unlike most families in Jessica's comfortable neighborhood, the Modines were coupon clippers, solidly middle class. But her parents did have a long marriage, and for Jessica, seeing them together, even in their formal, perfunctory way, had made up for other absences. Had they divorced years earlier, she might not have completely recovered, but now she felt it was too late to raise a protest, when she was supposed to be, at twenty-seven, all grown up.

A choirboy sang "O Perfect Love, All Human Thought Transcending." Gisele followed with a Rilke poem with the words "You, Beloved, who are all / the gardens I have ever gazed at." But instead of celebrating conjugal joy, the poem seemed more about an ethereal kind of love that was always out of reach. Reverend MacPherson followed Gisele's reading with a twenty-minute sermon about Cy and Ellen's commitment to the Kirk in the Hills, a place that before this weekend Jessica had never heard her father mention.

"I confess I did not know the bride and groom well when they began planning this wedding, but in a short time they have made themselves active members of our church community." He was a young minister, probably in his late thirties, with prematurely gray hair and small, accidentally hip glasses, over the top of which he would survey the congregation. In his sermon he attempted to explain the apostle Paul's unraveling of the "great mystery" of marriage:

"If the church is Christ's body and by faith a person is joined to Christ, thus a person becomes one with all believers. Christ is the husband and the church is the bride and conversion is an act of betrothal. Perhaps you're asking yourselves, 'Why wouldn't Christ be jealous of a new husband coming to take his bride?'" The young minister paused and looked up from the pulpit. "Ah, but jealousy is not a factor here, because God created human marriage out of the pattern of Christ's relation to the church, not the other way around." He smiled, as if pleased with himself for solving a riddle. "Husband and wife become one flesh just as Christ and the church become one body."

Jessica's thoughts swam in this eddy of language, as she remembered why she had avoided Christianity all these years.

"Cy and Ellen are one flesh in the church, married together and to Christ. The dedication they have shown to our mission here at the Kirk in the Hills augurs well, indeed, for the devotion they will have to each other from this day forward."

When Reverend MacPherson's oration came to its end, an acolyte brought out a stool and a guitar. To Jessica's surprise, Cy sat on the stool, ducked under the guitar strap, and began to play. This performance had not been discussed at the rehearsal, nor was it in the program, and the look on Ellen's face—a blend of fear, disapproval, and practiced good sportsmanship—suggested that Cy had put up a real fight for his moment onstage. Now he was singing:

Round and round the world I go,
the more I see the more I know.
You'll be traveling by my side,
come on, let's take the ride.

When I weary and times get tough,
you'll be seeing me through the rough.
We'll travel by each other's side,
come along, let's take the ride.

Jessica refused to catch her brothers' reaction, and focused instead on a little boy in the second row who made a face as if he'd tasted something sour. Cy played the guitar better than Jessica had expected, though the song required only three chords and a rudimentary strumming pattern. Her father had a decent voice, but he sang about two octaves higher than his natural baritone.

When the ordeal was finally over and Cy returned to his place for the ring ceremony, Jessica braved a glance at Ivan. Any thoughts of Gisele seemed to have drained from his face, leaving him pale.

Reverend MacPherson took his place between the bride and groom and an elaborate ring ceremony followed, with more prayers, off-the-cuff sermonizing, and the lighting of a unity candle. Jessica fast-forwarded to the moment when the wedding guests would leave the church and the acolyte would blow out that candle. What good was a symbol, she thought, when it was no more permanent than an inch of wax?

"You may now kiss the bride," Reverend MacPherson announced triumphantly, and Cy smushed his lips with Ellen's —a nervous kiss that had about it a slight tinge of embarrassment.

Soon the organist was playing "Let There Be Love Shared Among Us," and Cy and Ellen were walking up the aisle, joined in holy matrimony.

◆ ◆ ◆

Once outside, Jessica squinted in the bright sunshine. The bride and groom were down by the lake, talking to the wedding photographer. Ivan and Davy stood at the bottom of the church steps bending their legs.

"Good Lord," Davy said. "Could that have been any longer?"

"So, what's next?" Jessica asked. "Now that the tribe of Spivey-Modine has been officially launched."

"Pictures," Ivan muttered. "Then you're on Casper and M.J. detail. As for me, I've got to polish up my speech."

"Be nice." Jessica squeezed his shoulder.

Gisele, who walked arm in arm with Casper Spivey, joined them while M.J. trailed behind looking beleaguered.

"Excuse me for a second." Davy pulled a cell phone out of his jacket. "I should probably call Teresa. But don't let them do photos without me."

"So what did you kids think?" Casper asked, as Davy walked off.

"I think it's a good day to break my five o'clock rule." M.J. checked her watch. "A two o'clock Scotch would go down nicely today. Fortunately—" She gestured toward Casper. "I've got my designated driver."

Casper and Jessica laughed.

"Don't you worry about that," Gisele said, sounding patronizing. "We've arranged some drivers for you."

"Oh, thank you, dearest," M.J. replied, and winked at Jessica.

Reverend MacPherson came up to them then, mopping his forehead with a handkerchief, and shook each person's hand. "So happy you could come," he said, with his air of pleasant all-knowingness.

"Can I borrow you two for a moment?" He turned to Ivan and Gisele. "Excuse us, please."

"That minister is a horse's ass, but God bless him." M.J. started toward the lakeside, where people were gathering for pictures. She steered Casper in front of her. "What is it about the clergy, the police, and anyone who wears a uniform? You can't trust their motives."

Jessica followed along. "So, I've been wondering. I hope you won't take this the wrong way, but you don't seem especially thrilled about the wedding."

M.J. stopped and turned so she could look Jessica in the eye. "I admire your asking. But I'm sworn to secrecy, dear." She kissed Jessica on each cheek. "You'll understand sooner than you'd wish why a mother might have mixed feelings on a day like this."

5

AN OVERPOWERING SMELL of rubber and engine oil floated over from Uncle Ed's garage as Lydia stepped out of the Escort. She slammed the door shut, trying to assure herself that the car was fixable. Her focus had always been on the history of automobiles, not the intricacies of their engines.

She walked into the first open bay of the garage, and a crew of mechanics looked up, surprised. Over the loud *tock-tock* of an oil gun counting its measure, she explained how the wheel had tightened up, how the gauge had fallen so quickly.

"Sounds like an alternator problem," offered one guy in a shirt with cut-off sleeves. A toothpick moved in his mouth as he talked.

"Nah, it's the battery," shouted another.

Soon the whole team came outside to look under the hood of the Escort, each giving the engine a cursory once over.

"It may seem like the battery, but that's what happens when the alternator's shot," said the one with the toothpick.

"I'll give you four hundred dollars for it," came a voice from the pit. "The repairs on that thing will be more than it's worth."

The manager had come out to take a look, too. He was

someone who looked older than his years, Lydia guessed. His face was leathery, his hair smoothed back. He closed the Escort's hood and said, "Saturdays get busy around here. Not much we can do today. But feel free to use the phone."

In his office, he flipped through the yellow pages and slid his blackened fingers down to the listing of a nearby towing service. "This guy's the quickest in town—your only bet, really, if you want to get that thing on the road today." He left Lydia in the office and went back to the garage.

She began to sit down on a padded stool, but when she put her hand on the chair, her fingers came up smeared with grease. No paper towels or tissue in sight; the whole place teemed with dirt. Frustrated, she wiped her fingers on her gray skirt, leaving two black lines on her hip, like mini tire tracks angling off.

"Of course," Lydia said to herself, as an answering machine picked up at the towing service. She left her name and the number at Uncle Ed's, displayed in large brown type on a sign in front of her. She turned back to the phone book and began calling other towing services. No one had a truck available. The estimated wait was several hours. It was turning out to be, quite possibly, the longest day of her life.

She went outside and leaned against the Escort. The heat of the asphalt mingled with the warm breeze of cars rushing by on Washtenaw Avenue. The digital clock at the Comerica across the street read 1:55. Nearly an hour into the wedding.

There in front of her, almost beckoning across the four-lane road, was an Arby's. She hadn't eaten fast food in years, but on this day she suddenly craved it. She opened the front door of the car, slid her laptop under the passenger seat, and locked up. Then she hurried across Washtenaw, holding up the hem of her skirt.

Once inside, she ordered a large roast beef sandwich, curly fries, and, though it was the last thing she needed right now, a large cup of coffee.

"Do you want the horsey sauce or the Arby's sauce with that?" the pixyish woman behind the counter asked.

"What do you mean 'horsey' sauce?" Lydia pulled a five-dollar bill from her wallet.

"It's like horseradish, ma'am."

"Fine," Lydia said. "I'll have that." And before long she was sitting at a table by the front window, a paper napkin spread out on her lap. She ate some French fries and took a big bite of her roast beef sandwich. In front of the restaurant a cartoonish Arby's cowboy hat stood two stories tall, outlined with lights.

She looked down at her lunch. Her eyes welled up and the tears came. Maybe she *was* a pathetic, lonely person. Maybe Jessica was right: Lydia expected too much of her family; her hopes were absurdly unrealistic. How else to explain how thirty-three years of marriage had ended here, with her eating a sandwich, soggy with horsey sauce, while her children were celebrating their father's new life.

Pull it together, she thought to herself. She patted her eyes with the stiff napkins and got up to toss out the leftovers. In the bathroom, she splashed cold water on her face, then soaped a paper towel to clean the grease tracks off her skirt. But the stains smeared, of course—the skirt was probably ruined.

Davy had given her his cell phone number this morning, and though she'd promised herself she wouldn't use it, this did qualify as an emergency. She dug in her purse and found the slip of paper. She figured the service would have to be over by now. At the Arby's pay phone, Lydia took a deep breath and dialed.

Davy answered on one ring, his voice cross. "What?"

"There's been a problem," Lydia began.

"Oh, Mom. I'm sorry. I was expecting Teresa. She's been driving me nuts."

"Where are you, honey?"

"You don't want to know," he said. "I'm driving Dad's car to a place in Birmingham called the Casual Cactus. The wedding was interminable, and Dad played a ridiculous song on the guitar."

"He plays guitar?"

"Apparently. And before the reception is over I'm sure he'll wrangle me in for a jam session."

"Where's Jess?"

He hesitated. "Oh, she's in another car. Listen, Mom, how about I call you back? I shouldn't be driving and talking on the cell."

"Actually, I better call you—in about fifteen minutes?"

"Fine," Davy said. "Talk soon."

When Lydia returned to Uncle Ed's, the manager told her that the towing service had called and the guy was available if she buzzed him back within the next fifteen minutes. Lydia thanked him and said she just needed to get something from the glove compartment before calling.

Sitting in the driver's seat of her broken-down Escort, she allowed the minutes to tick by. She wouldn't call the towing service, not until after she had spoken with Davy, she decided. He could save her a lot of money that way. But when Lydia went back to the garage and dialed Davy's cell phone, she got his voice mail. She tried several more times before he finally picked up.

"Hey, Mom. We're just walking in to the reception now. What's going on?" He raised his voice over the noise of a crowd.

This time Lydia did not delay. "My car broke down."

"Jesus. Where are you?"

"Ann Arbor."

"Ann Arbor? What are you doing there?"

"It's a long story." She caught herself. "Research."

"Who is it?" Lydia overheard Jessica asking.

"It's Mom," Davy said, and then Jessica was on the line.

"What's the problem?"

"The car died."

There was a pause, just the din of the party in the background. Then, "Surprise, surprise. How perfect, Mother. What impeccable timing."

Lydia felt her calm slipping. "Is it my fault that the car died, Jessica?"

"I don't believe this."

"Perhaps you'd like to speak with the manager at this lube shop where none of these mechanics know how to fix it."

"You're amazing."

"Don't talk to me that way."

"Here we are, literally walking inside the restaurant to the reception and you call looking for a rescue. I honestly can't believe you sometimes."

"Jessica, I swear to God—"

"Maybe you'd like us to send Dad out there to fetch you."

"That's not funny."

"And you're calling from Ann Arbor. Taking a little drive down memory lane?"

"Forget it. You just go ahead and shower your father with all the affection in the world on his *special day*." She heard her voice crack. "Why am I always expected to make the world perfect for those who can't help themselves?"

"Those who can't help themselves? Look at you. Pulling a stunt like this?"

With that, Lydia slammed down the phone.

Why did her daughter hate her for caring? This morning had been fine. When had things gotten off track? Suit yourself, she thought. She would find her own way home. She had waited for eighteen months to see her kids. For this?

Just then the phone rang. Lydia picked up without thinking. "Mom?"

"Davy, how did you get this number?"

"Caller ID. Listen, I'm sorry about Jess." He was whispering. "She was nearly in an accident on the way over. Her nerves are frayed."

"Is she okay?"

"She's fine."

"What happened?"

"I'll tell you later," he said.

"Davy?" She could hear the panic in her voice, hoped he wouldn't notice.

"I'm telling you she's fine, Mom. Has someone come to tow the car?"

"I'm having a terrible time with that."

"Why don't you not worry about the car for now. We'll be at the reception until six at the latest. Then we can come and get you."

"I'll be okay," Lydia said. She was feeling better already. She hadn't meant to get upset with Jessica. It wasn't her fault that her father was remarrying.

"No, we'll pick you up. I'm so sorry this happened." Davy's phone was breaking up. "You'll have to take a cab to a coffee shop or have a glass of wine at the Earle."

Lydia knew that the last thing she wanted to do today was return to Ann Arbor. "I'll be at the car museum in Ypsi," she decided all of a sudden. It pleased her to think that she might actually be able to salvage this day.

"If you go anywhere else, I'll leave the cell phone on buzz." And with that, Davy hung up.

So her kids were going to pull through, after all. Cheered by this thought, Lydia retrieved her laptop, called a cab, and got the okay from the manager at Uncle Ed's to leave her car overnight. "We'll deal with it by the beginning of the week, I promise," she told him.

"Don't forget Marty's standing offer," the manager reminded her. "Four hundred bucks—no fuss, no muss."

Lydia remembered how, a few weeks after Cy had taken the job with Bobby Szoradi Ford more than fifteen years ago, Cy had surprised her with the Escort. "It's about time you switched from Chevy to Ford," he'd said. "I know it's not an LTD or a Lincoln, but I got a great deal and it's a fine little car."

Lydia had never been sentimental about the Escort. It was a lousy old tin can, as her kids were quick to remind her. But perhaps, she thought now, holding on to the car had meant more to her than she'd realized.

"Thanks for everything," Lydia said to the manager as the cab pulled up. "I'll think about that offer."

It was in the cab, riding to Ypsilanti, that Lydia finally admitted it to herself: Cy was never coming back. Even if he wanted to return, she realized, there would no longer be a place for him. They had given what they could to each other. And now Lydia had to focus on getting back on track. Her children were coming to pick her up, and she had a few hours to work, to lose herself in something she knew well—her research, after all.

Her history with Cy may have already been written. But she had another story—a hundred years of the car in America— that she knew she could study and, unlike the other, neatly revise.

6

THE CASUAL CACTUS was a Southwestern restaurant with dream catchers, Navajo blankets, and commercial art prints of desert monuments hanging on the walls. Jessica stood just inside the reception room, cross-examining her brother about his phone call. "You were talking to Mom, weren't you? I hope you didn't promise to drive out to get her. I wouldn't be surprised if she put peanut butter in the gas tank."

"Don't be so harsh, Jess. How is she going to get home?"

"I don't know. It's her problem. We've been telling her to junk that car for years." A waitress walked by, offering them a platter of grilled shrimp and red pepper skewers. Jessica helped herself to one. "You probably apologized for me, didn't you? What did you tell her? That I was having a terrible time at the wedding and not to take it personally? You always make up excuses so she feels better."

"I said it didn't help your nerves that you've been driving with the Spiveys."

Jessica pointed the skewer at her brother. "Don't blame the Spiveys. That last trip was a model in precision tandem driving. Mom is really going for it this time. She's probably wearing her wedding dress from 1965, expecting Dad to swoop into town, take her home, and start the whole dream over again."

Davy gave a tired sigh. "Come on, Jess. You've got to stop projecting everything on Mom. We see her about twice a year."

"Projecting? Don't get pop-psychy on me." Jessica folded the shrimp tail into a chili-pepper-printed napkin.

"I'm going to get a drink, and I'd highly recommend that you do the same."

While Davy went off to the bar, Jessica dropped the napkin into an empty wineglass on a side table and retreated to a quiet corner where she could scan the room. The wedding crowd seemed right at home in this *Love Boat* version of a Santa Fe restaurant. The wine, champagne, and margaritas were going around, and as people began to find their seats, the clubby atmosphere of the night before descended once again. A whoop went up as Ellen and Cy entered the room under a faux-adobe arch, then took their places at the front table alongside Gisele and the bridesmaids.

Jessica joined Davy at the next table over with Ivan and the Spiveys, just to the side of the evening's entertainment, a one-man-karaoke show called the Rick Stoker Experience. When Jessica sat down, Rick Stoker reached over, flashed a smile, and handed her his business card: *When a Band's Too Big and a DJ's Just Too Small.*

Davy leaned toward Jessica and whispered, "Somebody likes you."

"Just what I need. A swinging, singing DJ."

Rick introduced Mr. and Mrs. Spivey-Modine and cued up the first dance, which Jessica recognized with a cringe as Phil Collins's cover of "Groovy Kind of Love." As the couple swayed, Ellen pulled her husband toward her—no doubt to tie up his feet and hands, his knees and elbows. Cy had a habit of snapping his fingers when he danced, and at more than one party, Jessica had seen him trotting out strange moves as well—hands on hips, karate chop, wrist over wrist. Ellen was no fool, Jessica thought as she watched them dance close and slow. The song moved into its last bars, and the guests streamed onto the floor. Ellen helped her father to his feet, and Casper led her in a series of steps. No doubt sensing his audience, Rick sang Dean Martin's "Memories Are Made of This," Sinatra's "The Way You Look Tonight," then closed with Air Supply's "Two Less Lonely People in the World."

Casper bowed to the crowd's applause, then followed M.J. around the room to greet their friends.

After the Rick Stoker Experience turned off his microphone and left a CD of dinner music playing, Ivan said, "That was pure Velveeta."

"Are you disrespecting my man?" Jessica asked. "He's got a velvety voice, and that's not all."

A waiter brought their dinner plates: rolled chicken breast and a square of salmon; Mexican rice garnished with pico de gallo. "He's the perfect singer for Dad—a mimic, a follower, someone who buys the whole package, then claims that he invented it." Ivan took a fork and punctured the top of his chicken. A stuffing of pepper-jack cheese oozed from either side.

"That sounds like the ideal consumer." Davy ran his finger over an ear of dried corn, part of the table's centerpiece. "Make the consumer believe that the product was designed especially for him—so much so that he feels like he created it."

"Right," Jessica egged him on. She could tell that Davy was looking for a way to steer their brother off the subject of Cy.

"Bring the consumer into the fold—that's the trick," Davy continued. "Teresa and I were just arguing about that. Did I tell you she's come to work for us?"

"I thought she had been." Jessica took a bite of the salmon. Overcooked, of course.

"She's full-time now."

"That's great," Jessica said, though she was thinking it was a terrible idea.

"I wouldn't say great, exactly. We were cramped before—five hundred square feet in Lakeview. Now Sanjay's put us in the same office at work. We're on each other like sweat." He paused to pick at his meal. "Every day I wonder what I've gotten myself into."

"What are you talking about?" Ivan said. "You're a change insurgent. They'll be writing about you in fifty years."

"What's a change insurgent?" Jessica asked.

"Ask Davy—he's the dot-com survivor. I'm just the man in the gray flannel suit. Actually, I have no idea what a change insurgent is," Ivan said, then suddenly got up. "I have to go work on my speech."

After Ivan left, Jessica turned to Davy, whose fork was raised. "He must be freaking out about that toast."

"Well, anyway," Davy said. "About Lowball—basically, Teresa's freaking out, and I can't do anything right. Seems like yesterday we were flush, but today we can't cover payroll. I get quiet and she gets desperate. It's a bad combination."

"But what happened to that buyer? I thought you almost cut a deal."

"We did, too, but the guy was a flake. The fact is we're not selling a product, just information and research. Plus, we've made big promises as the 'lowest of the low.' People expect more than we can give them, which should be the truth right up to the minute. But at the moment we can't even offer that."

Davy continually surprised Jessica. She never would have pictured him talking about profit margins and how to reach the consumer. She had assumed he would stay in Ann Arbor after college, working at Schoolkids Records and picking up gigs in town or around Detroit. He loved recording sounds—creaky doors, truck horns and passing traffic, the Huron River after a thaw. As an undergraduate in the school of music, he had used these recordings to texture his compositions, and ever since high school, he had played drums for local bands.

Jessica's favorite of these was Queen Bee and the Drones, an R & B quintet more progressive than its name implied. Davy played with them his first two years in college before the gospel-trained lead singer of the group grew pregnant with twins. More than a year later, when it became obvious that Queen Bee would not be returning, Davy and the remaining Drones transformed themselves into a rockabilly band: two guitars, drums and a standup bass. Davy renamed the group the 57 Nomads after the beat-up station wagon in the Modine family garage. Jessica didn't much like the music, but Cy was the Nomads' number one fan, never missing a show and even proposing that the group take him on as manager. "They're playing my songs," he liked to say. "I remember when all the guys had pompadours."

Like everything else that was popular in the late nineties, rockabilly appealed to nostalgia, so the Nomads had gotten as many gigs as they could handle, and with a bit of organization could have probably toured. But just as their reputation was growing, Davy abandoned the group, moved to Chicago, and joined the Internet gold rush when nearly all the gold had already been found. Jessica wondered if her brother was not so much drawn to the siren call of wealth as he was unable to deal with his wannabe "manager."

Cy first took an interest in his son's music when Davy was fifteen and playing with his first group, a grunge band called Silent Thunder. They covered Pearl Jam and Nirvana at high school dances and wore the standard uniform of the day: flannel shirts, baggy jeans, and Caterpillar boots. Cy caught them at the Huntington High talent show, and over the next several months began to appear at all of their gigs. Davy would call Jessica in Ann Arbor and wonder out loud why Cy kept showing up, since their father's taste in music tilted toward the easy listening end of the dial. Jessica said some parents were late bloomers. "He's trying to bond with you, that's all. Better late than never." And for a while Davy agreed.

But soon Cy was subscribing to *Rolling Stone, Billboard, Modern Drummer, Entrepreneur,* and *Opportunity World.* He sound-proofed the garage, bought Davy a new drum set for Christmas, and recited over dinner the rags-to-riches stories of bands old and new. Davy, in turn, spent less time around the house. He moved the band's practice sessions from Franklin Street to the lead guitarist's basement. But for his sixteenth birthday, Cy gave him a four-track recorder. He said that if Silent Thunder made a tape, he would fly to L.A. to shop it around.

Even at sixteen, Davy was far more of a realist than his father. "Thanks, Dad," he said. "But we're just a cover band, you know. We're still in high school."

"Look how many groups got their break in high school. Frankie Lymon, the Osmonds. What about Green Day?"

It took the mother of the standup bassist of the 57 Nomads to bring Cy down to earth. At a dance they were chaperoning together, she told him that her son had joined the band for fun. He didn't want to be a rock star, and really, who was Cy kidding with his talk about recording contracts? "The woman tore into me," Cy had told Lydia, who immediately called Jessica at college. "She accused me of being a Svengali. I couldn't believe it. I just wanted to see the band succeed."

When neither Lydia nor Davy could muster a defense of him, Cy got the message, licked his wounds, moved on to new interests. Jessica remembered calling Ivan to give him the full update. "Dad's only out for himself," he'd said. "Quite a paradox, isn't it? He's out for himself, even though he has no self."

Though Jessica understood Ivan's anger at their father, she refused to place all the blame on Cy. That seemed too easy. All of the kids were complicit in allowing his misguided fantasies to continue. But to Jessica, nobody was more responsible than Lydia. *She* set the tone. Without saying anything, she made it clear that the family would not interfere with their father's business. They'd handle his pursuits with politeness and his defeats by looking the other way. Jessica knew she should be furious on Lydia's behalf about the end of the marriage. But in fact, she couldn't help feeling that her mother's approach had been self-serving. Maybe Lydia had *allowed* Cy to stumble, even welcomed his failures as a way to maintain control. Cy was the bad parent; she was the good one. He was the prodigal; she soldiered on. And so she ruled the empire.

As the waiters cleared the tables, Jessica came back to reality.

Rick Stoker tapped her on the shoulder. "Are you ready?" he asked. He picked up the microphone. "And now, ladies and gentlemen, the groom will dance with his daughter."

Before she knew it, Jessica was on her feet, with all eyes upon her, and her father was snapping his fingers, moving his arms back and forth as if drying his back with an invisible towel.

Soon the floor filled up again, and Davy mercifully broke in and danced Jessica back to the table. Between songs, Rick leaned over. "Hey, you're a good dancer."

"Thanks," she said, reaching for her glass of wine.

By the end of the set, Cy had taken off his tux jacket and vest, his back imprinted with a large sweat stain in the shape of a capital I.

Ivan returned, folding his speech into his pocket. M.J. and Casper were finishing their chicken, having arrived late to the meal after making their rounds. Davy leaned across the table and asked Casper if he had written a toast.

"It's all up here." Casper pointed to his head.

"Here would be better." M.J. put her hand over her chest. "But my daughter isn't making that easy. It would have been nice if we'd had some say in this wedding."

Before Jessica could consider M.J.'s comment, the waiters rolled out two cakes: the traditional three-tier white cake with buttercream frosting, and a cake shaped like a cactus, complete with green icing and black candy stipules.

"Why are there two cakes?" Jessica wondered out loud.

"It's a groom's cake," M.J. explained. "Ellen read about it in one of her wedding magazines."

The Rick Stoker Experience lifted his microphone out of its holder, smiled at the crowd and said, "Now the groom would like to make an announcement." He handed the microphone to Cy.

"Thank you, Rick, and thank you all for coming," Cy began. "Is this a great party or what?" He clapped his hands, causing loud thuds in the amplifier. The crowd, well into its cups, replied with a resounding, "*Bravo!*"

"Before we move on to toasts, there's a little secret that Ellen and I want to let you in on. What's the range on this thing?" he asked Rick, pointing to the microphone and beginning to walk around the first table.

Rick gave a thumbs-up.

Cy continued. "Perhaps you're wondering why we decided to hold our wedding at a Scottish church and our reception at a Southwestern restaurant. In fact, I'd like to personally apologize to those of you who had your hearts set on haggis for dinner. Nothing pleases the stomach quite like stomach." He laughed at his own joke and was quickly joined by the inebriated.

Cy stood over Casper Spivey, who glanced up and smiled politely. M.J.'s cheeks looked heavy, her expression flat as a horizon. Cy seemed to enjoy walking around with a microphone. He flicked it between two fingers like a fat cigar. Watching him, Jessica grew apprehensive.

"Maybe you're also wondering why this cake is shaped like a cactus and why the theme of the reception is Desert Southwestern." Cy moved from the front tables toward the middle of the room, touching people on the shoulder, giving a wave here and there. He looked more like Phil Donahue combing the studio audience than Jessica's father, his hair whiter without the beard, his features more bland.

"We chose the Casual Cactus to give the people we love — dear friends and family — a glimpse of the life Ellen and I are about to embark on together." Cy stood at the far side of the room now. "Ellen, honey —" He wandered back toward the wedding cake. "Come give me a hand with this."

Ellen floated toward him, and Jessica began to feel alarmed. She knew they were going to the Grand Canyon for part of their honeymoon, and assumed most of the guests were aware of this, too. Cy had never done surprises very well, and he had a remarkable way of de-dramatizing significant events. Jessica saw that her brothers looked worried.

Ellen took the microphone and held it chest high with two hands, an eager-to-please look taking over her face. She wasted no time. "Cy and I would like to announce that we're moving west," she said. "My maid of honor and best friend, Gisele, has found us terrific positions with Southwestern Cellular, and we're thrilled to tell you all that beginning next month our address will be Phoenix, Arizona."

The applause began slowly, a few hands clapping in the back of the room, and gradually moved toward the front. Davy clapped the loudest at table two. M.J. dabbed at her eyes. With a sinking feeling, Jessica wondered what her mother was going to think of this.

Ivan sat square as a soldier, one hand on the table, the other softly patting his chest, either to calm himself down or, more likely, to acknowledge that the best man's speech that he had worked himself into a dither over had become, with this latest news, obsolete.

7

ONLY ONE OTHER person was browsing in the converted showroom at the Ypsilanti Automobile Museum. Across the room, he held his glasses behind his back as he peered into a display case. No docents were in sight. Lydia had left her laptop on a desk near the back, and she turned around every so often to check on it. The "Heritage Collection," as the museum's neon sign announced, celebrated what its curator called the "orphaned car." No Chevy Bel Airs or Corvettes here. No Ford Thunderbirds or Mustangs, Chrysler Airflows or Lincoln Zephyrs—none of the classics from the Big Three automakers. The cars on display at this tiny museum had rolled hopefully off the line, only to be cut loose when the companies that had dreamed them up died.

She had been meaning to come here since the place had opened three years ago, but because her book was about GM, the trip hadn't been a priority. The cool darkness, the quiet buzz of the air conditioner, even the room's acrid smell of vinyl and Pine Sol were oddly soothing on this chaotic day. Lydia admired the plaid upholstery of a 1952 Henry J, the compact car made by the fleetingly solvent Kaiser-Frazer Company. Like the squat, orbicular 1946 Crosley, which hunkered next to it, the Henry J had gone on the market more than a decade too soon, well before the country showed any concern about emissions or fuel efficiency. In the 1950s, people had wanted styling and power, and GM had found a way to make them feel as if these features were indispensable: two-tones, tailfins, high-compression V-8 engines—each year's model a little different from the one before.

Lydia had always been fascinated with the period in the 1940s when the American car industry converted from a consumer market to a war supplier, then back again. She'd devoted several chapters of her assembly line book to this very subject, and she still wondered what might have happened had one or two of the smaller companies survived beyond that moment when the Big Three were shifting back from planes and tanks to cars.

When she looked up from the window of the Henry J, she realized that the man holding his glasses now stood beside her. He didn't smile or say anything, just put on his glasses, and followed her to the next display—a row of sedans from the forties and early fifties made by various companies like Nash, Hudson, Packard, and Studebaker. The struggling Nash and Hudson had agreed to a merger in 1954, creating the American Motors Corporation. AMC would update the economical Rambler, add the Ambassador, the Metropolitan, and later such seventies emblems as the Pacer, Hornet, and Gremlin, before being absorbed by Chrysler in the late eighties. Nineteen fifty-four could have been the year that Packard and Studebaker joined Nash and Hudson to create a powerful family of American Motors cars, with a full range of makes and models that might have even rivaled GM. But competition and clashing interests had barred the way. Packard and Studebaker held on too long to their independence, and eventually, unable to make it on their own, went the way of the Marvel, the Miller, the Flanders, the Hupp, the many thousand orphaned cars.

The man now turned to Lydia. She noticed he had gray hair pulled back in a short ponytail. Over his purple T-shirt he wore a vest the color of birch bark, and his sandals were made of hemp or some ropelike material. "These are beauties," he gestured. "But the prize of them all is over there."

Lydia followed him to another corner of the museum, where under the banner "Preston Tucker: American Dreamer" sat a shiny blue rocket on wheels, perfectly preserved from 1948, when it was billed as the original "car of tomorrow."

"The Tucker," Lydia said.

"The Tucker '48,'" he corrected her. "Now this is the ultimate. It's got an aluminum engine, in the rear so it held the road better. One of the first to do that, well before Volkswagen." He spoke as if he were giving a lecture or trying to sell the car. Lydia knew more about the Tucker than this guy could possibly realize, but for now she did not interrupt him.

At first she wondered if he worked for the museum, but he seemed too earthy to be a car fanatic. "And inside. Here, look." He peeked into the window, then stepped aside so Lydia could do the same. "See those crouch spaces under the dashboard? That's for when you're about to crash. Everything in there is padded—the dash, floors, doors, and steering wheel. It was the first car with seat belts, and that was just the beginning. It had disc brakes, a shatterproof windshield, side windows that popped out on impact. In terms of safety and engineering, this car was decades ahead of its time."

Lydia was used to men assuming that she knew nothing about cars. She'd been to scores of conventions and auto shows, had endured the double takes, patronizing voices, and predictable jokes about dangerous women drivers. They didn't understand that her interest had little to do with horsepower or intake manifolds, but with consequences, with the world the car had created.

"My favorite feature is the pilot ray headlight." The man knelt in front of the Tucker and explained how its third headlight, directly between the other two above the grille, moved in sync with the front wheels.

Lydia knew this, of course, and had it been any other day she might have spoken up sooner. The Tucker—called the "Torpedo" in its early stages and later the "48"—had pop-up taillights, an independent suspension, and a sticker price that would have made it one of the most affordable family sedans on the market. She knew, too, that by 1948, Tucker had raised millions in shares, bought a massive assembly plant in Chicago, sold more than two thousand Tucker franchises across the country on no more than a promise, and was on the verge of mass-producing his car when the government intervened and took him to court. For the next three years he was tied up defending himself against the Securities and Exchange Commission, which had charged him with stock fraud. By the time he had proved himself innocent, in 1950, his company had gone bankrupt. Only fifty-one Tuckers were ever made.

Car historians still talked about the idealist who had tried to challenge Detroit. Tucker's rise and fall was such a classic tragedy that Hollywood even made a movie about him. But Lydia had a special connection to this car because her father, Gilbert Warren, had worked for Tucker twice. It was Tucker who had first brought him to Detroit in 1935 to build race cars for Ford. Then ten years later, when Tucker started his own company, he'd persuaded Gilbert to leave Ford and help him design a brand-new car, a "torpedo on wheels" that would drive comfortably at 110. Lydia's father, not much of a risk taker, still felt a certain obligation to the man who had given him his first big break. He did many of the original sketches for the car and designed the lifelike one-quarter scale model that was used in the early promotions. "More like a Buck Rogers special than the automobiles we know today," read one of the ads Lydia had hanging on her office wall. "The Tucker Torpedo is scheduled to hit the road sometime in '47."

But by '47 the car had yet to be produced, and had begun to morph from the speedy rocket on wheels into the more practical "48" now on display at the museum. As Lydia's father had told the story, he'd grown frustrated with the project. He rarely discussed this chapter in his life, but Lydia still remembered the time around Christmas 1956, when Preston Tucker died of lung cancer and her father had sat at the breakfast table reading the laudatory obituary. "I felt bad for Pres, but if you say you're producing a car, at some point you've got to pull the curtain. Problem was, he couldn't make up his mind about whether he wanted speed or safety. He kept tearing up my plans and switching gears on me, all the while making a big ballyhoo and selling stock. I wasn't going to be under that house of cards when it all came crashing down."

There had been more than a touch of regret, even guilt perhaps, in her father's voice that morning. He'd repeated what Lydia already knew from talking to her mother—before resigning from the Tucker Corporation, her father had handpicked his own successor, Alex Tremulus, to carry out the final design. "I had a wife and young child. I couldn't risk staying there. So I quit." And it was a good thing, in the end, he'd added, since soon afterward Harley Earl at GM came calling.

Tucker was his own worst enemy, her father had said. A great salesman, bright and charismatic, but he had angered people in the government; he could be arrogant and uncompromising, railing against regulators and the "suits" at the big car companies. Tucker had won over the public by promoting his car tirelessly, taking out ads in newspapers and magazines, creating a swell of popular support and excitement. At the same time, he refused to work within the system. Gilbert Warren believed that what happened had been Tucker's own creation. Lydia had sympathy for Tucker—he was a visionary—but she understood that his project had more than likely been doomed to fail. It was one thing to start a small business in the "free enterprise" system, quite another to launch a car company.

Now the guy with the ponytail was reading the display copy out loud. He had somehow gotten closer to Lydia, and she took a step back. "It's a damn shame," he said. "What this doesn't mention is that the Big Three conspired to run Tucker out of business. There's the real story for you."

Before Lydia could decide if it was worth it to respond, he continued. "You think GM and Ford wanted to see a car like this on the market? It was cheaper, better in every way. They would have been playing catch-up for years." A few strands of hair fell over one eye, and he tucked them behind his ear.

She couldn't tell how old he was, probably in his fifties. But his clothes and his enthusiasm made him seem younger. "GM didn't care about safety. They knew they had to run Tucker out of business or spend a fortune to get up to speed. So what do you think they did but put spies on him? They paid people off to rat him out."

Lydia had heard this version before. It was the grassy knoll theory of automotive conspiracies, and most car historians she respected dismissed it. Lydia herself was plenty critical of the Big Three—she had made a career, in fact, of pointing out their offenses. Even though her father had worked for GM for fifteen years, she knew the company had cynical policies—out with the old, in with the new—and had contributed vastly to sprawl and scattered families. Her father had been just another moving part in that massive machine, and she didn't blame him any more than she blamed herself for owning a car. That same day at breakfast as he read Tucker's obituary, she'd asked her father if GM had helped destroy Tucker's company, and he told her that those theories were "nothing but applesauce." She had always believed him.

Remembering this now, she said at last, "The *government* certainly beat up on Tucker, but there's no proof that his competitors were involved." She didn't want to get into an argument, but it turned out the man was so impressed with how much she knew about cars that, when she finished debunking the conspiracy theory he backed off, quite literally stepping aside to give her room.

"Wow," he said. "Are you the curator or something?"

"No. I thought maybe *you* were the curator." She was suddenly conscious of the grease stain on her skirt. "I'm from Detroit. I have family in the industry."

The man introduced himself. "Norman Crawford." He extended his hand. "Norm. Pleased to meet you."

"Lydia," she said, and left it at that.

They talked casually about other car museums around town—GM World, the Walter Chrysler and Henry Ford Museums. Norm seemed friendly enough, and Lydia was getting ready to mention the automobile archives at the Detroit library, when an angular, gray-faced man appeared from behind a nearby door. "We're getting ready to close, folks," he said.

"Jeez, what time has it gotten to be?" Lydia asked.

"I don't wear a watch," Norm said.

"Five o'clock," the curator announced.

As they went outside, she stopped, still holding the door. "Shoot, I forgot something in there."

Norm, trailing close behind, almost stepped on her heels. "Sorry." He touched her shoulder. "Well, it's been nice talking to you, even if you're not buying my Preston Tucker theory." He laughed, then dug into his pocket and handed her his business card. "I'm just now putting up my web site. There's a lot about cars. You might be interested."

"I'll be sure to take a look." Lydia smiled and slid the card into her purse, then shook his hand goodbye. He waved over his shoulder and headed up the sidewalk. Strange bird, Lydia thought.

She went back into the museum and retrieved her laptop. Leaving her computer in Ypsilanti would have been the ultimate cap on this day. She thanked the gray-faced man and put a few dollars in the donation box.

Outside the streets were mostly empty. She walked over to a nearby bench and sat down. A few people clustered in the deli window across the street, while a tall man in an apron stood smoking in the doorway of a tavern down the block. It was still pleasant out. The warm air, the fading sun on her face, the knowledge that her children would soon arrive made her relax.

She opened her computer and returned to the book she'd been working on. She had done a great deal of research about the GM design team and its role in planned obsolescence, but she had yet to decide on the central figure around whom to organize the history. She had assumed at first that she would focus on Harley Earl, the master designer who had been her father's boss at GM. But after looking into his life over the years, Lydia had finally found him an unsuitable subject. Unlike Henry Ford and the Interstate designer Norman Bel Geddes, the focus of her last two books, Earl did not appear particularly complex. He knew what he wanted and acted on those desires, with seemingly few regrets. The letters and memos Lydia had seen revealed no great secrets or crises of conscience over the world he was setting into motion. She'd thought all along that she would need someone who was a struggle to understand, a sinner and saint wrapped into one fine contradiction.

But for all her searching she hadn't discovered that dark knight. Instead, she'd found herself thinking more and more about her father. He had worked for Preston Tucker and Harley Earl, two of the most influential figures in car history. He'd spent ten years at Ford, two at Tucker, and fifteen at GM. He'd arrived at the moment when planned obsolescence became institutional policy, and as much as anyone in the business, had contributed to the boom of the fifties. It could be one of those stories, in many ways emblematic of the transformation and transformative power of the automobile. For the first time in her career, Lydia allowed herself to consider her own personal stake in car history.

Like many men who rose in the auto business, Lydia's dad had come from a rural, working-class background. His father was a dairy farmer and sometime contractor who lived in the northern Michigan town of Oak Grove. Before going to school every morning, he milked the family's thirty cows. In the summers he sold Ford tractors, eventually saving enough money to buy a used 1918 Model T, his prized possession. After graduation, he took the advice of his tractor distributor and drove his Ford south to Grand Rapids, an important supply center at the time for the automobile industry. For five years, he worked for different auto body and parts suppliers, ultimately becoming a top designer at Peterson Coach & Body, the most successful custom car shop in town.

Lydia remembered the story her father loved to tell about meeting her mother. At an annual Christmas party, "in the blink of an eye," he'd said, he had fallen for his boss's only child, Ginny Peterson. She was a sophomore at Calvin College, nearly six feet tall, rich and beautiful, and so far out of his league that for the rest of his life he would tell people that pursuing her was his most daring act. Ginny had the stiff-necked self-assurance that came from her particular variety of Midwestern privilege, but as Lydia would later learn she had always dreamed of escape—out of the stifling confines of Grand Rapids society, out of what she believed to be the false promise of the Christian Reformed Church. She didn't intend to live by a set of impossibly strict rules for the reward of eternal heaven; her escape would be to an actual place.

"Your father went through hell to get me," Ginny would tell Lydia one evening over dinner at the Amberson Hotel in Farmington Hills. They had gone to the finest restaurant in town to celebrate Lydia's acceptance into the University of Michigan. Her father, who had promised to join them, had not yet arrived. He'd been finishing last-minute preparations for the GM Motorama, the traditional unveiling of the "cars of tomorrow." Over oysters Rockefeller, Ginny Warren was once again turning nostalgic as a way of forgetting her husband's absence.

"Imagine the nerve he had." She lit a Pall Mall and arranged her Scotch and ashtray in front of her. "Grandpa Peterson was no pushover, you know. Your father would deliver a dozen tulips each day to my dormitory, but your grandpa had tipped off the housemother. She'd intercept the flowers and send them to the school infirmary."

"So why didn't Grandpa Peterson fire Daddy?" Lydia asked.

"He couldn't fire him. Your father was a prodigy. Others knew more about engines, but no one before Gilbert had such a knack for marrying the machine to the body. Contracts doubled when your dad was there." Ginny inhaled from her unfiltered cigarette and lifted her glass. "Yes, your father was a great romantic."

"That's a little hard to believe." Lydia pushed aside the plate of oysters that her mother had offered her.

At the time, Lydia could not understand what she knew now: that her father *was* a romantic. Besides the flowers, he sent mash notes and countless drawings of young lovers driving down country lanes in long black cars of his own design. The best of these pictures had hung in Ivan's bedroom ever since he was a boy. At Peterson Coach & Body, Gilbert had suffered the wrath of his would-be father-in-law: longer hours, subtle acts of sabotage, public criticisms about his work. Only a true romantic would have continued to believe that a short, jittery, out-of-nowhere swain could win the heart of someone so seemingly unattainable. He must have known somehow that Ginny was a dreamer, too.

Ginny liked to tell the story about their secret marriage at the Grand Rapids courthouse, a week after Gilbert received a call from Preston Tucker, a salesman and engineer who had talked Ford into financing race cars for him to build. When Tucker invited Gilbert to move to Detroit and work under his guidance, Ginny, in particular, jumped at the opportunity. She left her family, her religion, and the social circle she had come to disdain, and never turned back. Four years later, Peterson Coach & Body would shut down, one of the countless casualties of Ford's and GM's decision to manufacture their own chassis and bodies. Lydia was not surprised to learn that her grandfather, who died at the height of the war with half a million dollars in debt, never forgave his daughter for marrying the country boy who had once been his star employee.

Ginny might have explained that her husband had just as much ambition as Peterson did, and that they had gone to the motor city not to spite him but to make the best for their family. But instead she hid away in a series of houses, in Dearborn when her husband worked for Ford and Tucker, in Indian Village and Farmington Hills when he moved to GM. And she drank. And smoked. She played bridge and took on civic projects with the wives of other executives.

It was as if, Lydia thought now, her mother had been too terrified to admit that something had gone wrong. She hadn't meant to marry an executive. She had married an agnostic, the son of a dairy farmer. Out of love? Out of rebellion? It didn't matter. All that mattered was her unwillingness to make peace with her past. And when her parents died within eighteen months of each other, any opportunity to do so vanished. As a result, Lydia had always thought that her mother lived out her days in a kind of perpetual mourning—for her parents, for the life she had imagined but never got to lead.

Lydia promised herself that night at the Amberson that she would not allow such sadness to descend upon *her* family. She would have more than one child, and those children would rally around their parents, and if they ever left home, they would go without anger or resentment. To Lydia, the past was sacred, as precious as any living thing. She would attend to it always. She would make it her life's work.

She was staring off into the bronze-lit afternoon when she felt a pair of hands cover her eyes.

"Guess who?"

Lydia started. "I know those clammy fingers." She bit her bottom lip, regretting her choice of words.

"Emergency rescue," Jessica announced. She took Lydia's laptop and helped her to her feet. "Will you be needing medical attention, ma'am?" She gave Lydia a hug.

"I think I'll be all right." She was still a bit dazed from snapping out of her memory.

"Sorry I was so obnoxious on the phone," Jessica said softly. "I've had better days."

"I know." Lydia had not received such affection from her daughter in what seemed a long time. "To what do I owe this?" She smiled.

"You're my mother. An old sage told me today that we ought to be good to our mothers, so look: I'm being good."

Davy and Ivan walked up behind their sister.

"I hope we're not too late," Davy said.

"No, no. The museum closed only a few minutes ago."

They were all still dressed in their wedding clothes. Jessica had on a green suit that Lydia hadn't seen before. Not the most flattering outfit, she thought, but she was not about to make a comment.

"So, how are you doing?" Ivan asked. He looked worn out.

"You know, I've actually had a wonderful time here. I got to do a lot of thinking." She followed them to the car.

For the first time all weekend, her three children walking beside her, Lydia felt as if her family was truly together.

"You're sure you don't want me or Davy to drive?" Jessica asked Ivan.

"I'm fine," he said a little brusquely, and unlocked Cy's car.

Jessica opened the door for her mother, then slid into the back seat next to her. "Ivan's not in the best mood today."

As Lydia reached for her seat belt, a sharp pain shot across her rib cage and into her stomach, like an arrow finding its target. "Ouch," she said out loud.

"What's wrong?" Jessica asked.

"I've been having some pain," she said, though she'd only just now gotten a stomachache.

"Have you seen a doctor?"

"I'm sure it's nothing." Lydia massaged beneath her rib cage, but the little arrow stayed in its place.

"You should get it checked out, Mom. You're nearing the age—"

"I know, honey. Don't worry, I'll see a doctor." Lydia felt foolish for wolfing down a fast-food lunch, but she wasn't going to admit it. "So how was the wedding?" she asked, the question she'd been thinking about for much of the day.

Ivan headed east on Washtenaw. Davy turned around and glanced at Jessica. "Just what you'd expect." He looked at his mother, then quickly away. "I told you about the guitar. Luckily, I managed to avoid a jam session. The karaoke guy took care of the entertainment."

"And people had a good time?"

"They were drunk," Jessica said. "It could have been a funeral and they'd have had a good time."

"It *was* a funeral," Ivan added.

"Yeah, we don't need to talk about it." Jessica rubbed her mother's arm, a gesture that seemed not quite patronizing, nor entirely honest, either.

"Don't feel you have to protect me." Lydia looked in the rear-view mirror at Ivan's eyes, but they gave nothing away. "I've let your father go, don't worry. I wouldn't mind having this car, however." She forced a laugh.

She wondered what had really happened at the wedding. Perhaps Cy and Ellen had fought or the reception had been filled with mishaps. The kids' behavior did seem funereal: respectfully calm, too sober and restrained. Jessica held her hand—so out of character these days. Davy seemed shifty—he was a peace broker, to be sure, but was usually up-front. And even Ivan, who couldn't stand his father and made no secret about this, seemed unusually quiet.

Lydia started to ask what was wrong, but stopped herself. There was something about driving in silence in this luxury car, cocooned with her children in the waning hours of a late spring day, that she didn't want to ruin. Nobody spoke as they passed Ford Lake, Romulus, Metro Airport.

Jessica squeezed her mother's hand. "Sorry it's been such a short visit."

"Well, at least we have tomorrow," Lydia said.

"Not much of tomorrow. My flight leaves at eight A.M. I won't get to Eugene until dinnertime. When are you guys leaving?" she asked her brothers.

"I tried to get an afternoon flight but couldn't. So I'm on your heels," Ivan said. "I wish we could stay longer, Mom."

"I'll be around through the morning, anyway," Davy put in.

Lydia sighed. "I guess it was your father's weekend, after all."

"We'll be back before you know it," Davy said.

Lydia leaned forward and patted his cheek. "I'm sure you will."

When she sat back, she felt the arrow again, a sharp pain this time driving up to her ribs. She took Jessica's hand and pulled it toward her. "Here," she said, and placed her daughter's palm against the ache in her middle.

8

ESSICA KNEW that her mother could have rented a car in Ann Arbor and driven home herself. But who could tell how she would react to Cy's picking up and leaving, not just out of metro Detroit, but clear across the country? Jessica had never been to Arizona, only knew of the Southwest from her ex, the ersatz Buddhist. Now she and her mother could commiserate: they'd both lost a man to the desert.

Blane had moved down to sell his amulets—Egyptian ankhs, Druid symbols, feathered necklaces, crystal-drop "energy" earrings and pendants. He had tried to make a go of it in Eugene, renting a kiosk in the Springfield mall, but he'd had more stuff stolen by doped-up teenagers than he probably ever sold. And the weather got to him, the unrelenting gray of winter, the slick and constant mist. Jessica was accustomed to demoralizing climates, but Blane, a North Carolinian, had to move to the far extreme to snap out of his daze.

Phoenix, of all places. A city of millions with no downtown that, thanks to the automobile and air conditioning, had metastasized into scores of exclusive communities that more or less governed themselves. In Oregon, people looked down on the

Southwest and Southern California, with their vulturelike water policies and desperate overdevelopment. Jessica would not follow a man down there, not to the so-called city of rebirth where retirees did anything but rise from the ashes. But now the Spivey-Modines were joining the mad rush for land. Their sprinkler systems would run all day to keep the desert blooming.

It had been Jessica's idea to say nothing about it to their mother. "She's not ready for this," she'd said during the car ride from the reception to the museum. "She'll chase after him, I'm telling you. Either that or she'll move in with me."

"She has to find out somehow," Davy said. "Shouldn't we tell her in person?"

"I think we should give it some time. Don't you find it strange that today of all days the Escort broke down? She's in Ann Arbor, for God's sake. Are you such a believer in accidents, Davy?"

"In this case, yes. It was only a matter of time for that car."

"Only a matter of timing, you mean."

Ivan accelerated past a car carrier strung with shiny Pontiacs. "It's only a matter of time before she finds out anyway," he said.

"Give it a couple of days, that's all I'm suggesting. That news would be too raw on top of what's already happened this weekend. You know Mom and Dad still talk. I think she imagined they'd get back together someday." Jessica looked out the window at the polluted landscape and pictured the Columbia River Gorge, the Cascades, the winding Oregon coast. As beautiful as it was where she lived, the West had done little to show her a way in the world. She would happily leave the place if there were somewhere else to go.

"When did you become so sensitive about Mom's feelings?" Ivan asked.

Jessica leaned toward the front seat. "I just know this isn't the day to tell someone whose life is tied up in history, who doesn't believe in endings, that her husband of thirty-three years is heading west."

"Literally and figuratively. He's going west to die," Ivan added. "Isn't that what people do?"

"Hey, I resent that."

"Not you, Jess. You're just hiding out there for a while. You'll come back eventually."

"For the record, I'm perfectly happy in Eugene," she said, though it wasn't true. "But how would you know? You haven't bothered to visit."

"*I've* been twice," Davy put in lightheartedly.

But Ivan was in no kind of mood. "You went on business," he shot back.

"Yeah, a lot of good that did me," Davy muttered.

"Forget it. Let's not keep score," Jessica said, though in fact she had. Davy had visited twice, and though he and Sanjay had had meetings with potential investors in Portland, her little brother had driven four hours round trip on two separate days to see her in Eugene.

"So, we've got a deal?" Jessica said as they turned at the exit for Ypsilanti.

"What if she finds out from someone else?" Ivan asked. "Like a friend, or the wedding announcements?"

"None of Mom's friends were there, and Dad told me they weren't placing a notice."

"What if he calls and tells her himself?"

"He's leaving for his honeymoon on Tuesday."

"That's seventy-two hours from now. A lot can happen in seventy-two hours."

"I'll tell you what, Ivan. I'll call her before the end of the week. By then she'll be back into writing her book and distracted enough to deal with it."

They passed the Ypsilanti water tower and made the turn for Depot Town, the old section where the train station had been converted into shops. Ivan parked at the end of the block in front of what looked like an old car showroom. "Okay, Jess. But when you call her, be nice. Even if she takes it badly, don't allow yourself to get mad."

"I love my mother." Jessica opened the door and got out

of the car. "I love my mother," she said. "This is my new mantra."

As she walked toward the museum, Jessica caught a glimpse of Lydia sitting on a bench halfway down the block. She seemed to be staring into the near distance, in her own private world. From this view, her mother looked at ease, her sharp features softened in profile. For a moment Jessica felt close to her in the way that she used to. If only she could keep this image of her mother—unguarded, lost in a daydream. She could have it stamped on a coin to carry in her pocket as a reminder that Lydia would be fine on her own, would allow her daughter to have a life, too. Holding this picture in her mind, as if trying to imprint it there, Jessica ran ahead quietly, put her hands over her mother's eyes and said, "Guess who?"

It was nearing evening, and Jessica was upstairs in her bedroom. Ivan and Davy had dropped her off at the house so she could pack her things and get ready, while they took Lydia to get a rental car. As Jessica collected her clothes and threw them on the bed she replayed the scene in front of the museum. She thought of the different possible answers to "Guess who?" other than the one her mother had given.

"I know those clammy fingers," she had said.

Over the years Lydia had offered plenty of guesses about who she expected her daughter to be: *You're a great beauty, so why do you hide it? Are you trying to scare men away? Are you worried that you'll end up like your grandmother Warren—a company widow? It's not the fifties anymore, Jessica. That would never happen to you.*

You have such a fine intellect. I don't see why you would waste it on politics. Politics is groupthink. You're too original for that. Why don't you come back to Ann Arbor, go to graduate school? You're unhappy because you're bagging groceries, dabbling in this and that. Your mind is turning on you, saying, Hey, what about me?

No one in this family is selfless. It's just not in our temperament. It's fine to experiment with doing for others, but genetically you're hard-wired to do for yourself. It's the family way. Look at your father.

Look at me, even. You just aren't made for causes. In the end the only kind of activist you could be is the one in charge, the one driving, not just echoing policy. Our family is incapable of working for other people.

Of all the sticking points, this one might have been the worst. This idea of the collective *we*. Her mother talked about her children's differences, but in the same breath she would push a communal rhetoric that never failed to put Jessica on edge. We, the family. Comrades Ivan, Jess, and Davy. Lydia had a romanticized view in which all of her children would one day live on the same street and share dinner together at a long table that stretched from the dining room to the foyer, and, as the family grew, it would keep on stretching down the street, on and happily on. It was a tribal fantasy or something out of a novel of manners in which the heart of human existence rested in the family. How quaint in this corner of the modern world, Jessica thought. Detroit, of all places, the Renaissance City, where people talked of rebuilding, but in fact could not wait to leave in order to reinvent themselves.

And how could Lydia accuse Jessica of groupthink when Lydia herself was dictating policy—in fact, had been defining who her family was from the beginning, writing up its corporate charter, its constitution, seeking no input whatsoever from the rest of the group. What kind of commune was that? There could be no all-for-one, when one was deciding for all. This family was not, as her mother would believe, a collective, but an autocracy.

And yet Jessica admired her mother, always had. In grade school she would donate Lydia's books to her school library and collect her mother's reviews and clippings in a shoebox under her bed. She used to boast to her friends about her mother's success. Embarrassing to think of it now, but she'd been an echo of Lydia's opinions, sounding off to her bored friends about the numbing effects of the suburbs. But she had done all this in secret, especially as a teenager. She'd idolized her mother, but only out of earshot.

Even now Jessica could scan her room for evidence of her

mother's influence, her driving need to shape her. Her desk had been transformed into a vanity table, the candles, books, and clutter put away to make room for moisturizers, scented soaps, a hairbrush and barrettes. At the back of the desk sat a table mirror that she'd never seen before, and in a frame above it, replacing an old photograph that Jessica loved, was her diploma, honors with highest distinction from Michigan. She had shoved the diploma away somewhere in her closet, but her mother had since recovered it to put on display, no doubt to beckon Jessica back for graduate school.

"Knock, knock," Lydia said, though Jessica's door was open. "Your worries are over, sweetheart. I have in my possession a reliable car."

Seeing her mother, Jessica remembered her father's sudden announcement and her own determination to keep quiet for now. "What kind?"

"A Chevy Corsica."

"What's a Corsica?"

"It's a four-door sedan, a basic car."

"But a Corsica, Mom? It sounds like a marine mammal."

"Or an island in Europe."

"But a car and an island don't jibe. One's on the move. The other stays put."

"I don't have an answer, sweetheart, but I'm sure there is one."

"Yes, look into it, please." Jessica rubbed her eyes, happy to be talking about nothing at all. *We should talk about nothing more often*, she thought, looking around for the fraying Guatemalan bag that Blane had given her.

"I hate it when you leave."

"Mom?"

"I know, I know." Lydia shook her head. "Well, we picked up a rotisserie chicken, unless you want to go out."

"No, that's fine." Jessica found the bag in a corner of the room and began stuffing her clothes into it.

Her mother looked at the unfolded clothes on the bed. "Do you need any help?"

"Where I live they don't care about wrinkles."

Lydia's eyes widened for a moment. "Okay, then. I guess I'll see you downstairs," she said.

Jessica changed into jeans and a T-shirt and hung the Lady Bird Johnson suit in the closet. It brimmed with her childhood things—stuffed animals, school notebooks, high tops and Nancy Drew novels, a deflated basketball and old clothes she'd never thrown away. She wouldn't be needing this suit in Oregon, that was for sure. She finished packing, then on the way downstairs, peeked into her mother's office for the first time that weekend.

On the wall next to the computer, her mother had hung the black-and-white photograph that used to be in Jessica's room: one of her parents' wedding pictures from 1965. In it, a young Lydia was tossing her bouquet from a balcony inside the Book-Cadillac Hotel. The bouquet hung in midflight, while the sea of faces looking on, even the bride herself leaning over the balcony, receded into a blur of black, silver, and gray. Only the bouquet was in focus, a tight spray of lilies of the valley in the center of the photograph. Jessica had always loved this image because the bouquet had seemed to be sailing toward her. But now Lydia was its recipient, as if by moving the picture to her office she hoped to recapture her younger self.

Closing the door behind her, Jessica suddenly felt sorry for her mother. She wished she could shake her, tell her that Cy was gone for good. Go downtown, she wanted to say. Take a look at the Book-Cadillac Hotel—thirty-two floors and twelve hundred rooms—for fifty years the jewel of Detroit, where presidents and movie stars once slept. Look at it now, its entrances and broken windows boarded up with plywood, furniture all sold at auction long ago, its lone security guard finally cut loose after keeping watch for a decade over an empty building. Sneak inside, as Jessica's high school boyfriend once did, to see where the murals and gilded moldings had been stripped by scavengers, the massive chandeliers denuded of crystal, the decorative doors and plaster details hauled away. The copper wiring, the plumbing, the galvanized pipe, even the radiators. All of it, gone.

Downstairs, Davy was talking to their mother about the wedding. "Just what you'd expect. Cheesy room, cheesy restaurant. They even put cheese in the chicken. We just wanted it to be over, Mom."

"What about Ellen's family?" Lydia asked.

"Oh, they're fine. The parents are cool," Davy said. Jessica gave him a sharp look to stop him from volunteering any more. "And Ivan had a thing for someone in the wedding party."

"One of Ellen's friends?" Lydia exclaimed.

"She's nobody." Ivan blushed. "The only sparks were between Jess and the wedding singer. Trust me, Mom. The whole thing was a nonevent."

"But your Dad must have been nervous."

"Yeah, I think he was." Ivan had carved the chicken and was spooning rice pilaf onto a serving plate.

"Anyway, it's over," Jessica said quickly, joining Ivan at the kitchen counter. "What can I do to help?"

"How about a vinaigrette?" Ivan suggested.

Lydia filled glasses with Chardonnay and brought the plate of chicken to the table. "I hear there's a new computer lab opening up at the library," she said. "I've been spending most of my time at the archives. The house is just too empty."

Here we go again, Jessica thought. Leave it to their mother to start talking about the empty house over the last dinner before everyone left. Jessica wasn't going to participate in this guilt ritual, not when she'd managed to avoid it all weekend. Instead she asked, "Have you seen that jam I brought from Oregon?"

Lydia looked startled. "Oh, that wonderful jam."

"I'd like to put a dash in the vinaigrette," Jessica said. "It gives it a nice balance."

Lydia started opening cupboards. "You checked the refrigerator?"

"Yes. I only just gave it to you."

They turned the kitchen over looking for the jam. "That's strange," Lydia kept saying. Ivan sat at the table. "Food's getting cold, ladies. Can't you make a dressing without the stuff?" He sniffed his wine, swirled it around in his glass. He had once taken a night class in viniculture.

"Maybe you've had a burglar, Mom," Jessica said. "That marionberry jam is gold to some folks."

Davy sat down next to his brother. "Come and eat."

"You know, I don't think I can. But you kids go ahead." Lydia held her stomach. "I don't feel so great. I've got to go in tomorrow and find out what's wrong. And, sweetheart, I still don't know where that jam is."

"Let's forget the jam, for Chrissake," Ivan said.

"It's just weird." Jessica whisked a dab of honey into the oil and vinegar and brought the salad dressing to the table. "Can I get you something for your stomach?" she asked.

Lydia sat down and seemed to force a smile. "Don't worry, darling. I can take care of myself."

But Jessica did worry, though at the moment she wasn't sure why.

PART TWO

More than anyone, Norman Bel Geddes was the true inventor of the Interstate. Visitors to his Futurama exhibit at the 1939 World's Fair took a tour of the America of tomorrow, a streamlined vision of broad highways, layered promenades, glass skyscrapers, and rooftop parks. At the end of the tour, spectators were given a pin that read "I have seen the future," not knowing how true this would turn out to be.

—From *The Magic Motorway: Norman Bel Geddes,
Maker of the Modern World* by Lydia Modine

9

LYDIA LOOKED DOWN Woodward Avenue from the huge windows of the public library's automotive history collection. The library was one of the few great buildings still habitable in Detroit, directly across the street from the Institute of Arts, and she had never grown tired of the place—so peaceful and majestic, almost ecclesiastical. Lydia sometimes thought a person could make a happy life between home and here.

It was Monday afternoon, and the children had all left. She knew she had to get back to her work. She sat down at the long table, took out her laptop and a pad of paper from her Mamarama case. As she rifled through her purse for a pen, a business card fell out on the table:

NORMAN CRAWFORD
www.nuplan.org

She had forgotten about the odd man from the Ypsi museum with his vest and ponytail, telling her about the Preston Tucker "conspiracy." Since she was here in the archives anyway, she figured she might as well leaf through the Tucker files.

Eventually she'd have to do some research about her father's years with Tucker, though she was sure it was only a small part of the larger story of car design. But when she looked over to the reference desk no one was there. In fact, the whole room was empty.

For now she plugged in her computer and opened the fragments of her book that she'd begun to sketch out, each focused on a division of General Motors—Pontiac, Oldsmobile, Buick, Cadillac, and Chevrolet. In the Chevrolet section she moved her cursor to the top of the screen and typed her father's name, Gilbert Warren, then a line about him: "He always stayed late at the Motorama."

Again she remembered how she and her mother had waited for her father that night at the Amberson Hotel. Ginny had said that Gilbert was once a great romantic, and Lydia had thought about how different her parents were. Her father, the dedicated company man, her mother ever wavering between duty, desire, and guilt over the parents she had left so abruptly.

"We're not ready," Ginny had said sharply when the waiter came by to take orders for the main course.

"Shall I return when the rest of your party is here?" The waiter stepped back and bowed.

"Our party *is* here," Lydia said.

"No, it's not." Ginny brought her hand to her lips. Her deep red lipstick looked lurid, almost bloody against her pale skin.

"The third chair will remain empty for the rest of the evening," Lydia pressed.

"It will not," her mother said. She twisted her rings with her thumb.

"Yes, it will." Lydia opened her menu. "I would like the filet mignon, medium, with asparagus and baked potato. Butter on the side, if that's possible."

Ginny grabbed her daughter's arm. "That's not possible. Please stop."

"I can come back," the waiter repeated.

"Yes, come back," Ginny said, letting go.

Lydia shut her menu with a loud snap that caught the attention of people at nearby tables. "Why do you continue to protect him?"

"Your father works very hard."

"My father is married to the General Motors Corporation. If it's not the Motorama, it's a progress report that interrupts Christmas dinner. If it's not the progress report, it's a fishing retreat in Canada, off with the rest of the seven dwarfs."

"Don't call them the seven dwarfs. You know your father hates that."

"There's Sleepy, Dopey, Happy, Sneezy, Grumpy, Doc, and Daddy. There, that's seven."

"Lydia—"

"Seven little henchmen all working for the great dandy, Harley Jefferson Earl. I don't know why they put up with it. And whenever Daddy's home he's out in the garage taking apart the latest Ford, trying to keep a step ahead." Lydia reached over and slugged what was left of her mother's Scotch.

"What has gotten into you? Have you gone mad?"

"I guess you were right after all, Mother. He is a great romantic. He's in love. That's why he works so hard."

Why did Lydia keep returning to that night at the Amberson? Perhaps she had felt guilty about leaving her mother to go off to college, and was acting out in much the same way that Jessica tended to now. It was also one of the first times she had seen, with the clarity that comes with imminent departure, the true picture of her parents' marriage. Her father had not lost his romantic urgency—only the object of his affection had changed. He was in love with cars, had poured all of his restless energy into helping create what many still considered some of the finest unions of beauty and machine: the 1951 Buick LeSabre; the 1953 "Blue Flame" Corvette; the 1955 Bel Air convertible; and the 1957 Chevrolet Nomad, "the Beauty Queen of All Station Wagons."

And, as much as designing cars, her father had loved to please his boss. The legendary Mr. Earl—as everyone, perhaps even his wife, was expected to call him—stood six foot four, towering over his immediate staff. He had originally come from Southern California, and Lydia remembered that he was always suntanned, with a winning smile and a perfect shave. His polychromatic linen suits always matched his two-tone shoes, and he looked as if he'd spent an hour each morning choosing which one to wear. In his office, which Lydia had once visited as a teenager, she'd caught a glimpse of the duplicate wardrobe he kept in his closet—on hand, no doubt, to keep him unwrinkled throughout the day.

GM chairman Alfred Sloan had hired Earl to realize his vision of offering a car "for every purse and purpose." Unlike Ford, who simply improved the existing model each year, Sloan and Earl would provide cars of unlimited color, style, and possibility. And GM, which had long held the second position, accelerated so far ahead of Ford in sales and profits that Henry Ford himself, after much resistance, adopted Sloan's "annual model" policy. Or what Lydia thought of now as planned obsolescence.

When the waiter returned, he took her mother's dinner order. Ginny managed to steer the conversation back to Lydia's acceptance into the University of Michigan. Neither of Lydia's parents had completed a degree, so Ginny had plenty of opinions on the subject. "Don't commit to a man before you've got your ducks in a row," she said. The waiter had brought her a second Scotch. Her mother had a poor tolerance for alcohol, but that never stopped her from drinking.

"You mean like you did?" Lydia asked.

"I'm not saying don't make my mistakes. I had choices. I made decisions. I'm not talking about myself. I'm talking about you." She swept her hand in front of her. "Leave Michigan if you need to, but don't follow someone out of here. Find your own way, that's all I'm saying."

Lydia backed off because she knew where this was going. Her mother once again teetered on that balance between pride and regret. She had not been wrong. No, ma'am. No decision she had ever made had had bad consequences. Yet what would have happened had she not gone to that Christmas party, had she not met the small, nervous man whose talents her father had praised? How would her parents have handled it had she finished Calvin College, one of the few to survive into gradua- tion unpinned, unattached? Perhaps over the years they would have given up, loosened their hold on her. She could have left, and who knew what she might have found in the world beyond Grand Rapids, Michigan? She was a striking beauty. She had intelligence, ambition. Who knew what might have been?

Lydia's father never did make it to dinner that night. When they got home he was asleep on the living room davenport, the Glenn Miller Orchestra playing on the hi-fi. As they ap- proached he still didn't stir, fully dressed in a gray suit and a thin silver-and-blue-striped tie, his top button undone. Lyd- ia's father lay there, soundlessly, his hands clasped over his stomach.

"There's the corpse," Ginny said.

Lydia laughed uncomfortably. In that moment, she felt ter- rible for her father. His small body fit so easily into the midsize couch, one of his hands clutching the other, as if frozen in the act of pulling himself to safety. His face in repose, he looked like family photographs of the farm boy from Oak Grove. Lydia pictured him speeding home, perhaps minutes after she and her mother had left for the restaurant. With time to spare, she imagined, her father had decided to unwind, put on a lively record so he wouldn't fall asleep on this night of celebration. He lay down, telling himself *only for a minute*, and then, in spite of his promise to his wife and daughter, he drifted off.

The next year, 1959, Harley Earl would retire, and with that the era of the dream machines would be over. Though her dad did not believe in economy cars—where was the beauty in these transport cases of reinforced plastic?—he would stay on and assist with the final stages of design for the Chevy Corvair. The sixties would mark a shift from styling back to engineer- ing, from romance to functionalism. Lydia remembered how her father seemed to lose his passion for the work he had loved for so long. He grew thin, pale, and forgetful, as if some heart- sickness were eating away at him. With the compacts came muscle cars—the Impala SS, the GTO, the Corvette Sting

Ray—340 horsepower with grilles like bared teeth. Gilbert had retired in the midst of all this, in the fall of 1963.

Lydia recalled her parents' wistful conversations about buying a house up north, out in the tall woods, across the Mackinac Bridge into the mysteries of Michigan's Upper Peninsula. Her mother liked the idea of going far away, of living in nature, which she had never had a chance to do. Her dad spoke vaguely of the fishing. But in the end he would make it no farther north than Oak Grove, to be buried beside his parents and his parents' parents.

It still saddened Lydia that her father never knew that she would spend much of her life writing about cars. Her mother, who did live to see Lydia's first book published, in 1976, had suggested around that time that she write about her father. "There's a story there. I'm sure you'll want to tell it one day," she'd said. Lydia didn't make much of it at the time. She had figured that her mother, like anyone, considered her own family more than worthy of a book. Lydia had thought of her father as just another man who got up at dawn and returned home exhausted, his dinner hardening on the stove. A company man. No great paradox. But now here she was, after all these years, trying out her mother's advice.

When Lydia looked up, she saw someone walk into the room and take his place at the reference desk. To her delight, she realized that it was her friend Walter Hill. Over the past few years she and Walter had shared the occasional lunch in the art museum cafeteria. Mostly they talked about their kids. His daughter and son both worked at Henry Ford Hospital, and lived nearby.

She closed her laptop and went over to see him.

"Lydia! What can I do for you?" He acted as if they'd just had coffee yesterday. In fact, she hadn't seen him in nearly a month.

"I've been thinking about Preston Tucker, actually," she said. "I wonder if there's anything new on that front. I ran into a guy a couple of days ago who gave me the grassy-knoll theory."

She thought about telling Walter that her father had become the focus of her book, but at the moment she still wasn't sure enough about her decision.

"Let me take a look." Walter went back into the archives and a few minutes later returned with a folder. "I doubt if anything in here will be news to you," he said. "But I'll make you a copy just in case."

"That would be great." While Walter ran off copies Lydia talked about her kids visiting for the weekend. "Not under the best circumstances," she added. She'd told him all about Cy's marriage plans. Walter's wife had died two years ago, so she was careful not to sound too sorry for herself. She didn't mention the Escort's breaking down, either.

"So where have you been lately?" she asked.

"I was out sick awhile."

She noticed that he did look a little ashen and seemed to have lost weight off his broad frame. Lydia wanted to ask what had happened, but she knew that he played his own life close to the vest. Every Friday after work he drove over the Ambassador Bridge to Canada to wager ten percent of his paycheck—never a dime more, he'd told her—at the Windsor Casinos. "You've got to have a vice," Walter liked to say. "Just as long as you keep it a hobby and not an occupation."

"As soon as I got back they sent me down to the new computer lab," he continued. "They're short-staffed." He placed a document on the glass and the light flashed. "I'm working half time here and half time there."

"I haven't seen the lab yet," Lydia said.

"Oh, that's where all the action is. You want to take a look?"

"Sure, if you have time."

Walter finished the copying and handed the pages to Lydia.

She went back to her laptop and slid the materials into her bag.

In the computer room, Lydia saw that there were as many people in this small space as in the entire rest of the building. Two kids in the back corner were laughing at something on their screen. Walter walked over to one of the terminals where a woman was standing up to leave. "Here you go, Lydia. Why don't you take station 8? And if you need any help, I'm always at your service." He spoke expansively now, returning to his official role.

"As a matter of fact," Lydia said quickly. "I do need some help." She remembered the address from the business card—www.nuplan.org—but she wasn't used to computers besides her own.

Walter helped her pull up a browser and type in the web address. The NUPLAN logo appeared at the top. A yellow daisy sprouted out of the letter u, followed by "think green." Under the logo was a link: *Click here to join me on a message board.*

"What's this all about?" Walter asked.

"It's the web site of a friend of mine. Well, not really a friend. Someone I met." Lydia clicked on the link and another web site—drive.com—came up.

"I've been to this one." Walter leaned over her shoulder and pointed to a section of the screen. "Is that your friend?" he asked.

The top message was from norm@nuplan.org. The subject heading read: *Wake up and smell the gasoline.*

"He just posted that this morning, I see. Looks like your friend may be a troll."

"Excuse me?"

"First you have to admit you're impressed with my lingo. Do I keep up or do I keep up?"

"I'm impressed. What's a troll?"

"A troll is a gate-crasher," Walter said. "Goes to a site and tries to stir up trouble."

I'm not here to talk about polluting the earth, Norm wrote. *You've heard that story before. But what about polluting yourself? Every time you get in your car you're inhaling benzene, carbon monoxide, toluene, and formaldehyde, at ten times the concentration.*

Norm's post had generated a page of replies:

Who is this asshole?

Is this how you ride out your unemployment?

"Your friend is definitely a troll," Walter said. "But I've seen a lot worse."

"He's not my friend."

Walter gave her what seemed like a knowing look. "Well, I should get back upstairs," he said, before she could fully gauge his reaction. He showed her how to refresh the page to see new responses and what to do in case she wanted to post a message. "Not that I would, what with all the crackpots out there. Just make sure you don't use your real name and don't give out your e-mail address," he added, then left the lab for the archives.

As Lydia read the replies and Norm's rebuttals, she saw that he held his ground against the herd of car fanatics. He cited statistics about runaway sprawl and misguided spending on highway projects—*adding more lanes is like trying to cure obesity by loosening your belt.* All the while, his enemies lined up to get into the fray.

How's the weather under your rock?

This isn't Greenpeace, dude.

But Norm was undeterred. *I'm not telling you to junk your cars or saying it's time to go back to the 19th century. We're stuck for a lifetime with the horse that never tires. But this needless waste is killing the earth and it's killing us as well.*

No, you're killing us with your bullshit.

Lydia had to admit she enjoyed the immediacy of this. She felt a little on edge, like a spy, and wondered about this missionary out in cyberspace. Was he really looking for converts? Or was Norm just a saboteur, a grown-up kid who rang the neighbors' doorbells, then ran away?

Let me tell you what's possible, he continued. *A car that would never be obsolete but eternally recyclable, with a supercharged hydrogen engine. It would run on solar energy, far more efficient than fuel cells, and every bit as fast as a standard V-6. It would use sunflower oil as a lubricant, and nearly all the components—roof, dash, seats, body panels—would be made of biopolymers: corn-based or soy-based foams and plastics. The new car of tomorrow would look just like the ones you're driving now, only most of the materials would come from the earth. Everything on the planet should be green or reusable, cars included. I want to see a day when you can plant a hubcap and it'll grow into an herb garden.*

Norm carried on in this manner, talking about eco-friendly buildings and closed-system roads. And though others continued to give him a hard time, their language softened a bit. Not that they seemed convinced. But over the course of his spiel he had managed to disarm them somewhat.

Let me leave you in peace, my friends, he wrote. *I didn't mean to interrupt your board. But if we're going to turn things around we have to let the car companies know that this is a new century and we deserve a whole new way of thinking. If you want to find out more, go to www.nuplan.org or write me at my e-mail address: norm@nuplan.org.*

And with that he was not heard from again. The insults faded and new subjects turned to upcoming auto shows.

Lydia had read more than her share of articles about emissions and environmental waste, and much of what Norm had written was no different from the current literature. She found it a bit bizarre that he would take his case to an Internet message board. But his earth-to-earth idea did have a certain grassroots appeal.

She left drive.com and typed in www.nuplan.org. But the message on the screen read "Web site not responding." She tried again, and still the page came up the same. It crossed her mind that she could send Norm a note of support. *Neat ideas,* she might say. Or *You really know how to stir up a crowd.*

But just as she was trying to figure out how to access her e-mail, Walter returned to the lab to check on her.

"So how's your friend?" he asked as he approached.

She closed the window on the screen. "They chased him away," she said. "Just as well. I ought to be getting back home."

10

T HE CAR ARCHIVES closed early, so Lydia thought she'd
spend the afternoon at the house, sorting through the
Tucker articles and her father's papers. But when she
pulled up to 309 Franklin she was surprised to see, parked
right in front of her walkway, as if the hours had wound back to
the weekend, Cy's new Infiniti sedan. Thinking that it must be
Ivan, though she knew perfectly well that she had driven him to
the airport yesterday, she got out of her car and walked toward
the Infiniti.

The driver's side door opened and out stepped Cy.

"Lydia," his voice slid down to a melancholy register. "It's
good to see you."

"What are you doing here?" she managed. "Aren't you supposed to be on your honeymoon?" And in that suspended moment, as Cy brought his hand to his face and clasped his jaw,
her heart jumped as she wondered if perhaps he had abandoned
his new wife, if the marriage had combusted within the span of
a day. Or maybe Ellen had left him standing at the altar. Could
that explain the children's curious behavior when they returned
from the wedding?

"We leave tomorrow morning." He rubbed his chin. "I wanted to ask you a favor."

"Of course." Lydia looked at the ground. A root system from the large oak tree in front of her house had pushed up on the sidewalk, leaving a jagged edge where one block of concrete connected to another. "Would you like to come in?"

"I don't have much time. I know this is awkward."

Lydia noticed that Cy's shirt was open at the collar. A gold cross lay halfway visible beneath the loose, silky fibers. He'd never worn a cross before. "You left some things in the basement, you know. I haven't touched any of them." As she said this, she focused on his neck, which looked sunburned. She couldn't bring herself to look him in the eye.

"Yeah, it's been a while. I don't remember what's down there." He followed her up the walk to the front porch, held open the screen door while she rummaged in her purse for her keys.

Even now, Lydia realized that she'd never been angry with Cy. Hurt, yes. Exasperated, constantly. But never truly angry— because she had not allowed herself to care for him with the same intensity that she reserved for her children. Yet she could imagine now, as he stood there holding the door for her, his voice in perfect control as if tuned to the sympathy channel, that as the months and years accumulated, as he drifted away and became unrecognizable, she could become angry, even bitter. She told herself never to let this happen, not to become one of those divorcées.

"Well, there's some exercise equipment down there, for starters. Plus books and various things you've probably lost interest in." Hobbies, she might have said, that you took up for five minutes then ditched at a ridiculous cost. When he moved out he took almost nothing, and though she had mentioned these things to him a dozen times before, he had never wanted them back. "And there's that expensive camera I used the other day."

"That other stuff you can probably chuck," he said as they walked into the house. "I'm not going to have time to go through it before we take off. But I think I would like that camera."

For a moment Lydia regretted mentioning it, but then she thought of Cy's developing the roll and seeing the photographs of the kids lined up on the front steps of her house, the house they had bought together. "Here." She picked the camera up from the table in the front hall.

"How old is this thing, anyway?" He took it from her.

She had bought the camera for him for Christmas maybe twenty years ago, when Cy was interested in lighthouses. "Pretty old, but it still seems to work perfectly well." They crossed through the dining room into the kitchen. "I'll just grab the zoom lens from the basement," Lydia said.

She was glad that she'd cleaned the place again after the children left. My house is in perfect order, she thought. Take a look around in case you're wondering whether I'm doing okay. She had mopped the kitchen floor, even swept the basement stairway. Cy would find all of his old hobbies arranged along a shelf in the small room at the bottom of those stairs. His fishing rods were in cases; books upright and neatly arranged; rowing machine and stationary bike dusted and pushed to the wall.

"I think I'll stay up here in the kitchen," Cy said as Lydia stopped in the middle of the basement stairs.

"You're sure you don't want to take anything else?"

"I shouldn't." His voice had a slant of humility, as if staying upstairs was the honorable thing to do.

Lydia couldn't tell if he was trying to be generous by allowing her to keep his discarded projects or if he just didn't care enough to take them off her hands.

She fetched the lens off the shelf and brought it up to the kitchen. Cy took it out of its case and looked it over, twisted off the 35-millimeter lens and fitted the zoom in its place, then tested it out. He panned around the kitchen, moved up to the large window at the back, aimed the camera at the garden outside. He looked out onto the patio. "I forgot how nice the lilacs are here."

"Yes, they're my favorite." It was strange to be carrying on a conversation like this, and Lydia wondered what Cy was doing here.

"You have tulips, too."

"Can I get you something to drink?" she asked.

"Maybe some water."

She filled a glass with tap water and placed it on the kitchen table, then sat down. "You know, the Nomad's still in the garage. Do you want me to give that away, too?"

"It's your car, Lydia. You could probably get a pretty penny if you sold it." He came back to the table. "Thanks." He sat down and sipped the water. For the first time, Lydia noticed his wedding ring. For thirty-three years he had worn a plain gold band, and she wondered what he had done with it. His new ring was large and platinum, etched with a faintly Celtic design. He fiddled with the camera's shutter release. "I've been thinking about getting into nature photography. All those desert flowers and cacti. It should be amazing."

"What do you mean?"

"The place we bought is about fifty miles northwest of the city, near El Mirage—an easy trip to the mountains. The light out there is supposed to be spectacular."

Lydia leaned back in her chair and looked directly at Cy for the first time that day, into his unfocusing eyes. "You're moving?" she asked.

"The kids didn't tell you?"

"No, the kids didn't tell me."

"Huh. I assumed they would." Cy looked genuinely surprised.

She crossed her arms and held her elbows, as if they were wings she was trying to bind.

"Yes, we're moving to Arizona. Right after the honeymoon. Most of our stuff is already tagged or in boxes. We should be settled there by June." He slipped the camera into its case. "I thought you already knew."

"Well, I didn't."

"Ellen and I both got jobs at the phone company. It just

made more sense. Except for college she's lived in Detroit her whole life, and so have I, pretty much. We thought we'd try a new adventure."

Lydia could feel the blood rush to her face. So this explained Jessica's sweetness, her courtesy in the final hours of her visit. *Better take care of Mother. Boy, is Mom going to take this hard—all alone now, no reliable help for miles.* Lydia hated nothing more than being pitied. And now she felt foolish that no one had told her about this. Foolish and furious with her children, Jessica most of all. Did they think that she couldn't handle the news? Then why did they leave her to find out on her own?

Cy checked his watch. "About that favor." Lydia tensed. What next, she wondered. "I'm not sure if the kids told you about Ellen's parents, Casper and M.J.? They're delightful people—Casper worked his whole career at Ford, might have known your dad, as a matter of fact. Anyway, they're taking all this very hard—the move, I mean—much harder than we thought. Ellen's an only child. You know how that goes. They live in Royal Oak, and I wondered if we couldn't get you all together."

"What do you mean, exactly?" Lydia asked.

"You know, I thought you could meet them, check in on them every once in a while."

"You're joking, right?"

Cy looked a little sheepish. "Well, no."

"They must have friends in the area."

"Of course they do. This is for me. I feel responsible, that's all. It would mean a lot."

Here was a new twist, Lydia thought. Cy felt responsible for once in his life, so he was calling upon his ex-wife to soften the blow for his new wife's parents. What a fine arrangement! He wanted her to take care of his in-laws. "Well, this is something, all right," she managed to say. "Sure. Go ahead. I'll give them a call."

"Great. That's wonderful. I really appreciate it." Cy took out a pen and wrote the Spiveys' number on the back of one of his Michitel business cards, then stood up from the table. "I should go." He handed her the card, then rubbed his hands together. "We have a million things to do before tomorrow."

"Of course." Lydia followed him to the door, where he stopped and held his arms out. "You've been a great support." He hugged her, his loose shirt soft against her arms.

"So this is it?" she said.

"Hardly. This is our city. We'll be back all the time."

"Well, enjoy Phoenix."

But he was out the door without another word—not even *we'll be in touch*. He probably believed that she wished him well. Down the steps he went, into his shiny car. And with a wave out the window, he was gone.

Upstairs, Lydia lay down on her bed and stared at the ceiling. She thought of Phoenix, that ready-made city, thought of her kids now torn between there and here. Where would they go for Christmas? How often would she see them now? Half as much? One time a year? Already she saw them so seldom. She wondered what enticements Cy and Ellen would lay before the children. Free flights. Sunshine and swimming pools.

From Lydia's office, the phone rang and Jessica's voice floated over from the answering machine. "Mom? Are you there? Hello. Hello. If you're there, come talk to me."

Lydia got up and hurried to the phone. "Hello."

"Hi, Mom. What's wrong? You sound weird."

"It's been one of those afternoons. Guess who I ran into today."

"Who?"

"Your father, as a matter of fact."

Jessica paused, then said, "I've been meaning to tell you—"

"No, let me finish," Lydia interrupted.

"We were going to tell you after the wedding. It just wasn't right. We were shocked."

"I don't think so." Lydia was starting to feel hysterical.

"We were. We had no idea how you would react. We hardly had time to react ourselves."

"Isn't that the problem? It's always us and you. *We* had no idea how *you* would react. Why does it have to be that way? Why the separation? When I created this family I expected us to be great, which meant we had to bond together. What kind of a family is this, all stretched out to the far points of the globe? You wanted to leave me out, didn't you?"

"What are you talking about?"

"You always leave me out. Don't you think you've isolated me enough, Jessica?"

"We weren't isolating you."

Lydia was thinking two could play at this game. If you're going to isolate me, I can isolate you as well. Walter was right: everyone needs a secret life. Perhaps that had been the problem all along.

"A family that goes around whispering, keeping others in the dark, is not a family," she said. "How would you like it if I had news that I kept to myself? That's called betrayal. Plain and simple."

"We were trying to protect you."

"Well, I don't need protecting," Lydia said, and in spite of how hard she was trying to hold herself together, she hung up.

Jessica called back right away, but Lydia let the machine answer. She walked away from the phone, glimpsed the photograph of her wedding bouquet, and grabbed it off the wall. She went to the back of her closet and gathered up her old wedding dress, which for some crazy reason she'd brought down from the attic the week before. Jessica was still pleading for her to answer the phone.

Down in the basement, Lydia found a half-empty box in Cy's shop of discarded projects, and stuffed the picture and her wedding dress inside. Grabbing the packing tape from the shelf, she felt an odd rush, almost as if she needed to have that secret she'd been thinking about—and right away. She sealed the box, and considered mailing the whole package to Cy, a housewarming gift. She wondered whether her children had enjoyed keeping their secret from her.

She went back upstairs to her office, where she signed on to her e-mail.

Dear norm@nuplan.org,

We met the other day at the museum in Ypsilanti. You might recall that we talked about Preston Tucker. I was interested in what you had to say, so I signed on to your web site this afternoon, which led me to the chat room of drive.com. That was quite a lively discussion! As an industry-watcher, I'd be interested to hear more about your plans.

Yours sincerely,
Lydia Modine

She read her note over and deleted her last name. He had looked like a perfectly gentle aging hippie, though, and he might prove useful for her research. She typed out her last name again, read the message over. What could be the harm? And with that, she pressed "Send."

Later that afternoon, sitting on the living room couch, she looked through the Tucker papers that Walter had copied for her. The top article, from the *Detroit Free Press*, covered an early appearance of the Tucker prototype at a parade in Detroit in early 1948. Under the headline COULD THIS BE THE CAR OF TOMORROW? Tucker waved from the window of his car, his bow tie slightly askew. Over his shoulder, his wife flashed her best Jane Wyatt smile. Vera Tucker, the article went on to say, couldn't wait to see her husband's car available for every American, especially in her favorite color: waltz gown blue.

Beneath the first article were advertisements and newspaper clippings, a random sampling of Tucker history. Though Lydia had come across much of this material before, it seemed worth reading again. Here was the same ad that hung on her office wall of her father's early design—"more like a Buck Rogers special than the automobiles we know today"—plus other ads for the '47 and '48 proposed models. Each looked less and less like a "torpedo" and more like a streamlined family sedan. Lydia remembered her father's frustrations with Tucker, who couldn't decide whether the focus should be on speed or safety.

She looked through the articles: a couple of early briefs mentioning her dad when the design was still "shrouded in mystery"; a big story in the *Chicago Tribune* covering the launch of the first actual prototype in late 1947, not long after Gilbert had left for GM; another in the *New York Times* about Tucker's approved purchase of an assembly plant in Chicago, the biggest one in the world, where he planned to build his car once the financing came through. Underneath all this was a transcript of the famous broadcast announcing that an investigation by the Securities and Exchange Commission "would blow the new Chicago auto firm higher than a kite."

Lydia knew that this broadcast, by the respected newsman Drew Pearson, in June 1948, had been the first and most devastating setback for Tucker. It had been known within the company that the government was looking into its books and records, but SEC officers had promised that the investigation would remain secret so long as Tucker complied. But someone had apparently leaked the information to the press, and immediately after the broadcast, public confidence in Tucker collapsed. Lydia checked the articles for any indication of the source of the leak. But she found nothing, certainly no proof that anyone in the Big Three had been involved.

She got up from the couch and put the clippings into a new folder marked Tucker/Dad, then filed it in her office with her latest research. She thought of what her father had said, that those theories were "nothing but applesauce." If there had been anything to them, surely Lydia would have known by now.

Toward dusk Lydia sat outside at the patio table, sipping a glass of red wine. Surrounded by the sounds of zoo birds and crickets, she let her mind wander from conspiracy theories to Norm himself. There had been something exciting about sending him an e-mail this afternoon. Sure, Norm was a rabble-rouser and not exactly her type, but she had this rare feeling that here she was, waiting for a man to pursue her. There'd been no waiting with Cy. The very day they'd reunited at the Brown Jug, he had called to ask if she would like to see *Butterfield 8* at the Michigan Theater that evening. He admitted to having a crush on Elizabeth Taylor—"Meow," he'd said. In the days that followed, they saw each other again and again, falling into a comfortable routine, as if the whole affair had been prearranged. Theirs was less a romance than a pairing, and it had remained that way throughout their marriage.

But on this particular spring evening, Lydia let herself imagine Norm as that companion who steadily burned the days with his work, came into the kitchen to cut vegetables, pour wine, and sit kitty-corner at the table, where they'd talk until late.

She picked up her glass and went inside, sliding the door behind her. Upstairs, she checked her e-mail again, and, on her screen, as if she had wished it there, was a message:

Dear Lydia Modine,

Imagine my surprise to open my e-mail and find a note from you. You hardly have to be so formal. I know who you are. I've read your books. If I'd known you were the Lydia of *Together on the Line* and *The Magic Motorway* I would have talked your ear off at the museum. I do have a bone to pick with you, though: I could have used a little help on that message board. Next time I crash a party will you be my date?

I'd love to hear what you're working on next. Nobody has handled such important subjects with as much grace. You truly showed why "I" is the first letter in "Interstate." The most massive public works project in human history proved just how destructive the myth of American individualism has always been.

But I won't step up to the pulpit now. My recently ex-wife used to tell me that I never know when to stop preaching. A couple of questions: are you still living in the same place? It says here under the picture that you live in Detroit with your three children. What do you think of the city these days? Is the latest renaissance showing any promise?

Would love to chat.

With admiration,
Norm

Lydia stood up and leaned over her chair, wondering about the words *will you be my date?* Her ex-husband was about to fly away to Phoenix, and now, out of the noplace of the Internet, here was a note from a stranger suggesting—friendship? Company? *I know who you are. I've read your books.*

Lydia had received her share of letters, mostly praise and the occasional critique, but never something like this. *Would love to chat.*

She looked out the window toward her front yard. The dogwood wavered in the breeze. Reading back over the e-mail, and seeing the invitation half buried in his words—*my* recently *ex-wife*—Lydia felt a flutter of possibility.

She found the number for Uncle Ed's in her wallet, picked up the phone and dialed.

The manager answered, "Hello, sweetheart."

Lydia paused. Had a love bomb detonated over southeast Michigan, and she was the last to know about it? "I was wondering if Marty was there?" she asked. "I'm the one whose car broke down in your parking lot."

"Oh, I'm sorry. Thought you were my wife. We closed a couple of hours ago. I'm doing the books, running late for dinner."

"So Marty has left?"

"Yeah, he's long gone. Can I leave him a message?"

"I've been thinking about it," Lydia said. "And I'd like to sell him my car."

"You sure? That beautiful Escort? It's just sitting out there saying 'Take me home.'"

"Yes, I'm sure."

"Well, I'll pass on the message."

"I appreciate that."

"And sorry about answering the phone that way. I could have sworn you were my wife. That woman is like clockwork. As soon as we hang up, I'll bet you she calls."

"I don't mind," Lydia said, which was true. It had been a long time since a man had called her sweetheart. "If you could tell Marty I'm sending him the title, I think we have a deal."

She got the address for Uncle Ed's plus Marty's last name, which was none other than Rose. She hung up the phone and dug out the Escort file, wrote a quick note, and signed a letter passing ownership of the car from herself to Marty Rose. She wouldn't even bother to wait for the check.

She went outside and walked down to the end of the block, where her neighborhood met the fence line of the zoo. A mailbox sat there, and beyond it Lydia could see the shelf of rocks and man-made caves where the sea lions often gathered to sun themselves, though none were there now in the day's disappearing light. She opened the creaky mouth of the mailbox, slipped the letter in, and listened to make sure that it slid to the bottom.

11

LYDIA WAS SURPRISED by how much willpower it took not to write Norm back immediately. She drafted a letter and revised it over the course of the evening, tinkering with every word:

Dear Norm,

Many thanks for your note. How nice it is to know that community does still exist—at least the community of ideas. In the motor city, as you might imagine, I have to proceed with caution when expressing my views.

Yes, I'm a Detroiter, born and raised. Little has changed—this is still the city of tomorrow. But I love it and have lived here all my life. I'm no longer married, only to my work. I'm more or less the same person in the photograph, only the bio has changed. My three kids have scattered east and west. I wish it were temporary.

Where do you live? Do you have children? Are you on the design or the engineering side of car-building? And why the interest in Preston Tucker? Might you be the next incarnation?

Always nice to find an ally in this world.

Sincerely,
Lydia

After debating whether to send the message, Lydia decided to wait until the morning. She saved the letter in her draft file in a new folder called Norm. Crawling into bed, she wondered if he lived in Ypsilanti. Tucker himself had lived there in the early 1940s, and though it was hard to merge the two characters in her mind—one a bow-tied salesman, the other a pony-tailed activist—that's what Lydia was inclined to do. Maybe Norm was a scientist or an architect, an environmentalist or a designer. She pictured him hunched over a drafting table, working out the details of his own prototype. She lay there imagining what it would be like to have Norm living here in her house, setting up his shop out back, filling the empty space of her bed.

But the next morning, she woke up tired. Cold weather had returned, and overnight a sheet-metal gray had dropped over the city. Lydia got up, made herself a cup of coffee, and reread her note to Norm several times. It seemed too serious, too flirty, too strained, too playful, a little desperate, and somehow just wrong. She tried recasting the note entirely but only made it worse. She felt embarrassed by last night's fantasies. So, for the rest of the day, and through the next, she told herself to forget about Norm.

Thursday she awoke to the fourth straight morning of gray weather and made up her mind to deal with the task she'd been looking forward to least: calling the Spiveys.

"Bonjour," answered a woman in a throaty voice.

"Is it too early?" Lydia glanced at the clock: eight-thirty.

"Depends on who you are, my darling. If you're wondering whether I'm happy with my long distance, yes it is too early."

"This is not the phone company."

"Good. On the other hand, my long-distance bills are about to go up."

"This is Lydia Modine."

Just then, another voice came on the line. "Hello." It was a soft-spoken man.

"You're five minutes late, Casper. Pardon my husband. He's stuck in a lower gear."

"Goodbye." The phone clicked as the man hung up.

"Now what did you say your name was, again?"

"Lydia Modine. I'm Cy's ex-wife."

"I see." Ellen's mother seemed at a loss for words, which Lydia guessed did not happen often.

"Cy told me to call you."

"He did?"

"I'm sorry. I thought you knew."

"No, this is the first I've heard of it. What did he want you to call me about?"

"That's a fine question," Lydia said. "This is awkward. I honestly thought he had told you."

"It seems that my daughter and your ex-husband have made surprises a hallmark of their new marriage. Did it come as a surprise to you, too, that they were moving to Arizona?"

"As a matter of fact, yes."

"So this is very much in keeping with their style. It's nice of us to accommodate them, don't you think?"

Actually, Lydia was thinking that she'd like the Arizona earth to open its dry mouth and swallow the city of Phoenix.

"I have an idea," the woman continued. "Let's meet for lunch today. My name is Marie Jeanette, but please call me M.J. My husband is Casper. You can call him what you'd like."

Lydia had not expected to meet so soon, if at all. She had only been following up on a promise. "I'm not sure. I've only just—"

"Come on, it'll be good to talk."

"Well—" Lydia hesitated.

"Where do you go for lunch?"

"I don't usually."

"How about a for-instance? Where was your last lunch out?"

Lydia thought of Arby's and could almost feel the bile rise in her stomach. "The café at the DIA. I work nearby."

"Casper, pick up the phone," M.J. yelled. "Casper!"

After a moment Ellen's father was on the line again. "Hello," he said. "Make up your mind. Do you want me or not?"

"Better leave that one alone," M.J. said. "We're going to the DIA for lunch. Now be a good boy and dig up the exhibition schedule."

"Right away." Casper fumbled the phone.

M.J. continued. "We're lifetime members. We have three permanent tickets to special exhibitions. Me, Casper, and Ellen. We were about to buy a fourth for Cy, but I guess that's no longer necessary."

"Probably not." Lydia tried to sound as if she didn't care.

"Remind us and we'll lend you two of our tickets. Maybe you can take a friend. Are you seeing someone?"

This conversation was growing more personal by the minute. "Me?" Lydia said. "No, I don't think so."

Casper got back on the line. "So here's what's showing: it's called 'Abelardo Morell and Camera Eye.'"

"Yes, tell us about it, dear."

"It says here, 'Abelardo Morell explores the basic principles of photography and human vision.'" Casper read slowly. "'His subjects are familiar—ordinary domestic objects and interiors, illustrated books and maps, children's toys—yet his photographs reveal the extraordinary found in the commonplace.'"

"Well there we have it," M.J. said. "How does that sound, Lydia?"

"Okay, I guess." Actually, it seemed pretty interesting. "Lunch would be fine."

"How's noon?"

"Shall I pick you up?"

"How about we get you?" M.J. asked.

And because Lydia was not about to be her ex-husband's new in-laws' keeper, she said, "Sure." She gave M.J. directions to Franklin Street, adding with a certain pride in her voice, "My house is the only one on the block with a front porch."

"Au revoir," M.J. said and hung up.

Oddly enough, Lydia found that her spirits had lifted. She signed on to her e-mail account and sent her reply to Norm.

The Spiveys arrived in a long black Town Car, promptly at noon, and Lydia climbed into the squeaky back seat.

"Is that the zoo over there?" Casper nodded in its direction.

"Your old home, dear," M.J. said before Lydia could reply. "My husband is a fugitive—broke out of his cage."

Casper looked over his shoulder. "Hardly a fugitive. I live with the zookeeper."

"A left turn will do now." M.J. made a motion like steering, as if by doing this she could keep the car steady. Casper turned left, then followed his wife's direction—she seemed compelled to narrate the drive—turning right at Lincoln, then right again onto Woodward and down from there, somewhat precariously, to the DIA.

It turned out, though, that Casper had read the exhibition dates wrong. The Abelardo Morell photographs would not be shown for another month. When M.J. scolded him, he said, "You should have looked it up yourself."

"I'm not your seeing-eye wife. Can't you tell May from June?"

"You pressured me. I don't do well under pressure."

"Oh, for God's sake. I ask so little."

Lydia quickly said, "It doesn't matter. I love the permanent collection."

And so they spent more than an hour wandering the cool halls of the museum. M.J. took Lydia to her favorite places: the sixteenth-century chapel from Château de Lannoy, with its flamelike window tracery; the French Impressionist room with

Seurat's *View of Le Crotoy, Upstream*, and to the Thomas Germain silver collection, once the table settings for eighteenth-century French royalty.

"What period do you like?" M.J. asked Lydia, and she told them about the Detroit Industry Frescoes, how the Rivera room had become her sanctuary.

"I haven't been there in a while," Casper said. "All I remember are these great machines and a lot of gray, yellow, and blue."

When they entered the room, Casper squinted up close to the main mural and walked from factory worker to factory worker, as if he were the foreman scrutinizing their productivity. He stepped back and faced the north wall. "So what's going on here? Describe it to me," he said.

Lydia thought of her father, who had been so proud of these murals because Ford had commissioned them around the time he had been working there.

"Yes, Lydia, tell us what we're looking at," M.J. said. "We understand you're the resident authority."

Lydia did not wish to say anything critical about cars, just as she had kept quiet when her father brought her here. Diego Rivera was a Marxist, so of course he had been fascinated by machines, seeing technology as a way of freeing the working class from exhausting menial labor. It was the most unlikely partnership: Edsel Ford, the son of the twentieth century's great industrialist, calling upon a Communist to render the assembly line.

As Lydia described the harmony between worker and machine, she couldn't help being amazed all over again by the frescoes. As often as she came here, the power of this room's idealism never diminished for her. Where else could the world's conflicting ideologies come together to make something beautiful? Where else could a believer in the commune, like herself, stand next to a Ford pensioner, like Casper Spivey, and be equally moved? Here was Detroit as it might once have been—Ford Rouge, 1932—but also Detroit as it could become again. Like the Renaissance art that inspired the frescoes, like the renaissance that Detroit was forever promising, this was a celebration of both the past and the future.

"It's really something how those images have come back to me," Casper said.

Above and set away from the main walls were the smaller panels, the green-hued warning signs: syringes and skeletons, warplanes next to predatory birds, scientists working on a chemical bomb, an embryo suffocating in clouds of poisonous gas. Even Rivera had to concede that as progress created, it also destroyed.

"So—" Casper interrupted her thoughts as they walked out of the room. "Where did your interest in cars begin? The second I get started on the subject, M.J.'s eyes glaze over."

"Like this?" M.J. tilted her head back and demonstrated.

Casper peered closely at her. "That's it," he said.

Lydia explained who her father had worked for. As an only child of one designer, she said, and the granddaughter of another, she'd grown up with gasoline in her blood.

"What was your father's name?" Casper asked.

"Gilbert Warren."

He put his hand on his cheek, and an odd look crossed his face.

"He was at Ford for a while, but probably before you got there," Lydia added. "He worked for Preston Tucker, then he went to GM."

"The name does sound familiar." Casper fiddled with a button on his shirt. "Small world, isn't it?"

They had lunch in the DIA's Gothic courtyard. Casper chose a Salisbury steak, M.J. a fruit cup and a bowl of cottage cheese. Lydia had a salad and a cup of tired-looking minestrone.

"You know why I like you," M.J. said all of a sudden. "You've raised good children. I had a nice time with Jessica. She's a gem."

"So people tell me."

"She gives you a hard time?"

"She's twenty-seven, still finding herself." Lydia opened a package of Italian dressing and drizzled it on her salad.

"There's no end to people finding themselves. The shame of it is, they'll keep searching, and one day they'll look up and what they thought they had, what they took for granted for so long—you, me—we'll be gone." M.J. looked up toward the ceiling for a moment, then down again. "What I'm wondering is, why now? I honestly thought we'd never lose Ellen. Foolish me," she said. "So, why is your daughter angry with you?"

Lydia was taken aback by M.J.'s bluntness. She was still plenty wary to be having such a conversation with these people whom she didn't know. Still, she answered the question. "I think she's just angry, and here I am."

"Angry with her father, I assume."

"She wouldn't admit it, but you're probably right. There's plenty of rage headed Cy's way already. Ivan has that territory well occupied, so I guess Jessica has to look for other battles."

"So it's misdirected?"

"For the most part, yes," Lydia said, though she hadn't considered it in quite this way. "Maybe she wishes that I had taken Cy on."

"What do you mean?"

M.J. had an almost eerie way of putting her at ease, and Lydia wondered how many jobs Cy had gone through since they'd been together. Twelve? Fifteen? More? Bringing up such details with his new mother-in-law hardly seemed fair, though. "I put too much time into my work," Lydia offered instead.

"There's always a reason for not wanting to fight for your marriage." M.J. dug her spoon into the cottage cheese and took a large bite. "I don't mean to pry. I'm trying to figure out why Jessica would be angry with *you*."

"You and me both," Lydia said and laughed a little.

"Do you want my theory?"

"Sure."

"Be a dear, dear," M.J. said to Casper. "Grab me a cheap

white wine and maybe a sandwich. Who am I, pretending to have no appetite?"

Casper stood up and made his way back to the food line, as though accustomed to taking such orders.

"Should I give him a hand?" Lydia asked.

"He sees much better than you'd think." M.J. finished the cottage cheese and scraped the bowl with her spoon. "You and your daughter are too much alike, that would be my guess. Granted, I've known you all of a couple hours, but my intuition has been hailed as legendary from here to Montreal."

"I might have said we were too much alike when Jessica was a girl, but not anymore. I can hardly get in a word without her taking me to task."

"That's because she's patently antagonistic where you're concerned. You could tell her the sky is blue and she'll say red, just to choose a different color. People should always come back to who they were as children. And as a child, like you said, she was mother's helper."

M.J. theorized that people came up against a few crises in life, and those who made it through preserved their true identity. "Everyone comes up against something," she said. "The ones who make it, who find some measure of happiness in the world, don't run away. I worry for my daughter. I don't think she realizes what a major step she's taking."

Lydia wanted to ask, *What's the crisis?* But she could just as easily guess. Ellen, the only child, had not left gracefully. She had lingered around home for thirty-five years and her parents had grown used to her company—so settled into the habit of having her nearby that this departure must have felt like a desertion. Ellen had waited too long, until her parents could no longer imagine life without her. Lydia's children had left one by one. When Ivan went off to college, two kids remained in the house, which made the separation bearable. When Jessica left, Davy was always around to help out. And by the time her youngest was gone, Lydia had grown to expect that her children would split off in all directions for a while. But they would come back. They had to come back sometime.

Lydia told M.J. about the ersatz Buddhist who rolled into Royal Oak one day and slid open the door to his van. "Just like the sixties," she said. "And she followed him to the coast."

"She's waiting for a test, something to challenge her," M.J. said.

"The divorce has been a test."

"Yes and no. It's a late divorce, so she probably feels awkward raising a fuss about it." M.J. polished off the fruit cup. "She needs a bigger test, I think, something that pits her against her own resistance."

Casper returned with two mini-bottles of wine, plastic cups, and a turkey sandwich.

"I think I will have a glass of wine, after all," Lydia said, and began to get up from the table.

"Here, have mine," Casper offered.

Again M.J. saw through Lydia's motives. "You're right," she said. "We can't have him drink and drive." She poured wine for herself and Lydia. "Just as well. This means more for us."

"So what did I miss?" Casper asked.

"The eternal mystery of mothers and daughters," Lydia said.

"Parents and children should aim for zero friction. It's impossible, of course, but this should be the goal." M.J. bit into her turkey sandwich and continued talking. "In a marriage, on the other hand, friction is essential. Isn't that right, mon cheri?"

"I suppose you'd like me to disagree," Casper said.

"Exactly. We agree to disagree, and therein lies the secret. This turkey sandwich you brought me, for example, is wretched. Processed within an inch of its life. Soggy bread, lettuce from last week's salad bar. Is this the best you can offer? Is this what forty-five years of marriage has come to?"

"You are what you eat," Casper said.

"So tell us, Lydia, about this man you're seeing?" M.J. asked.

"Did I say I was seeing someone?"

"That's one of her old tricks." Casper laughed. "I knew you wouldn't fall for it."

"Well, it does so happen that I've been corresponding with a man through the Internet," Lydia found herself saying. She didn't know whether she was sharing this because the Spiveys had a way of drawing her out or, just as likely, in the hope that the news would reach Cy.

"The Internet? How terribly modern you are," M.J. said. "Tell us about him."

Lydia took them back to five days ago, when she had seen Norm at the museum, then visited the message board and sent him a note. His response, she said, had in its tone more than a small hint of the possible. She recounted from memory, almost to the word because she had read the note over so many times, the reply letter she had sent earlier that morning.

"It was a little forward, I have to admit," Lydia explained.

"You don't know what forward is," M.J. said. "If you think that's forward, you'll be alone for the rest of your life."

"But I asked him where he lives, what his work is. I pretty much said I was lonely."

"He started it, darling. You gave him far less than you think you did. I think we should write your new friend a spicier note."

"Oh, no—"

"I think it would be a marvelous way to spend an afternoon. We're done here. Casper, why don't you ask the lady at the register where we can use a computer."

"The library has computers," Lydia said, before she could stop herself.

M.J. lowered her head and leveled her eyes at Lydia. "I'm beginning to think you like my idea of sending your boy a note."

"I didn't say that."

M.J. smiled. "Oh, but you did."

12

J ESSICA STOOD on the fourth-floor deck of her apartment in Eugene, just back from a long walk with the dog up Hilyard to Alton Baker Park. They'd strolled along the Willamette River through the bright, clear morning. As usual, Bedlam had flown off the path, found the nastiest muck by the riverbank, and dug in with his paws and snout. Now he slumped at her feet languorously cleaning his long fur.

Today was her day off and she wanted to get out of town, leave her tiny apartment, just go somewhere. She lived in one of the most beautiful states in the country, but since Blane had left with the van, she'd been more or less stranded in Eugene. She rode the bus to work, relied on friends to shuttle her around. But nearly all of them, graduate students at the University of Oregon, had gone home for the summer. She wished she had a car, but she couldn't afford one.

She remembered it was Void's day off, too. He worked part-time at a head shop and hung around cafés and a comic-book store near the University. He'd once mentioned that he'd gone to Stanford for a while but had found Palo Alto so bourgeois that he'd dropped out and moved to Alaska to work on a trawler for a couple of years. He talked nostalgically about the ocean. "Let's go to the coast," Jessica said when he answered the phone. "I've got my day bag packed."

Void sounded as if he had just woken up, but within an hour there he was below her balcony, waving from the window of his old red Civic. Jessica filled Bedlam's food bowl, kissed the dog goodbye, and locked up her apartment.

She and Void had been seeing less of each other lately, which was fine with her. The mystery of Void, which had drawn her to him in the first place, had been steadily eroding over the past month. Now he seemed less the inscrutable rebel and more the self-obscuring lost soul, and her patience was wearing thin. Recently, without any prompting, he'd said that his real name was Kevin and that he'd borrowed his moniker from a Seattle alt-radio DJ named Void Oblivion. "But don't tell anyone. I need to be able to trust you," he'd said. "There are people who don't like me, you know. I've got reasons for keeping things under wraps."

"So where are we going?" Void asked as Jessica climbed into the car.

"It's a surprise. You just do the driving."

"Look at the adventuress," he said.

They drove on 126 west from Eugene, into the countryside of old farms, trout ponds, and bright green fields. Outside Noti, the road began to wind; the terrain turned rugged. Void pointed to a general store with a red gas pump out front and said he'd stopped in there once. "I got into a long conversation with a fourth-generation logger. He told me people don't *neighbor* like they used to. What do you think, Jess? Do you still *neighbor*?"

"I called you, didn't I?" She looked over at him, and he gave her a little pout. She hadn't seen him in more than a week, since before her father's wedding and hadn't even bothered to call him when she got back. He looked even younger than usual today, reedy, with pale, almost bluish skin and deep red lips. From the first time they'd met, Jessica had felt old around him, and she wondered now if he weren't making everything up, from his name to his age to the Alaskan trawler story. He'd probably dropped out of high school and come to Eugene, like others she knew, to blend in with the scenery. She didn't know how old he might actually be. Certainly not twenty-eight, as he'd claimed.

She was waiting for him to ask about her weekend, was all prepared to tell him what had happened at the wedding. But Void was saying something about old-growth forest, pointing out the wild blackberries growing along the side of the road. Jessica realized that she had barely mentioned her family to Void in the four months since they'd met. So why begin now?

Their relationship was marked by a desire for company, not necessarily companionship. They tended to meet in busy places where they didn't have to pay close attention to each other. They went to art films and danced at the Workers of the World meeting hall, once a hotbed of labor activism, now boasting "the best hardwood dance floor in the Pacific Northwest." They had cheap drinks and free food at happy hour in noisy bars and after dancing would go back to her place, always her place. Unlike Blane, whose three hundred daily prostrations to Buddha made him sinewy and pliant, Void felt fragile when she held his narrow shoulders. Looking into his face in the murky light some evenings, she had the odd feeling that she could have been seeing her own face, a bit unsure, searching for approval. Bedlam would come up and nudge them with his nose, wanting to go outside. Later, Void would drive back to his own apartment, a place that Jessica wondered if she'd ever see.

"Up or down?" Void asked at the intersection of 126 and the Oregon coastal highway, and Jessica said north. She breathed in the salt air, watched the gulls and cormorants swoop and dive, and thought for a moment that she might like to live here, in the seaside town of Florence. They drove past the marina and chowder joints, Mo's and Captain Jack's, and started up the coast, which was more breathtaking on this cloudless day than the one time Jessica had driven the same stretch with Blane.

Void looked as if he'd seen it all before. He had an annoying habit of weighing every experience against one that he'd had in the past, and always the present paled in comparison. Jessica could almost feel him getting ready to gush about the scenery in Alaska. Anticipating this, she said, "So I've been thinking about applying to graduate school." In fact, she had only really considered the possibility over the past few days. Something about her father's leaving made her realize that time was slipping by. She'd come back to a quiet town, a more suburban city than she wanted to admit. Eugene was no nirvana, no perfect solution, and with her friends gone and the campus mostly deserted, she'd found herself, to her surprise, actually thinking a year ahead.

"Grad school?" Void sounded disapproving. "In what?"

Yesterday she'd gone to the library after work to look into some programs. In the back of her mind she'd always figured she would do something similar to her mother. But she knew she couldn't be a historian; she had no desire to trespass on that territory. For all Lydia's speeches about politics and group-think, Jessica still believed in that unfairly tormented idea: "making a difference." She had looked up programs in Urban and Regional Planning, vaguely recalling that her mother had taken a similar degree but hadn't pursued a career in the field. "Urban planning," she said now, as if she had given it real thought.

"What are you doing living in Eugene if you want to be an urban planner?" he asked.

"I did grow up around Detroit. And my mom went to grad school in regional planning. There was a lot of talk about cities around the house."

"I don't know." Void hesitated. "They'll brainwash you in grad school. You'll think you're working for the greater good. But follow the paper trail, and some oil company is paying for your research."

"These are public universities," Jessica said.

"Public, private. It's all the same these days. Everyone's getting paid off." Void seemed about to cook up one of his diatribes when Jessica saw the sign she'd been looking for.

"Turn here," she said.

◆　◆　◆

Atop a high cliff sat a small building overlooking the Pacific. "So is this your big surprise?" he asked as they reached the entrance.

"You'll see." She opened the door and hurried him in.

When she and Blane had driven the coast on a rainy weekend in late fall, the sea lion caves had been closed, and she'd regretted missing out ever since. At the admission desk she bought two tickets.

"Seven dollars a pop! What do you get for it?" Void asked, loud enough for the woman at the desk to hear him.

"My treat, okay?" Jessica said sharply and took Void's hand, leading the way out of the building. They followed a path to an elevator, which they shared with a father and son who wore matching Seattle Mariners jerseys. The son, clearly excited, read from a brochure as they slowly dropped two hundred feet toward the water. A recording announced that they were entering the largest sea cave in the world. "The length of a football field and twelve stories high," Void repeated in a faux radio announcer's voice.

The elevator doors opened to an observation area surrounded in chain-link fence. The boy shot ahead, his father trailing.

Void held his shirt over his nose. "More like the largest natural toilet in the world. Help, we're trapped."

"It's not that bad," Jessica said. "Look," and pointed to a sea lion pup slapping its way onto a basalt rock ledge. A green translucent light poured in from the mouth of the cave, brushing the walls and playing on the water's surface. She and Void took a path along the edge of the vast grotto, a good distance from the herd of sea lions, all necks and noses, splashing and diving, sitting high and queenly on the rocks. Void nuzzled up next to Jessica, kissed her on the temple. "Aaarf, aaarf," he said loudly in her ear, but she shrugged him away.

The few people gathered behind the fence, even the boy in the Mariners jersey, spoke in whispers. The tinny whistle of the wind, with the surf, the bird cries, and the guttural moos, had an otherworldly sound.

"I can't tell which is worse." Void stepped away from Jessica and crossed his arms. "This place or the zoo. At least in the zoo everyone knows it's artificial. But here we are, in their natural environment, and we turn them into entertainment. Seven bucks a show." His voice echoed off the walls.

Ordinarily Jessica might have agreed or even gone one further. Void was always expressing his outrage over some new offense, but it occurred to her now that he exhausted her. He spent all of his energy reacting. "This is what sea lions do," she said. "They eat fish and sit on the rocks and couldn't care less if we're watching them."

"How do you know what they think?" Void asked, and caught the attention of the boy in the baseball jersey. The kid had probably heard similar logic on the playground.

Jessica didn't want to get into this. "Look, we're the ones behind the fences, not them. This is nothing like a zoo."

Void continued to pontificate—on whale watching, safaris, the circus, petting zoos. He stopped and leaned against the chain-link fence, the green light throwing a lattice over his face.

"How about we just go back to the cliffs? Would that be better?" Jessica asked.

"If that's what you want." Void seemed to miss the disillusionment in her voice.

They took the elevator back up to the surface, went out to a scenic point overlooking the steel-blue ocean. Tourists fed quarters to coin-op binoculars and watched as more sea lions sunned themselves on the rock shelves outside the caves. Void stood with his hands in his pockets, the wind pasting his hair to his forehead. Jessica wondered what it meant that she was standing at the edge of the United States, as far as she could possibly go to get away, yet the only words that came to mind were *What now?*

When Void pulled up to the curb outside her apartment, he leaned over to kiss her. Jessica turned away. It was six in the evening and they'd spent half the day together.

"So? Do you still *neighbor?*" Void gave her his best puppy dog eyes.

"I don't think so," she said.

He put his hand on her leg. "Oh, come on."

She unlocked the car door.

"Let's go out and get some dinner. It's still early," he said. "Don't you want to dance?" But his voice had already trailed off. On the quiet drive home, he must have lost what nerve he had.

"Maybe I'll see you at the checkout." She got out of the car.

"Well, I'll call you," she heard him say as she reached for her keys.

Inside, Jessica lay down on the couch. She had taken Bedlam for a quick walk, and now he trundled up to her and licked her face, then rested his head on her lap. He looked into her eyes, as if no one else in the world mattered.

She must have drifted off to sleep when Davy called. "Well, the inevitable has happened," he announced. "We had a meeting last night and Lowball's shutting down." He told her about their unsuccessful scramble for more investors and their last, depressing meeting.

Jessica put aside her own lousy day with Void. "I'm sorry, Davy. How's Teresa taking it?"

"We aren't talking. I can't imagine packing up is going to be much fun."

"But *she* decided to give you that money. She took that chance."

"I don't know, Jess. I can be really persuasive when I believe in something. And I was sure at the time about Lowball. She lost forty thousand dollars. Half of what her mother left her. I don't know if we can ever get over that."

"So what are you going to do?" she asked.

"An Oregon vacation sounds like a nice idea. I've got frequent flier miles if you've got room on the couch. I clean. I do dishes."

"Are you serious?" She got up and looked out the window. The streetlights had winked on.

"Just for a few days? A long weekend? I need a break, Jess. For now, anyway, I haven't told anyone but you."

She couldn't imagine a worse time. But what else could she say to her little brother but "Of course"?

Later that night, though, she started to get excited about the idea of having Davy visit. As awful as it was for him to face the end of Lowball and, perhaps, of his relationship with Teresa, at least he'd be free to start over, do something new. Jessica wondered what *she* was waiting for. She had come out here to begin her own life. But something was holding her back. It was as if she had never gotten away. She and Davy could rent a car, go places she'd been meaning to see. Together they could talk about *What now.*

13

L YDIA WAS FEELING tipsy by the time she and the Spiveys entered the library's computer lab. Walter happened to be working the desk and she worried that he would notice. But his attention was entirely on Casper. "I'm a great admirer of yours," Walter said, introducing himself to the Spiveys. He mentioned some of the ad campaigns Casper had shepherded through at Ford. "My favorite, 'Quality Is Job One,'" Walter explained to Lydia, "turned the focus from cars to the people who built them. Mr. Spivey is the guy who brought Ford out of that long slump."

"That's very nice of you," M.J. said before Casper could get in a word. "But take care with my husband's ego. It's already overtaxed."

Walter looked unsure about how to take this. "So what brings you here?" he asked Lydia.

"Our friend is showing us the wonders of the Internet," Casper answered.

"Well, not exactly," Lydia said. "We're just doing e-mail, that's all. Thank you, by the way, for the Tucker information." She turned to the Spiveys. "Walter put together some Preston Tucker clippings for me."

"Not much of a conspiracy, is there?" Walter added. "Not until you can show me a smoking gun."

Casper gave a little smile. M.J. put her arm around him.

Walter found an open computer terminal and pulled up extra chairs. "So you're all fine here?" he asked. "I'm doing double duty. I've got to run upstairs in a minute."

Lydia thanked him and signed on to her e-mail account. When she saw that a message from Norm was waiting, her pulse quickened. M.J. pulled her chair up closer. It might have been the wine or her own newfound desire to shake up her life, but Lydia didn't mind M.J. leaning over and reading the note out loud.

"'Dear Lydia,' it says. 'I know all about Detroit's latest plans, and as usual they're going for the temporary fix. The only way they'll pull themselves out of this moribund state is to aim for a sustainable economy rather than the exhaustive one they've been so committed to for the past hundred years. And you can't have a sustainable economy unless you create a physical environment that supports and nourishes it.' My, my," M.J. said. "This is some racy stuff. Are you sure you want us to read this sizzling billet-doux?"

"It gets better," Lydia said. "Look at the next paragraph."

"'The city is pawn to the highway,'" M.J. continued. "Something about casinos. Baseball. The Renaissance Center. Etcetera. Aha, here it gets interesting: 'So you're married to your work?'" he writes. "'That's a line I'm all too familiar with, one I used to hear at home on a regular basis. I've often wondered what might have happened had I married someone else who was married to her work. If two people are married to their work, it wouldn't be so bad, would it? They could come together at the end of the day and have an affair.'"

Lydia stopped on that line. "That's something," she said. "You know when my ex-husband—"

"Our son-in-law," Casper put in.

"When I met Cy for the first time he used a line much like this one."

"So it's auspicious," Casper said.

"I don't know about auspicious. We are divorced, after all."

"But your marriage lasted a long time. Thirty-some years is a good ride in this day and age. What else does the letter say?" Casper asked.

"He talks about his children," M.J. said. "A son and a daughter. Both in college."

"Do you think he's younger than I am? Two kids in college. I bet he's not yet fifty."

"I thought you saw him."

"I couldn't tell. Honestly," Lydia said.

"Men always start late. I'm sure you're contemporaries."

"How does he close the letter?" Casper asked.

"'Warm regards.'"

"So let's hop to that reply," M.J. said, and soon, with the Spiveys' help, Lydia had written a follow-up:

Dear Norm,

I once had a professor in graduate school who used to keep her married life interesting by giving her husband a new name every few months.

You'd think after a while this might get confusing, particularly when they went out in public. I remember meeting her husband on several occasions and under a variety of noms de guerre. It was hard for the rest of the world to keep up with the many names. But it worked for them, and who needs the rest of the world when life at home is never dull?

So, where are your children in school? You forgot to tell me, also, where you live.

Enjoying the distraction from work,
Lydia

Norm replied within five minutes, generating a cackle of glee from M.J. He lived in Windsor, where he had just joined the faculty in Urban and Environmental Planning at the University of Windsor. Both of his children went to the University of Minnesota, where he used to teach.

"So, he's just across the bridge." M.J. rubbed her hands together.

"I don't know," Casper said. "You've got to watch out for those Canadians. They'll eat you alive. Look at me. A shell of the man I was when I met this woman."

"I don't think he's a Canadian." Lydia turned serious. "He just moved to Windsor. I wonder why. Minnesota's a better school and closer to his kids." But she was pleased that they both had a background in planning. And Windsor was less than a half hour's drive away.

"So let's ask him more questions," M.J. said. And Lydia began typing.

The day, like the Internet itself, had an unreal quality. She felt safe sitting behind the hard glass of the computer screen, sending out her queries to Norm, safe also in the company of Casper and M.J. To think that she had dreaded calling them at all.

If Jessica had been witnessing this, she might have called it desperation. But in fact here was a man interested in Lydia—waiting on her every signal. Norman Crawford, professor of urban and environmental planning. At fifty-four, a touch on the young side, but as M.J. said, definitely in range. Lydia had never liked Windsor, but the place seemed almost exotic now: Ontario. Canada. Another country.

After they had at last signed off, Casper and M.J. drove Lydia home.

"I had a wonderful time. I'll call you soon," she said through the passenger side window.

"Thanks for taking care of us." M.J. grabbed her hand.

"I should say the same to you." Lydia waved goodbye and went up the steps to her house.

Jessica, Davy, and Ivan had each left a message on the answering machine.

"I'm calling to check in on the patient," Jessica said.

Lydia had forgotten any conversation she'd had about being sick. She'd eaten a roast beef sandwich that one afternoon, for God's sake. She didn't need to see a doctor, didn't need her children checking up on her to make sure she wasn't wasting away. No, she was the author of four reputable books, a sixty-one-year-old divorcée who had a younger man in the wings, someone with ideas and energy, swooning over her.

Lydia thought about calling her kids back and setting the record straight. She also had an urge to tell them about Norm, let them know that their mother still had certain charms. But secrets could carry even more of a thrill. She wouldn't mention her new admirer, not just yet, and she could play out this so-called medical problem a bit longer, too. She liked hearing from her children, and if a mysterious stomachache could hold their attention for a while, was it a crime to let them worry, just a little?

Over the next two weeks she exchanged several e-mails a day with Norm. Even when he visited his kids in Minneapolis, he managed to dash off a couple of notes to her. Lydia pictured him wandering the hidden metropolis of malls, tunnels, and skyways, telling his children to hold on; he was expecting an important message. She imagined his kids—Jeremy, who was soon to go to Yellowstone to volunteer in reforestation, and Tracy, who planned to waitress another summer at Pizza-delic—sitting in a cybercafé, waiting for their father to write her back. Norm had already told them about Lydia. And while it seemed quite early to her, she wondered if his children had pulled up chairs next to him and, like the Spiveys, dispensed advice.

She had spoken with M.J. several times in the past couple of weeks as well, mostly about Norm, but also about Cy and Ellen. The movers had arrived in Phoenix with their things and soon Cy and Ellen would start their new lives, which at the moment did not bother Lydia. Her days were beginning to fill again. She told the kids that she'd seen a doctor, who thought she looked fine but was putting her through a series of tests.

"Just to be safe," she said. "It's probably a dairy allergy or something." She felt a little bad for carrying on like that, but then again, they were far away and would never find out.

They called—that was what mattered—and once on the phone she could catch up with their lives. Ivan's work at International Trade looked quiet until late fall when he would lead a business development mission to Brazil. He was taking classes in Portuguese, looking to buy a condo in D.C. Davy said he was wining and dining another investor, while Teresa complained about being neglected. Jessica was having her own relationship trouble. She'd even volunteered that she might have seen the last of that anarchist, Void. Lydia felt for the first time in a while that she could cheer her kids up for a change, not the other way around.

From the attic she had brought down a dozen boxes of her father's notes, drawings, and correspondence, which now sat open in her office. It had taken an hour just to find them, wading through all the boxes of children's clothes, her parents' antique furniture, forgotten chairs with broken arms. There were Jessica's crib and rocking horse, the dollhouse she had ignored, Davy's red and yellow Big Wheel. To make a path, Lydia carried down some of the kids' boxes to Jessica's room. She couldn't help opening them and having a look—at Davy's baseball cards, Jessica's ribbons and trophies, Ivan's Evel Knievel Stunt Action Play Set. It had been the germ of Ivan's alter ego, Ivan Knievel, who used to set up ramps around the neighborhood, crash his bike, and return home with a fake limp claiming multiple fractures.

Over the next few days she organized her father's sketches, photographs, and internal memos from the GM Art & Color section. Unlike his daughter, Gilbert Warren had not been fastidious, so all the makes and models in his files—dream machines and chromed-up coupes, wagons and convertibles—were mixed together, as if, like memory, no boundaries existed between the years.

Amidst the GM materials, scraps of Tucker history kept turning up as well. Apparently, her father had never quite let the man go. One document, in particular, Lydia set aside. It was an ad that Tucker had taken out in all the major newspapers proclaiming his innocence. Tucker's "Open Letter to the Automobile Industry in the Interests of the American Motorist" ran only days after Drew Pearson's announcement about the SEC's investigation. In the ad, Tucker claimed that certain powerful people had "carried on a carefully organized campaign to prevent the motoring public from ever getting their hands on the wheel of a Tucker. These people," he wrote, "have endeavored to bribe and corrupt loyal Tucker employees." He went on to promise the two thousand Tucker franchise owners and fifty thousand Tucker stockholders that he would fight and prove that he and his company were victims of sabotage and unfair competition.

But Tucker's open letter had all been for naught. The stock in his company had continued to drop, and the grand jury overseeing the case against him soon called for an indictment. Lydia slid the letter into a folder along with a newspaper photograph she had found among her father's things: Tucker emerging from the courthouse in 1950, cleared of all charges, but with his company bankrupt and shut down.

With a twinge of guilt, Lydia remembered her book; she had no reason to be thinking about Preston Tucker at the moment. His story was mostly a distraction from the actual work she had to do. If anything, he'd take up only a small chapter in her father's history. The arc would mostly cover Gilbert Warren's years at GM, his behind-the-scenes influence during the golden age of car design. Resolving to get some work done today, Lydia packed up the Tucker clippings. But she couldn't resist checking her e-mail once more. Waiting for her was a message:

Dear Opal,

I'm trying out your old professor's technique: Remember? I call you Opal. You call me Stan. Sorry for the delay. I believe it's been a day and a half. But I'm back in Windsor now and had to catch up with end of the semester meetings. There's so much I wanted to get done this summer and it already feels half over.

I see the weather is cloudy today. Cloudy all week is what the weatherman says. Which is hardly fair—it's June! So what would you say to correcting this injustice and trying to brighten things up? How does lunch on Thursday sound?

Yours,
Stan

For this one, Lydia needed help. It was Tuesday already, and she had to speak to someone about this. Oddly, she could only think of M.J. Her book would have to wait.

"Am I interrupting dinner?" she asked when M.J. answered the phone.

"Let me guess," M.J. said. "You have a date."

"How did you know?"

"Oh, please. It's about time."

"He wanted to know if I'd be free for lunch."

"Well, of course you're free for lunch. Let him sleep on it tonight, so to speak. Wait until morning to write him back," M.J. advised. "Now that he's on the scent, you can retreat a little. This is fine news. Aren't you pleased?"

"I haven't been on a date since college. I almost wish it were happening sooner, so I wouldn't have to think about it for two days."

"Why not swing by tomorrow morning and pick me up," M.J. said. "No better time to shop than the middle of the week." She gave directions to the apartment in Royal Oak. Lydia was glad for a chance to get out of her house. She could imagine herself pacing for two days, worrying over what to talk about at lunch.

The next morning Lydia e-mailed that she would be happy to join him for lunch on Thursday, but only if he called her

Lydia and she could call him Norm. He replied quickly, suggesting a tapas restaurant in Royal Oak, and Lydia marked the details on her calendar.

At the Spiveys', Casper answered the door in a golf shirt, red pants, and slippers. M.J. insisted on showing Lydia around. Besides the very French decor, the apartment was a portrait gallery celebrating the freshly hyphenated Ellen Spivey-Modine.

"I've never seen a picture of your daughter," Lydia said. And suddenly she felt a surge of competitiveness.

"Well, you've come to the right place." Casper sat down on the love seat and crossed his long legs.

M.J. gestured toward an oil painting over the mantel. "There she is at eight years old in her Mary Janes. That's Snowy, her beloved bichon. He was a noisy and spastic dog with a taste for ladies' underwear that eventually did him in. But Ellen loved him. At night he slept on her head like a barrister's wig."

In the portrait Ellen's posture was perfect, her dark eyebrows knitted over her plain and serious face. The Easter-theme backdrop and the fluffy white dog in her lap only heightened the sense that this girl took no joy in childhood. Lydia wondered if this was her natural temperament. Cy needed joy in his life, needed to keep his senses refreshed. What disappointments lay ahead when the honeymoon was over and the daily sunshine of Arizona felt as monotonous as housework?

There were photos of Ellen at her senior prom. She looked pale, and though she was smiling, the staidness lingered in her slate eyes. M.J. pointed out the curving line on the right hand side where Ellen had used a pair of scissors to cut out her high school sweetheart. "A lifeless, adenoidal youth," M.J. said.

Casper countered, "Nice boy. His father worked in finance at Ford."

"And this one by the window we took at Ellen's thirtieth birthday party. That's when Casper had his silly mustache. You'd think at sixty-six a man would be able to grow facial hair.

But not old downy lips." M.J. blew her husband a kiss. "I had to shave it off for him."

Imagining the scene, Lydia realized that a couple had to endure a great many years to know that kind of trust and inseparability. No wonder Casper could drive nearly blind. M.J. was not just seeing for him; she had become his eyes.

Could this ever have happened with Cy? Could they have merged into one, a kind of ego/alter ego, as often happens in long marriages? What if, instead of losing herself in research, Lydia had suggested a long vacation? She could have applied for a residency in Rome, Paris, New York, or taken a fellowship at one of the great libraries. Or better still, they could have gone, as a friend of Lydia's had when her children left home, to Latin America or Africa, on a working, humanitarian mission. Cy would have been game for this. Maybe she had been unfair to disparage him for wanting to try something new. She had always seen this as a weakness. Instead, she might have accepted his adaptability—embraced it, even, allowed herself to be led wherever the road took them. What if, for once, she had stepped outside of her comfortable, tightly controlled space, the Empire of Lydia, as Jessica called it, and let external forces guide her?

M.J. was still talking about her daughter, explaining that Ellen had wanted to get married a decade ago. "She had a couple of boyfriends, but you know the story—they were young and had commitment problems."

So she went for Cy? Lydia's fantasy of running away with him suddenly seemed ridiculous. Capricious, wayward Cy. If Ellen was worried about commitment in her twenties, she had another thing coming with the man she had just married.

"By the way," Casper said, "We should thank you on Cy's behalf for taking such good care of us. He called last night to say, among other things, that you might be stopping over."

Lydia hadn't talked to him since his visit to the house. She wanted to know if the Spiveys had mentioned her new epistolary romance, but instead she asked how the newlyweds were doing.

"Not so well, it turns out," Casper said. "They had to cut the honeymoon short. The movers returned to find that a pipe had burst in the basement and the whole place was flooded."

"That's awful." Lydia held a five-by-seven head shot of Ellen in her early teens.

M.J. peered over the half-glasses that she wore on a long chain and smiled a little, as if to say, but doesn't it give you a *modicum* of satisfaction?

Had it been two weeks ago, Lydia would probably have allowed herself pleasure at the news, but Norm's sudden appearance had given her a new degree of empathy, almost a lofty feeling about Cy's misfortune. "I think it's terrible," she said. "They haven't been married a month."

M.J. rested her glasses on top of her head. "Awfully ironic, don't you think? They left a place that's surrounded by water and arrived in a place where there's no water at all—except exactly where they don't want it, rising up the walls of their living room."

"Irony is rarely generous," Lydia said. "I hope they can move in soon."

"I hope they take the flood as a sign."

Casper squeezed M.J.'s hand. "The girl's got to have a life."

"She had a life, and you know it." M.J. walked back toward the bedroom and returned with her purse and a wide-brimmed hat.

On the way out of the apartment, Lydia noticed another photograph on the wall. It was a picture of Casper when he was young, keen-eyed and dashing, standing between two older men, one of whom Lydia did not recognize, but the other she most certainly did.

"Is that Preston Tucker?" she asked, surprised. Tucker smiled boyishly, his bow tie slightly askew. He seemed to be following her everywhere these days.

"The very one. He was the greatest car salesman that ever lived, any ad man's idol."

"When was this picture taken?"

"Nineteen fifty-three. My first year at Ford. That's my boss, Mickey Gibson."

"Not the same Mickey Gibson from the Tucker Torpedo days. The PR guy?"

"That's him."

"My father did some of the first designs on the Torpedo. So he certainly knew your boss. I've got an ad on my office wall that Gibson probably wrote." Lydia could hear the excitement in her voice. She felt connected to her father standing here, just one person removed from him.

"Detroit can be a village," Casper said.

"Well, enough talk about cars," M.J. broke in. "We have some shopping to do."

M.J. took Lydia to a series of boutiques in the center of Royal Oak. She sped through the racks as if she'd been put in charge of quality control. She must have ran her hands over every garment and pulled out two dozen dresses, skirts, and blouses, all of which she held up against Lydia's body. "This one seems fine," she'd say. "Too sexy . . . Not sexy enough . . ."

At a store called Pull My Daisy M.J. held up a black and white dress. "This would look smashing."

Lydia fingered the thin, slippery material. "I don't know. Norm's kind of earthy."

"Who's leading who here? *You* set the pace, and don't forget it. If he's earthy, clean him up; give him some grooming."

Lydia tried on three dresses and two skirts and each time stepped out from the dressing room with a bit less apprehension. There was something freeing about the way these clothes, much lighter than the cotton knits she usually wore, felt on her shoulders and skin. And though she had never been comfortable in sleeveless shirts, her change in appearance seemed much less shocking with M.J.'s urging her on.

Before lunch she bought a pair of eighty-dollar slingbacks.

"Are you sure about heels?" she asked.

"Absolutely," M.J. said.

"But Norm's kind of short."

"Short men are drawn to tall women. It's the law."

Lydia examined the pointed toes. "Are these shoes too sexy?"

M.J. eyed Lydia's own nondescript flats with an arched eyebrow. "Don't even ask that question."

After lunch they tried a boutique in Birmingham, one of the ritzier suburbs.

"So you won't wear black?" M.J. asked.

"Isn't black for dinner? He's taking me on a lunch date."

"Black is for always. I'll tell you what. We'll compromise. You can wear a gray skirt. But let me help you with the top."

To this, Lydia agreed, and soon she was standing before the mirror at the Stitch-in-Time in a pencil skirt with a side slit and an embroidered white boat-neck shirt that seemed to ride the crest of her clavicle.

"The shirt seems awfully bright," Lydia said.

"It's summer. Liven up."

"And the slit. Look how high it goes. Are you sure this isn't for a much younger woman?"

"You can pull it off, honey. Look at your legs. They're gorgeous. I would kill for legs like yours."

M.J. stepped back from the mirror and thumbed through a display of floral print scarves that rested on a nearby table. "Look at this beautiful silk twill." She held one up. "Here, lean down," she said, and when Lydia bowed her head M.J. tied the scarf adroitly around her neck. "Voilà! You're perfectly radiant."

The outfit, including the shoes, cost three hundred dollars. Lydia couldn't remember the last time she had bought a piece of clothing that wasn't on sale. It was strange to see herself like this. She was beginning to enjoy the idea of having a whole new look; it would give her a chance to hide if she needed to or, better yet, to begin all over.

14

T HE NEXT MORNING nothing looked right. The skirt was too short. The bright top seemed more appropriate for a thirty-year-old. What on earth had she been thinking?

To break in her new shoes, Lydia strolled down a few blocks to the zoo entrance. The clouds hung low and heavy and showed little promise of burning off. Walking back to the house, her feet throbbed, blisters already beginning to form.

She dressed in front of her bedroom mirror, berating herself for buying a white shirt. With her nerves what they were today, of course she was going to spill something on it. And this damn scarf—Lydia tried to recall how M.J. had looped the ends around each other. But no matter how many times she tried to tie it, the knot resembled a mongrel dog—cock-eared, as if listening to two masters at once.

She should have known that she was not the type for overnight transformations. Her whole life had been devoted to making things last. But here she stood in a three-hundred-dollar ensemble, trying to look like someone else. It was eleven-thirty, and she had half an hour to get to the restaurant. She started to panic. The shoes were pinching her feet. She would trip on the steps leading into the restaurant. Rummaging through her closet, she found a pair of sensible, reliable flats. They could have used some polish, but at least they were black. Would Norm really notice her shoes, anyway? Lydia was long and slender, even elegant. With any luck, he would be focused on her eyes, not on what she was wearing.

Her face looked unfamiliar this morning—waxen and severe. She put on a bit of blush, lipstick, and mascara, then went to Jessica's room. Standing before the full-length mirror, she untied the dog-eared scarf and tossed it into a corner. Now the shirt seemed to wash out her features. So obvious that she was trying to appear younger. She decided to go with an old standby: a short-sleeved button-down with a Peter Pan collar. The gray-blue color was a bit too close to the gray skirt she had on, but at least she was looking a little more like herself. The slit skirt stood out now, but she'd run out of time to bring the outfit together. She was already late.

When she got to the restaurant, Norm hadn't yet arrived. Lydia sat at a table by the window and watched the passersby, trying to pick him out of the crowd. Teenagers with tattoos and Day-Glo hair passed mothers pushing babies in double-strollers. Lydia fiddled with the collar of her shirt, soft from so much laundering. Her skin felt loose on her face, as if she were aging by the minute. She was still looking out at the street when a chair scraped the floor, and there was Norm, sitting across from her.

"Did I surprise you?" he asked.

"There you are." She smiled.

He looked different from the man she'd met at the museum. His hair was down, over his ears, and it seemed shorter, shoulder-length. He had on the same glasses as before and a white shirt with a mandarin collar. On someone else it might have seemed studied, but Lydia got the sense that Norm had always been able to carry off a look. He was probably the kind of professor whom women fell for and men described as "cool." Lydia suddenly felt off balance.

"Some drivers you have here. They're out to kill. I'm still not used to it," he said.

"They have a reputation to keep."

"Well, it's an honor to meet you officially now." Norm reached across the table and shook her hand.

"Same here." Lydia felt vaguely disappointed by this greeting.

"Has someone come by for drinks?"

"I told him to wait," Lydia said. She felt awkward and provincial, regretted changing out of the new clothes M.J. had picked out. What had happened to Norm's aging hippie look?

"So, how was your flight back from Minneapolis?" she asked. A stupid question, but the only one that came to mind.

"It was a nonevent."

"I haven't flown in twenty years." Lydia tried to break the ice. "I'm terrified of getting on a plane. There's something unnatural about loading into a giant dart and praying that it finds its target."

"That's kind of extreme, don't you think? I fly all the time."

"It's just not for me. I'd do it if I could get up the nerve, believe me. I have kids on both coasts, and I hardly ever see them."

"Fear of flying. We better not get into that conversation." Norm relaxed in his chair and beckoned a waiter over. "Two sangrias," he said. "You want a sangria, don't you?"

"That would be fine." Lydia was searching for something to say. She hated herself when she was nervous, and here she was going on about her fear of flying. Norm was not the talker that he'd been before. She could sense herself growing anxious, eager to fill the silence. "I hate bridges as well," she said. "One time when my daughter was barely a teenager I refused to cross the Mackinac Bridge. We had been up north visiting my father's side of the family—it was just us girls—and we decided since we were up there, we might as well keep going and cross into the U.P. Have you ever been to the Upper Peninsula?"

"Can't say that I have. I hear it's rather dead."

"The fact is, neither have I," Lydia said. "Just as we approached—it's one of the longest suspension bridges in the world—I panicked. I told my daughter, 'Jessica, just wait here;

I'm going to find a policeman to drive us across,' but she was at the height of adolescent self-consciousness and the idea of someome seeing us out there—she just couldn't take it. So we turned around and drove home. I still think about that moment when I pulled over and knew I couldn't do it. Five miles across. I can't tell you how impossibly far that seemed. And it gets windy. You hear stories about gusts throwing people over the edge. And the bridge is so close to the water. The cars looked as if they were driving right into the Straits of Mackinac, about to be swallowed up and lost forever. Jessica hardly spoke to me on our drive back to Detroit. Still, I can't remember feeling more relieved or closer to her. It's strange. There she was, hating me for freezing up, but I felt this intense bond, for having survived a trial together."

Lydia broke out of her reverie and saw that Norm was looking away. He seemed distracted, perhaps wondering where the waiter had gone. "I don't know why I'm talking about this," Lydia said with a little laugh.

"We've all got our quirks." Norm took off his glasses and set them on the table.

In the uncomfortable pause that followed, Lydia felt foolish for having said so much. She worried that Norm had lost interest the moment he'd seen her again, and wondered whether her clothes did matter, after all. Or maybe she was so poor at flirtation that she had stunned him into silence. He had conveyed such energy in his e-mails. But already he seemed weary, could barely meet her eyes without looking away.

"Have you had a chance to check the menu?" he asked.

"I don't know much about tapas. I'm counting on you."

The waiter came by with sangrias, and Norm ordered a variety of dishes for the two of them—jumbo shrimp, andouille sausage, baby lamb chops, and new potatoes in tomato sauce. Lydia rarely ate meat other than chicken, and she had guessed, quite wrongly, that Norm would be a vegetarian. She also couldn't remember, except for that time with M.J., when she'd last had an afternoon drink. But she was in new territory now, she reminded herself, trying to keep an open mind.

When the bread and olives arrived, Lydia ate to settle down. Norm was describing his former position at the urban design center and his new job in Windsor. As he talked, he kept pulling his hair behind his ears. It occurred to her that maybe he was as nervous as she was.

"After this, we should go downtown and tour the Necropolis," he said.

"Necropolis?"

"Detroit, where the dream began. It's a cemetery now. I thought we'd pay our respects."

"Be nice. That's my hometown you're talking about."

When the tapas arrived, Lydia had a few bites of potato and more bread and olives. Norm ate all the shrimp and sausage.

"Wasn't it Henry Ford who said the best way to solve the city problem was to leave the city?" Norm gnawed at a lamb chop.

"That's our Henry."

"And Detroit is the result."

Lydia did not want to get into this conversation on what she had hoped would be a date. Save your lectures for the classroom, she thought.

"I love the utopians in particular," he continued. "So many of them were so wonderfully wrong. I teach a seminar on the utopian planners, and my favorite is Le Corbusier." Lydia knew all about the modernist architect who, like Bel Geddes, had influenced the expansion of the suburbs. She had written about him in *The Magic Motorway*, but Norm nevertheless went on. "You've got his Radiant City right here in Detroit. The highways shoot off in every direction, like spokes from a wheel, radiating out like sunbeams. In the Radiant City the idea is to drive on your radial tires as far away from the center as you can. I mean, who can survive in the middle of the sun, where it's hot, crowded, and treacherous?"

"My ex-husband moved to Phoenix." Lydia tried steering Norm off the topic. She was happy to talk about highways and cars—they were her subject, after all—but not here in a public place, with him growing louder and more didactic. And not today, when she'd had every reason to expect that she and Norm would continue where they'd left off. What had happened to the pet names, the wordplay and innuendo? Where had that person on the computer screen gone?

"Phoenix? Now, there's a Radiant City," he went on, and Lydia felt her patience slipping. When the waiter returned, she ordered another sangria and finished it off before the bill arrived.

"I've got this." Norm reached for his wallet. "I've been meaning to bend your ear."

"Sure," Lydia said. She thanked him for lunch, feeling more frustrated by the minute. She wished he had warmed up right at the moment when she confessed her fear of bridges. She had given him an opening, a personal insecurity. Perhaps she should have said more. Or maybe that was the trouble. She had talked too much about her own family.

She was too old for this nonsense.

Lydia followed Norm out of the restaurant to his car, a small green convertible with a long rounded nose and short rear end.

"So is this your 'car of tomorrow'?" she asked.

"It's a fuel cell. I've got it on loan from a firm I do research for. These are my summer wheels."

"Nice," Lydia said.

He surprised her by opening the passenger side door. So their date was continuing? She had a moment's apprehension about getting into a car with someone she barely knew. But since this was her day of adventure, she decided to go through with it. Surely Norm would soften up once they spent more time together. And she didn't want to tell M.J. that she'd been the one to cut it short.

"So I assume that you're working on your own designs as well?" she asked, getting in.

"I don't like to talk about work in progress."

She wondered what he'd been doing on the message board if he didn't talk about his work. "I know what you mean. I'm the same way." She was trying so hard to be agreeable.

"I've got a lot on my plate," Norm said. "Mine's a whole-model approach. The car is just one component. Then there's the city, the highway, products in general. And all the various materials that go into making those products."

"When do you sleep?"

"Not often." Norm turned the ignition. "So what do you say we tour the ruins?" But he didn't wait for her reply.

They took Woodward Avenue south toward downtown. The day was growing chilly. With one hand Lydia held the knot of her hair in place, and with the other she clutched her shirt collar to keep warm. They didn't speak again until they were parked in the underground garage of the Renaissance Center, the half-billion-dollar mall and office tower complex that Henry Ford II had helped build to revive the business district. It was just Lydia and Norm in the near-empty garage under the massive downtown structure, and she felt that note of unease again. She wondered what her children would think if they could see her now.

They approached a sign to one of the towers. "It's easy to get lost in this place," she said. "That might as well read, 'Abandon hope, all ye who enter here.'"

Norm laughed, which made her feel a little better.

The Renaissance Center, originally built for shoppers, businesspeople, and conventioneers, was a colossal failure in design. From the outside it looked like a glass fortress—built to keep "undesirables" away—and inside was a concrete Inferno, a dark maze of connected circles, with levels of footways and blind alleys. Nearly all the stores were vacant or empty. As many policemen wandered about as customers. There was no center, no gathering place, only a huge concrete column rising from the middle of a ground-floor wishing pool.

Lydia and Norm had been following a path of red floodlights but found themselves back where they had entered. They took several wrong turns before finally making their way through a tunnel and onto the People Mover, the aboveground train that looped three miles of downtown. The only other passenger was a solemn-faced security guard. "Listen to this." Norm laughed. He had picked up a People Mover brochure and as the two-car train departed the Renaissance Center, he began to read out loud:

"'You'll board the People Mover at one of thirteen attractive, conveniently located stations—some of them actually inside downtown buildings.'" His mocking voice filled the small space. Lydia was trying not to catch the security guard's eye. Below them, though it was the middle of a workday, the sidewalks and buildings were empty. "'You'll enjoy a breathtaking view of the city as you move quickly, quietly, and safely above the streets on one of the most technologically advanced transportation systems in the world.'"

A minute later they were already at the next stop. An elderly woman stepped onto the train and smiled at Lydia. Within the next six minutes, the People Mover had stopped at six more stations, including Greektown, Cadillac Center, Grand Circus Park, and Times Square. Norm seemed to get a great kick out of Detroit's Times Square, a couple of burnt-out buildings and a weed-filled lot with a rusted sign: PARK HERE $2.75 ALL DAY. Not a single car sat in the lot.

"So I have this idea that I wanted to run by you," he said as the train pulled into Michigan station. "I've been studying this place for years—it's one of the reasons I moved to Windsor. Let's face it, there's no more devastated city in America. Newark is bad, but Detroit is hopeless. I mean, look out there; it's like Dresden after the firebombing."

"You could keep your voice down," Lydia whispered. The elderly woman still smiled, a few seats away. She held an aluminum cane in front of her, both hands resting on top.

"I was listening to Click and Clack on *Car Talk*," Norm continued, a bit softer. "Click asked Clack in his funny accent: What's the cushiest job in America? Answer: Working for the Detroit Bureau of Tourism. Well, they had a big laugh at that, and I guess it must have been funny, though I was thinking at the time, if it weren't for Detroit, you two wouldn't be on the radio. But I wondered: What if Detroit actually *did* reinvent itself as a tourist town?" Norm held his finger up as if anticipating a response. "I know it sounds outrageous, but hear me out."

A trio of teenagers got on at Joe Louis Arena, which did nothing to deter Norm. He talked about black empowerment and economic pragmatism, the different approaches of the city's mayors, and he said downtown didn't stand a chance unless someone did something radical. "Making Detroit a tourist mecca—now that would be dramatic. And not just a tourist town, but an environmental wonderland. So—" He clapped his hands. "I'm devoting the next issue of Nuplan to something I'm calling the Emerald City Project."

Lydia looked around, as if for support. The old woman still seemed lost in her own world, and the security guard focused on the teenagers, who were laughing and talking among themselves.

"Mayor Young was halfway there with this People Mover. It's like a toy train tootling around a war zone," Norm continued. "But he was trying to lure traditional business. As I see it, the only way to use these abandoned buildings is to turn them into greenhouses. Look." He pointed to a high rise with moss and ivy growing on its walls. "The earth's already taking Detroit back. Why not showcase the organic city?"

"The organic city?" Lydia asked, incredulously.

"Let's face it. The most successful tourist destinations find a way to create fun for their visitors and along the way shake them down for a few dollars. Look at Orlando, Anaheim, Las Vegas. I'm no fan of kitsch, but people spend money there and that money goes into the city's coffers."

A computer-generated voice announced the approach of the Renaissance Center. Lydia stood up but Norm stayed where he was. "Let's go for another loop," he said. "I haven't told you my plan yet."

"I doubt I want to hear your plan." She began to move toward the doors.

"Oh, come on." Norm grabbed her hand and squeezed it.

He hadn't touched her since the beginning of the date, but now she felt like pulling away. This was not the beginning of something, as she'd actually believed it might be. "Am I embarrassing you?" he asked.

"There's a time and place."

He gave her a look that seemed to say *What, you don't like me?*

She had liked him on the Internet—a crusader on the message board, a charmer over e-mail—but in person he had the balance all wrong, at turns noisy and dispassionate. "It was different on the message board," Lydia whispered. It was all she could say. *You* were different. She'd built him up, just like Cy, let him grow in her mind into an ideal. She wondered how she'd set herself up for this.

The teenagers got off at the Renaissance Center, replaced by a policeman and a young couple who seemed to lean into each other to keep upright. The woman with the cane stayed on. Perhaps she would ride all afternoon.

Norm let go of Lydia's hand. She sat back down and half-listened with increasing agitation as he pointed out the dilapidated buildings they passed. "There's beauty in wreckage—just look at Rome," he said as they passed Greektown and the boarded up windows of the Book-Cadillac Hotel. "I've always believed that one person's trash can be another's treasure. I love eBay," he said. "And I still check the papers every Saturday, get up early to go looking for yard sales. One of my favorite things to do is to take something old and give it a new life."

He talked about the way Disneyworld and Las Vegas combined the past with the future. "Nostalgia has never been more chic than it is today, but I see domes of glass and steel, too, futuristic sculptures with moving parts and lights dancing all around them, geometric shapes juxtaposed with the rubble in strange and beautiful ways. And all of it would run completely clean. No pollution. Solar power. Everything that goes out comes back in. It would be the perfect closed system. And what a symbol! Imagine making Detroit—birthplace of the car and highway—the new ecological model for the world."

He drew shapes on the train window with his fingers, as if to superimpose his blueprint over the city. His voice rose with excitement. "The roofs would be made of grass, all the parking lots would be porous. There'd be wetlands over there by the Cobo Arena that would filter into the Detroit River and make it run as clear as rainwater. I see canals with tourist boats crisscrossing the city, trains like roller coasters running in wild patterns underground, in the air, through tunnels, into buildings, sweeping through the streets like benign demons. Come on, Lydia. Don't be a skeptic. Imagine the rides, the thrill spaces. People will flock here, as if it's the new Eden."

Lydia looked for an escape. The policeman and the young couple were staring at them now.

"I see indoor stages and amphitheaters," Norm went on. "Detroit would become more than just a stop for the major acts. It would be a northern home for long-run shows."

"People *live* in Detroit," she said now. "Have you considered that in your crazy scheme?" And right away she regretted asking another question.

"I'm talking about jobs here. The Emerald City would lower unemployment dramatically. The people of Detroit would make decent salaries at the restaurants and stores, work on grounds crews tending all the greenery, and I guarantee that when a critical mass occurs, other businesses would open up downtown: a coffee bar in place of that old wig shop, an organic clothier over there at Jefferson and Woodward. The trickle-out theory at work. Tell me, how is that not a benefit?"

Once again the People Mover pulled up to the Renaissance Center. "Excuse me," Lydia said. She couldn't go another loop or stand another minute. The train felt like an airless capsule, and Norm's voice positively boomed. How in the world had he turned out this way? *Nostalgia is chic. Everyone loves a ruin.* She wondered if he'd even noticed her, or if he saw her as nothing more than an audience.

"Where are you going?" he called out. But Lydia had already stepped onto the platform. She moved briskly in the slit skirt that she had bought for her own humiliation. Her heart raced as she hurried into the tunnel, then rounded the corner.

At the darkened window, Lydia stopped and looked back toward the train. Norm was still standing at the open doors, a confused look on his face. From a distance, with his odd Prince Valiant haircut, he looked less the mad scholar than the lost boy. As the doors began to close, he stepped off the train, and Lydia rushed into the labyrinth of the Renaissance Center.

15

T HE CAB DROPPED Lydia off at the tapas restaurant, where
she picked up her rental car and drove home. She had
walked inside the house and put her keys on the kitchen
table when the doorbell rang. For a moment she worried
that Norm had followed her, but when she opened the door,
there was M.J. "I was in the neighborhood," she explained,
stepping into the foyer.

Lydia was not surprised to see her. She wondered how long
M.J. had been staking her out, awaiting a full report. "Well, it
could not have been worse," Lydia began. "He's just awful. I
can't tell you how angry he made me. He wants to bring earth
movers into Detroit and turn the city into an ecological Disneyworld."

"What exactly are you wearing?" M.J. asked.

"I can't explain it. I just had to get out of there. I left him on
the People Mover."

"Running away isn't the worst strategy." M.J. followed
Lydia into the living room, and sat on the couch.

Lydia sat down on an ottoman. "It wasn't a strategy."

M.J. offered a butterscotch candy to Lydia, who shook her

head. "Let's talk about your outfit," M.J. said. "Do I see a Peter Pan collar and flats? What happened to that beautiful scarf?"

"I couldn't tie it."

"You should have called me."

"I panicked. It hardly matters now."

"You look like an airline stewardess, Lydia. And no offense, but the old kind that sues for age discrimination."

Lydia ignored this comment. "You should have heard him go on. He was practically yelling inside the train, insulting the city, dismissing self-government."

"He's an academic. Isn't that his job, to come up with schemes that never amount to anything?"

"He was completely ignoring me, lost in his own stupid fantasies."

"It's your life," M.J. said. She seemed irritable, and not in her characteristic bantering way. Was she upset that Lydia had ditched the Parisian clothes? "I don't need to tell you how difficult it is for a woman in late middle age, even one as smart and attractive as you, to find a suitable man," M.J. continued. "I know a number of such women, professionals mostly. Intelligent, independent mothers of grown children. In a couple of years they'll be at retirement age, so they're looking at a future with no company at all. These women try, Lydia. They go on dates and stick it out for a while with men a lot worse than your urban planner. You can't imagine the aging Lotharios some of my friends put up with. Players and obsessives, the kind that fancy themselves potbellied sex objects or, worse yet, the ones that label their socks, wash their hands forty-five times a day and make a great fuss in the checkout line."

M.J. recalled one older man, the owner of a Ferndale photography studio, whom a friend of hers had been dating for a few months. One evening, after a romantic dinner at his apartment, he unveiled his life's great project. He had taken more than a thousand photographs of people's feet—eleven by seventeen close-ups, nearly always without shoes. The feet of the famous, like Aretha Franklin, Lee Iacocca, and Detroit Tiger legend Mickey Lolich. The feet of the infamous, like Jack Kevorkian and Leonard Tyburski, the one-time dean of students at Mackenzie High School in Detroit who hid his wife's body in a freezer for three years. Most of the subjects were unaware they were being photographed; a few had consented. Over the course of thirty years the man had taken pictures of celebrities, civic leaders, ordinary citizens, the old and the young, strangers, friends, and former lovers. "After showing the woman a series of toe-tag photographs that he had shot at the Dearborn morgue," M.J. said, "the creep asked my friend if she wouldn't mind removing her shoes."

"Why are you telling me this story?" Lydia asked. "First you say I have to make an effort, and now you seem to be scaring me off men for life. Some decent ones must still be out there." But as soon as she said this she had her doubts.

"I don't know." M.J. sat back in the couch. "I'm flummoxed by the math. Every divorce involves one man and one woman. Why, then, is the ratio of middle-aged singles one lonely man for every ten lonely women? Where do the worthwhile men go, the ones who have no feet in their closets? Do they walk into some river and disappear?"

Lydia knew where they all went, and she nearly said so. They had married younger women. They'd all gone, not into the Detroit River but to the altar with thirty-five-year-olds, to the suburbs of Phoenix to start new lives. Lydia considered for the first time the real possibility that Ellen and Cy would have children. She would be thirty-six soon, and he would be sixty-two, pushing eighty by the time the first child—who knew how many Ellen wanted?—would go off to college. Suddenly she felt a chill sitting in the living room with M.J., the mother of her ex-husband's wife, an only child. Of course M.J. would want grandchildren. She was in her seventies, and deserved grandchildren. Cy and Ellen were her only chance.

Lydia stood up and went to the window. "Did they happen to buy a big house?" she asked without thinking.

M.J. sounded confused. "Who are you talking about, dear?"

"Cy and Ellen," she said, and then unconvincingly, "I'm trying to figure out how many rooms were flooded."

"It's only the downstairs. They have three bedrooms upstairs. What an odd question to ask."

"Well, I appreciate your stopping by. You really didn't have to."

M.J. seemed to get the hint, standing up from the couch. "I'd love to take a look around," she said. "You've never shown me your house."

Lydia resisted. "Oh, I don't want to keep you."

"You're not keeping me. I'd love to see where you live."

Reluctantly, Lydia gave her a tour of the downstairs. M.J. complimented her garden, the daffodils and magnolia, the crabapple tree, the potted pansies on the back patio, and the scattered blue hydrangeas.

"I miss having a garden," M.J. said. "I used to love the endless projects around the house. I imagine it must be difficult without someone around to help."

Lydia would not allow herself to be provoked. "I manage."

At the foyer she went to open the front door, but M.J. insisted on looking upstairs. "I'm sure it's a mess," Lydia said.

"I doubt that." M.J. already had one foot on the steps.

They went into every room, even the bathrooms. Lydia found herself standing in front of closets, worried that this nosy woman would open them and start pulling out her clothes and shoes. In Jessica's room, M.J. picked up one of the floppy dolls now lined up on the bed. "Adorable." She stroked its orange hair.

"My daughter calls them my substitute children," Lydia said automatically.

"I don't know. I think *we're* the dolls, all ragged and diminished. I remember when Ellen was a girl she was my mirror. I saw myself in her eyes. When she was proud of me, *I* was proud of me. When she looked at me as larger than life, *I was* larger than life. But over time, I guess I've realized I'm not quite the figure I'd thought myself to be. And now with Ellen gone it feels as if she's taken part of me with her. So I want her back, though I know it's not right. I want *myself* back because I'm too old to start over. Do you know what I'm talking about?" M.J. returned the doll to the bed.

Lydia couldn't help wondering how much of this was meant for her. "You don't seem diminished to me."

On their way downstairs, M.J. insisted on looking into Lydia's office, even though the door was closed. Lydia knew she should just refuse, but the hostess in her had to be polite. She apologized for the scattered papers as M.J. studied every picture on her office wall—of the children, of Lydia's grandparents, of the old house in Indian Village—her eyes wide, as if absorbing it all. "When did you live in that lovely Tudor?" "Oh, look at Jessica. What a stunner," she said, and with each question and comment Lydia tightened up, spoke more tersely. What was M.J. looking for? She seemed to be scouring the house for clues. "Who's this?" she asked, finally, pointing to a photograph of Gilbert Warren standing next to a dapper Harley Earl.

"My father," Lydia said.

"So that's what he looks like."

"What do you mean?"

M.J. brought her finger to her lips, as if she'd said something by mistake. She turned to the framed ad on the wall of the Tucker Torpedo, Gilbert Warren's original design: *More like a Buck Rogers special than the automobiles we know today.*

"Did you know my father?" Lydia asked. "Or did Casper know him?"

"Oh, I really shouldn't say."

"What is it? Tell me."

"Well." M.J. crossed her arms. "As a matter of fact." She looked down at the floor, not meeting Lydia's eyes. "I didn't exactly know your father—I just know *about* him. Casper told me not to tell you this, and I realize it's none of my business. But as a historian—as anyone, frankly—you might as well know the truth."

Lydia didn't like the sound of this. The office suddenly felt stifling.

"You've heard the talk about moles at the Big Three who helped bring Preston Tucker down," M.J. continued. "Even *I* know those stories, and I've never cared much for cars. Well, Casper's old boss Mickey Gibson told him something that he made him swear he wouldn't tell anyone else—the people at Ford don't like generating controversy if they can help it. He said he knew the mole, in fact used to work with him; he was a designer who had been at Tucker, then later GM. Gilbert Warren was his name. He ruined Tucker out of revenge because Tucker fired him."

Stepping back, Lydia bumped into the doorknob. "You're wrong," she said. She felt faint. "My father did no such thing. I should know, for God's sake. I've only been studying this my entire career. And anyway—" She gathered herself. "My father wasn't fired. I know for a fact that he quit."

"Are you sure?"

"He told me."

"What does it say in the history books?"

"It says my father left. There's no mention of the circumstances. But I've never seen anywhere that he was fired. That's ridiculous."

"Is there any record that he quit?"

"I'm sure there's a resignation letter somewhere."

"That's because he was asked to resign."

"Look, M.J. You're right about one thing: this isn't your business. But about all the rest, you're wrong." Lydia heard her voice rising.

"I'm sorry. I shouldn't have said anything. Sometimes I talk too much." M.J. backed off. "Maybe we should go downstairs and sit down."

"I don't need to sit down! I'm fine. Why should I defend my father in my own house? I don't know where Casper got these ideas, but I shouldn't have to listen to this. My father quit the Tucker Corporation. He handpicked his successor."

"I'm only the messenger, Lydia. Mickey Gibson had no reason to slander your father, and Casper trusted him completely. He said that Tucker asked for Gilbert's resignation because he wasn't happy with his work. I don't know the first thing about car design, but Mickey said that your father was pushing for speed and Tucker wanted safety. He brought in Alex Tremulus to make it more of a family car."

"I know what Tremulus did," Lydia said. "But my dad had already put much of the design in place."

"I'm no expert. I'm just telling you what I heard. Your father was furious about being fired, so he went to GM and said he knew all the details about Tucker's business methods and if they wanted to stop the Tucker '48' before it took the country by storm, they ought to hire him right away."

"My father was a great designer. There's no secret about that," Lydia said, but she felt as if the wind had been knocked out of her. She thought of the papers that Walter had copied for her, with all the assorted history minus the smoking gun; she thought of Tucker's "Open Letter" complaining about certain people trying to bribe his employees. She remembered the edge of guilt in her father's voice that morning after Tucker died. She'd been struck then by what had seemed like unusual wistfulness for a man who tended never to look back. Reading the obituary pages, he had seemed almost angry that his old boss had passed away. Now Lydia wondered if her father might have regretted something far worse than parting ways with Tucker. But even if he *had* been fired, she could not believe he would have been that vindictive or helped destroy the man who had given him his start. "Harley Earl brought my father on for his talent, not for espionage," she said, but with less certainty than before.

"You don't have to believe me, Lydia. I understand and I'm sorry. I guess I couldn't help telling you what I'd heard, that's all."

"If you were looking to make a bad day worse, you've succeeded."

At the front door M.J. tried to change the subject. "I know your date was disappointing. Still, I hope you'll consider giving Norman another chance."

"We'll see." But Lydia had no intention of meeting Norm

again, and she was thinking, too, that after today she would spend no more time with the Spiveys. As she said goodbye and watched M.J. descend the steps one at a time, carefully, a little sideways, she couldn't help feeling that something was deeply wrong with this friendship. She didn't understand M.J.'s motives. It occurred to her now that the shopping, the matchmaking, all the big-sisterly advice, couldn't be simple generosity. Maybe she wanted to annoy Ellen by befriending her husband's ex-wife. Or perhaps she hoped to learn some unpleasant secrets about Cy. Lydia wondered if M.J. took satisfaction in telling people's secrets, regardless of their veracity.

But Lydia did not want to think about this now. She would go to the car archives first thing tomorrow and find her father's resignation letter—or something from Tucker himself that proved M.J. wrong.

Lydia fixed a potato in the microwave and poured herself a glass of water. Once again, she thought of Cy in the desert, wondered what kind of a place it was. His Infiniti would sit in the garage, beside the rakes, tools, and weed trimmer, the chemicals and console for the sprinkler system that snaked under the yard. He'd have a high adobe wall and an iron gate blocking out his neighbors and a rock garden with flowering cacti. Inside, the track-lit rooms would have wall-to-wall carpeting, the pale kind that he'd always wanted. He would ask visitors to take off their shoes upon entering the house.

Ellen and Cy would file a homeowners' claim to cover the flood. Out to the curb would go the too-dark sofas and heavy wood tables, into the living room a teal leather couch, glass table and a Navajo rug. On the walls they would hang black-and-white photographs of Hopi women from the end of last century and close-ups of Georgia O'Keeffe's hands. They'd buy knickknacks from Robert Redford's catalogue and play CDs of wolves and coyotes, night sounds of the desert.

Upstairs, the master bedroom would be more or less complete—a king-size bed spilling with overstuffed pillows, and, Lydia imagined, a fat white teddy bear with a big red heart that read "Love me" in bubbly letters. In the guestroom they'd have a daybed and wicker furniture and a television and VCR where Cy could watch sentimental movies about aging baseball players and conflicted lieutenants, dramas of initiation into the world of men. And the third room, the one at the end of the hall—at the moment Cy would keep his treadmill there, and perhaps a radio, where he would play what the locals listened to, easy-listening country tunes for commuting professionals. Some day soon the exercise equipment would go down to the basement, and Cy would take a health club membership, because with a baby on the way they'd convert the room to a nursery.

A baby, Lydia thought now. Cy and Ellen were going to have children.

Lydia cut open the potato, salted it, and took the plate upstairs. Her office desk was stacked with papers, many of them Norm's e-mails, which she'd printed out and collected, as if she were an eighteen-year-old courted by an eager paramour. She gathered them up and tossed them in the wastebasket.

When the phone rang, she hesitated to answer it, thinking it might be Norm.

"Morning, Mom," Jessica said.

"Afternoon." Lydia sat down at her desk, relieved to hear her daughter's voice. She thumbed through the color copies of Harley Earl's dream cars, her manuscript pages covered with notes.

"It's still morning in Eugene." Jess seemed in a good mood. "I figured you'd be at the library."

Lydia shuddered as if she'd been found out. She wondered if Norm had driven to the library to look for her. She'd said that she did research there, had even told him about the car archives. Would he have tried to find her, or given up by now and gone home? "I'm *often* at the library." She considered for a moment mentioning Norm. "But today I'm not."

"So what have you been doing all day?"

Lydia pushed the potato aside. "Why does it matter?"

"Come on, Mom."

She paused, thought better of saying something, then changed her mind. "I met a man. There. Now you know."

"A man? You're kidding."

"No, I'm not kidding."

"Where did you meet him?"

Jessica's disbelief spurred her on. She did not want to say that she'd met Norm at the car museum on the same day that her ex-husband was getting married—that would have sounded desperate. "Lately I've been spending a lot of time with the Spiveys." She explained how Cy had stopped by the house to see if she'd look after his in-laws.

"Isn't that weird?"

"In fact, M.J. acted as my matchmaker."

"Now that's definitely weird," Jessica said. "And he's a friend of Casper and M.J.'s? He must be old. You're not dating a widower, are you?"

"No, he's divorced. His name is Norman."

"Norman? You mean like Norman Vincent Peale or Norman Schwarzkopf? Is he a man of God or a man of war? Norman Rockwell or Norman like the conquest? What kind of a Norman is he?"

"I'd rather not say."

"Come on, Mom. You can tell me."

"Do you tell me everything about your life?"

"How many times have you been out with him?"

"Is this twenty questions?"

"How about a hundred and twenty?"

Lydia was beginning to lose her mooring. As if to anchor herself, she pulled her office chair up close to her desk. She had been on one bad date and had no plans to see Norm ever again. But at the same time she felt a tremor of possibility—she liked being asked so many questions. "We've seen a lot of each other lately," she said all of a sudden. "I know him much better than you can imagine."

"And what exactly does that mean?"

"We've been friendly for a while."

"I thought you said you just met him."

"Actually I've known him for months, but the Spiveys helped to accelerate things."

"What do you mean?"

"They pushed me along, you know, told me to let my guard down. And it seems to have worked," Lydia said.

"You've known him all this time? Why didn't you tell any of us?"

"I wasn't sure it would go anywhere."

"Still." Jessica paused for a moment. "So how did you meet him in the first place, if not through the Spiveys?"

Here, she could only think to say that she hadn't actually *met* him in those early months and wasn't sure for a while if she ever would. She went on to explain that you can't know someone based only on words on the screen. There was no way to anticipate how two people would get along until they met, face to face, and had actual contact. "M.J. kept pushing me to meet him, so just after you all left I finally did."

"Wait a minute," Jessica said. "You're not saying that you found him on-line?"

Lydia was silent.

"I thought you could hardly use the Internet."

"Well, I've gotten better."

"Do you read the papers, Mother? Young girls aren't the only ones getting lured off the web by psychopaths. You have no idea what you're doing. There are freaks out there who prey on people like you."

"Norm is not a freak, for crying out loud," Lydia said. "And what do you mean 'people like you'?"

"They don't call it a frontier for nothing. You have to learn how to protect yourself."

"I know what I'm doing. I'm the mother here."

"Are you trying to make me nervous?"

"Why don't you calm down."

"Why don't you get some sense!" Jessica was yelling now. "You got lucky this time. He *could have been* a monster, and you know it. If I had done something as stupid as meeting a stranger on the Internet, you would never let me hear the end of it. Did you answer a personal ad? Did you meet him in a chat room?"

"We're not talking about this anymore, Jessica."

"Just last week I saw in the *Oregonian* that a woman got in a chat room and next thing she knew she was boarding a plane to Las Vegas with her purse stuffed with cash. Her new love interest had talked her into a gambling weekend. I'll spare you the details, but she never made it home to Portland. Strangled in the hotel bathroom."

"Don't get dramatic on me," Lydia said.

"Spoken like a true expert."

Lydia felt lightheaded, as if she were caught in the shadow world between waking and sleep. She got up and opened a window to let air into the room. "I can't believe you," she said. "I was going to let you know, and this is just proof that you'd rather I have no life."

"What are you talking about?"

"I don't think you understand what I'm telling you," Lydia continued. "You don't realize how serious this is. Norm and I have written every day, several times a day since—the end of last year. It's been many, many months, and it seems like forever to me."

"I can't believe I'm hearing this," Jessica said. "I can't believe you didn't tell us."

"How much did you keep me in the know when you went off with your Buddhist friend?" Lydia recalled bitterly. "Weeks passed by after you climbed into that ridiculous van and drove out to Oregon. You certainly didn't care what anyone else thought."

"And how many dates have you had with Norman the conqueror?"

"I didn't think it was right for us to meet until after your father's wedding. Norm wanted to. I wanted to, believe me. We waited out of respect," she said. "Listen, I've never known any man better in my life, and I hate to tell you this but that includes your father. It's been one of those amazing, inexplicable things." Jessica had stopped speaking now, so Lydia kept going: "I read a line in a poem once that I haven't forgotten: 'love is a deeper season than reason.'"

"What do you mean, 'love'?" Jessica sounded distressed. "You're telling me you love this man and you've only met him once? Twice?"

"We've seen each other every day for the past two weeks. So, yes, that is what I'm saying. And there's something else—" Lydia knew even as she spoke that she was being reckless. She could sense her words were expanding in the air, setting changes in motion. But she felt separated from the words, as if someone else were saying, "It just so happens—he's planning to move in."

There was no sound over the phone line.

"I'm happy," Lydia said, because that was all she could think of. "And you should be happy for me."

16

B Y THE TIME Davy arrived in Eugene, Jessica had spent a week thinking about her mother's news. In subsequent calls, Lydia had grown more reserved about her mystery man, whom she described as younger, a career academic who had emigrated to Canada. Jessica knew he shared some of Lydia's interests, but beyond that she couldn't grasp the appeal. She was convinced that her mother had pursued Norm just to keep up with Cy. Some of her friends' divorced parents had gotten remarried within months of each other, as if from the moment they'd signed the papers the race was on to get to the altar first. Perhaps this had hurried her mother along, too.

Still, as many times as Jessica went over the scenario, something didn't add up. Her mother seldom acted so rashly. Better to bring the world to you than to go out into the world, was one of her guiding principles. Everyone who crossed her porch was carefully screened, and Jessica had watched more than one boyfriend get interrogated at the border. Even more baffling was the idea of Lydia's throwing everything into a relationship. She had long been critical of the kind of woman who put a man first. "Do you want to be like your Grandmother Warren?" she'd asked when Jessica moved west. "When the going gets tough, you can always hitch up," she'd said sarcastically. But here she was now, seeming to ignore her own warning.

Davy had rented a car at the airport, and soon after he arrived Jessica took him to The Buzz, a coffee shop and cyber-café down the street from her apartment. He looked tired, but seemed sanguine about their mother's news, maybe for no better reason than to take his mind off his own. "I think it's great," he said, sipping a black coffee on the terrace. "If you weren't Mom's daughter, you'd call it kismet. You'd say this proves there's an order in the universe."

"You sound worse than the ersatz Buddhist."

"The Internet really does put everything in order. You can find a match without even looking for it."

"I don't know. I think she was looking for it."

"That's not what she told me. She was hanging out on a message board and this troll came along, who just happened to be the troll of her dreams."

"But people can create 'kismet' out of anything if they want it bad enough."

"Hey, if she's happy, we should be."

"You sound just like her."

"Come on, Jess. Get on board the love train. She hasn't been this upbeat in a long time." Davy stood up and excused himself to make a phone call. "Long flight," he said. "Better check in with Teresa. And yes," he added, taking in her look. "We're still together. I'll tell you about it later."

Sitting alone, it dawned on Jessica that if Norm did move in, a certain burden would be lifted. She wouldn't have to deal with expectations or disapproval or worry over her mother day to day. No more guilt trips or regressive holidays at home. How open her life would be if she no longer felt responsible.

She looked over the railing of the terrace and saw Davy pacing on the sidewalk below, talking on his cell phone. She made a mental note to give him some time before asking about Teresa; he had come to Oregon to get away, after all.

When Jessica got home from work the next day they stayed in to make dinner. While she chopped zucchini and mushrooms for stir-fry, Davy told her about the basset hound Bedlam had met on their walk in Alton Baker Park and the Lester Bangs compendium he'd read on the terrace at The Buzz. "It was nice just to be by myself for a change, not a care in the world." He checked the pot of rice and added, "Oh, and I got a couple of e-mails from Mom today. She asked how you were doing, wanted a full report about life in Eugene."

"I hope you didn't tell her anything."

"Don't worry. I dug out your diary and sent along only the choicest bits."

"Thanks," Jessica said.

"I hadn't realized that Norm had been married twice before. Apparently his other wives had no interest in his work."

"What do you mean, 'other *wives*'?" she asked over the hiss of onions in the frying pan.

"Oh, he's no stranger to marriage."

"She never told me that."

"Maybe she just found out."

"Maybe. Either that, or she's telling us different things." Jessica slowly stirred the vegetables. It wasn't like her mother not to call her right away about something like this.

"Sounds like Norm married his high school sweetheart. They never had a chance to grow up." Davy seemed to be trying to appease her. "According to Mom, they had a couple of kids, then realized they were different people than they'd been at sixteen. Norm's mistake was rebounding too quickly after the divorce. The kids had just started high school so he thought he could make a new family for them."

"You sound like you're reciting Mom, word for word."

"Well, I strive for accuracy," Davy said.

Jessica scooped the rice and stir-fry onto plates and brought them to the living room table. "So what was the problem?"

"She said his second wife made the classic mistake. She asked Norm's kids to call her Mom." Davy grabbed a couple of pilsners from the fridge and sat down on the couch. "She went to all their events at school—their plays and baseball games. She called them on the phone, tried to make friends with the ex-wife. She tried so hard to win everyone over and when they kept pushing her away she gave up, became bitter and took it out on Norm."

Jessica sat down cross-legged on the floor. "How long did that marriage last?"

"Ten years." Davy shrugged. "Some people can't change the way they are."

The news still bothered Jessica, especially the fact that she'd gotten it secondhand, when she and Davy set out the next morning on a day trip. She wanted to ask more questions but Davy said, "Can we make a pact not to talk about this Norm situation, at least for the ride?" Jessica had to keep reminding herself that this was his vacation.

Recent forest fires had cast a haze over the sky, but the temperature was perfect, just above 80. Davy drove east on Route 126. They cut through mountains along the McKenzie River, and Jessica pointed out the lava beds curving around stands of pine. But soon she realized that both their minds were elsewhere. She fought back the urge to borrow Davy's cell phone and call Detroit.

The snow-capped peaks of the Cascades came into view as they approached the town of Sisters. "Look at that," Davy exclaimed, and Jessica remembered how lonely she sometimes felt in Oregon.

When his cell phone rang, Davy said, "If it's Teresa, just tell her I'm driving and I'll call her back."

But it was their mother, and Jessica couldn't hide her annoyance at being left out of the news about Norm's marriages.

"I assumed Davy would tell you," Lydia said.

"I'd rather hear it from you, Mom. This is a big deal, you know—falling for a guy and letting him move into the house. I don't know the first thing about him."

"So what do you want to know? I'll tell you anything."

They passed the WELCOME TO SISTERS sign and Jessica motioned to Davy, who pulled over at a city park where a Conestoga wagon sat at the entrance.

Jessica did have some questions for her mother, as a matter of fact. She wanted to know, for starters, why Norm had moved to Canada. In the back of her mind Jessica wondered if he had been running away from something in the States. After hemming and hawing, Lydia admitted that Norm had resigned from the University of Minnesota under pressure. "But there's a good explanation. He's an idea man. And his plans were too big for the academy." She went on to say that universities had become too specialized, and Norm's ability to see the big picture, the way whole systems worked, must have been threatening. Lydia, who sometimes taught adjunct courses at Wayne State, empathized with his frustrations.

"So they forced him out?" Jessica heard the alarm in her own voice.

Lydia hesitated. "He's so charismatic. He fills up a room."

"And how is that a problem?"

"It's great in the lecture hall. He uses the entire stage," Lydia explained. "I sat in on his summer school class and he was up there pounding the podium, pacing back and forth, coming down and walking the aisles. He's very entertaining. You'd like him."

Everything about Norm sounded larger than life. He had a booming voice, big ideas. He was a "man of appetites," Lydia had said.

"His voice travels. Maybe his colleagues didn't like that."

"That seems unlikely. He must have done something." Jessica rolled down her window.

"Well, he did get some complaints from students. But what professor doesn't? You have to be so careful these days. You have to watch what you say. Even body language."

"Are we talking sexual harassment here?" She shot a look at Davy, who raised an eyebrow.

"No, no. Nothing like that. He's totally harmless. Norm has a big heart, too big a heart to be teaching in a university. So he runs into problems sometimes. This happens when you've got new ideas. People misunderstand you." Lydia continued to downplay it. "I trust him, so trust me," she said, as if she had known Norm forever and was the only one who could make sense of his eccentricities. "He loves his new situation. He's here to stay."

But for the rest of the afternoon, these words took on the ring of foreboding. "He's here to stay" reminded Jessica that Norm was actually moving in. She imagined this overbearing "man of appetites" stalking into her mother's life, demanding to know everything about her, making her fall in love with him only to use her and disappear.

Davy had a sunnier outlook. While he and Jessica walked around Sisters, went into the shops, and had lunch, he shared all the good things he'd heard about Norm: how he taught free seminars at community centers, took on extra work to put his kids through college. Without fail, apparently, he flew back to Minnesota to see them every couple of months. He had recently driven with his son, Jeremy, nearly a thousand miles from Minneapolis to Yellowstone, where Jeremy was working for the summer. Davy said that Norm liked to surprise their mother with wildflowers. He'd cleaned the gutters at 309 Franklin, cut away some low-hanging branches that threatened the roof, fixed the ceiling fan in the dining room that hadn't worked in years, was now pulling up the rotten planks on the front porch. It all sounded too conveniently good, Jessica thought.

After lunch they drove to the Cascades and hiked up a trail crowded with gnarled vine maples. In a clearing they looked up at Proxy Falls, where lavender shifted to silver over the mossy rocks. Davy picked up a walking stick and scraped off the bark. Jessica took off her shoes, walked a little way into the pool at the base of the falls. "I still don't like it," she said after a while.

Davy knew just what she was talking about. "Relationships are hard, Jess. You've got to support Mom on this. It's almost impossible to find the right person, you know." Since the day he'd arrived he hadn't wanted to talk about Teresa, and it reminded Jessica that everything he said, all of his wishful thinking about Norm, was being filtered through his own unhappiness.

Two days later, on Davy's final night in Eugene, Jessica splurged for a farewell dinner at Patsy's in the Fifth Street Market. "I'm sorry I've been talking so much about Mom," she said over fried oyster salad. Davy's trip had been too short, and now she felt guilty for monopolizing the conversation. She had tried to bring up Teresa, but it was clear that Davy still wasn't ready to deal with the fallout.

"Sounds like he's had quite an influence," Davy said. "Ivan told me today that Mom bought a car, too. A Corolla station wagon, only slightly used. She even got a cell phone. She's joining the modern age."

Jessica was annoyed again to be the last to know. "How's she affording all this?"

Davy took a bite of Chinook salmon. "I don't know. He's probably helping her out."

But Jessica couldn't erase the picture of Norm sleeping in her mother's bed, clearing out all the closets in the house, tossing clothes, mementos, photographs into boxes and stuffing them in the attic to make room for his things. He'd move in his oversized coats and furniture, clear out Jessica's room to set up his own private office.

By the time she brought this up with Davy, he was already into his third glass of Pinot Noir and asking if next time he visited they could go out to wine country. "I could get used to these Oregon wines," he said. For the rest of the evening he continued to shut down, as if preparing himself for what he knew he'd have to face tomorrow, back in Chicago.

After Davy left, Jessica felt at a loss, as though she'd missed out on a chance to really talk to her brother. When she called home, Lydia reported that Norm had bought planters for the front walk, repaired the backyard fence, and was priming all the downstairs rooms to repaint. She e-mailed news of other projects, too: replacement pipes for the shower, a new transmission for the washing machine, repairs and new fixtures, and soon it occurred to Jessica that in fact Norm was not moving in. Worse than that. He was sprucing up the house to sell. He'd fix it up, put it on the market, then somehow take the equity and run. Jessica had seen stories like this on the six o'clock news. Sure, the victims were usually grannies, but the rest of the warning signs were all there: the charismatic seducer, the hasty affair, the lonely, smitten divorcée.

Then one morning, less than a week after Davy had gone back to Chicago, Lydia left a message on Jessica's answering machine: "Things have been so hectic here, I almost forgot to tell you—Norm wants to elope."

Jessica had just returned from her morning walk with Bedlam, but when she tried to call back, telling herself, *Don't panic,* Lydia wasn't home.

A minute later she tried again. No answer. She kept hitting redial until finally she left a message. "I'd love to hear from you." She kept her voice at an even pitch. But Lydia hadn't called back by the time Jessica had to leave for work.

All through her slow Sunday shift stocking shelves and bagging groceries at Oasis, she worried. She had left messages for Davy and Ivan. On break, she tried her mother's new cell number, but a phone company recording said the person she was trying to reach was "out of the Michitel calling area." She thought of her father, who used to work for Michitel, even considered ringing him in Arizona. What did it mean exactly that she was "out of the calling area"? Had Lydia left town? Had they eloped *already?*

When Jessica returned to her apartment at seven o'clock that evening, her mother still hadn't called. It wasn't like her to go anywhere without telling one of the kids. Ivan hadn't heard from her either, but he was taking it all in stride. "On her message she said Norm *wants* to elope," he reassured her. "That doesn't mean they ran off together. She'd never do that, Jess."

"Then where is she? It's past ten o'clock Detroit time. She's never out this late."

"Maybe Norm's using a power sander on the kitchen walls and they can't hear the phone."

"I've been calling pretty much on the hour."

"Stop getting hysterical."

But nothing Ivan said made Jessica feel any better. And Davy was no more helpful. *They're out to dinner. A movie. She hardly knows how to work a cell phone. You know how it is when you fall hard for someone—you forget about everything else.*

"We're talking about Mom here. This is the woman who would rush us to the emergency room at the slightest fever, who made us call from parties to say we'd arrived safely. She never takes chances."

"Our mother has not eloped," Davy said. "And she hasn't been abducted, either."

But by nine o'clock—midnight in Detroit—Jessica was not so sure, and she was exasperated with her brothers for taking it all in stride. After walking Bedlam around campus, she furiously cleaned her apartment, imagining the worst. This grifter had taken all he'd wanted from her mother and was now looking for a way to get rid of her. Perhaps he'd lured her over the border and the next time the phone rang it would be the Ontario police saying they'd found a station wagon registered to a Lydia Modine. Or maybe Norm himself would call from a pay phone saying he wanted ransom money within twenty-four hours. But Jessica couldn't pay ransom, nor could her brothers. Where would Norm get the idea to kidnap their mother, anyway? What, exactly, did he want from her? She thought of the vast wilderness of Canada with so many places to hide a body, thought of her mother leaving home to "elope," unaware of what was coming. Sitting on the deck looking up at the ash gray sky, Jessica wished, for the first time since she'd moved to Oregon, that she weren't twenty-five hundred miles away.

At ten o'clock, she picked up the phone and dialed Huntington Woods 911.

Twenty minutes later, Lydia finally called. "What exactly were you thinking, Jessica? I'm in my nightgown, for Chrissake!"

"Why didn't you return my messages?"

"I didn't check the machine. Do you know what it's like to see the police at your door at one A.M.?"

"We were worried about you."

"*You* worried about *me?* What do you think went through *my* mind when I opened that door? Don't you ever scare me like that again!"

"Look, I've been trying you all day."

"Well, I was out. We had errands."

"Do you realize you left a message this morning and said you were *eloping?*"

"I didn't say that." She lowered her voice, as if she didn't want Norm to hear. "There's been talk, but no plans have been finalized. Is that what this is about?"

"I'll tell you what it's about, Mom. You're not yourself. This guy is taking over your life. Have you ever considered that you're moving too fast?"

"Is this your concern?"

"One day you're the smart, sensible mother I've always known and the next you're throwing yourself at the feet of an Internet loiterer. Yes, it's my concern."

"I don't have to listen to this. You're way out of line."

"I just want to know what's going on. Are you eloping? Are you selling the house?" Jessica could hear the sound of rustling sheets on the other end of the line. She pictured a big ape of a man sprawled across the mattress where her father used to sleep. He'd reach for the phone, urging her mother to hang it up and come back to bed.

"Not right now, Jessica. We'll have to talk tomorrow." Lydia's voice lowered to a whisper.

"Fine," Jessica snapped, but when she hung up she did not feel fine. Her relief that her mother was safe quickly gave way to the steady dread she'd had ever since Norm stepped foot in the house.

That night she slept fitfully. In the morning she waited for the fog to burn off, but the clouds only settled down further over the western ridgeline. The smell of burnt pulp from the

Weyerhaeuser mill seemed particularly sharp in the dewy air. She walked down to the Buzz Café, logged on to the Internet, and searched for discount airfares.

She wasn't sure how long it would take to figure what Norm was up to and sort things out with her mother. The ticket, costing more than she could afford, was a one-way flight leaving in a week and a half, the last Friday in June.

She had planned to tell Steve, her hippie-techie manager at Oasis, that her mom was sick with an undiagnosed stomach ailment. In fact, Lydia had sent the kids an e-mail just a few days ago reporting that at long last the doctor had given her a clean bill of health. But sitting down in Steve's office, Jessica could tell that he wouldn't mind her absence. The summer had been slow, and he'd been in a good mood lately. So, she told him the truth. She explained how her mother had been acting freakish, and said she had to go home to see what was up.

"Sounds like she has symptoms of early onset Alzheimer's," Steve said. "Inattention, shift in personality. She could be right at the front of the curve." Alzheimer's was like a life in reverse, he explained, a speeded-up backward fall that ended with a literal second infancy, the patient helpless, empty of thoughts, with no control over her functions. "It's why I got into homeo-therapy. If it happens to me, I can self-prescribe." He listed the anti-inflammatory drugs and new treatments on the market when Jessica interrupted him: "Thanks, but I don't think my mom has Alzheimer's."

But riding the bus back to her apartment, Jessica allowed that it might be possible, that anything was possible at this point. She realized that the longer she went without seeing her mother, the more her imagination would look for new terrors. She couldn't get home soon enough.

Her excuse when she e-mailed Lydia to tell her the plan was that she wanted to sort through her things, *just in case* her mother decided to sell the house. At the current pace, she thought, 309 Franklin would end up on the market in a matter of days.

"Great!" Lydia had replied. "We've been sorting through your stuff anyway. Norm thought it would be a good idea if we had a yard sale. But you shouldn't put your life on hold," she added. "Still, I'm always glad to see you."

What life? Jessica wondered.

At the checkout on her last day at Oasis she finally talked to Void, whom she'd been dodging since the sea lion fiasco. He tried to apologize for that weekend—they hadn't spoken since—but Jessica brushed it off. Too little, too late. He looked regretful, told her he wished he could see her again. "I'm sure I'll catch you here or there," Jessica said. She hadn't missed Void exactly—maybe his company, anyone's company. But this pallid figure seemed even more remote to her now than Blane.

Later that evening, she sat down at the Buzz Café and surfed the web for information about graduate schools. The most interesting programs happened to be in Norm's field of environmental planning. Here was a way to make cities and roads work with the natural world. She ordered a dozen catalogues, mostly from West Coast schools. Walking back to her apartment, she was struck with the feeling of having something of her own to look forward to.

From a window seat of the 757, Jessica thought of Bedlam in his cage in the belly of the plane. She had asked a flight attendant to check on him during the Salt Lake City layover, and a baggage handler on the ground reported back that the dog seemed happy and hydrated. Now they were flying over the northern Midwest. "If you're on the left side of the plane you'll see the Badlands in the distance, thirty miles to the north," the captain announced. But Jessica sat on the right, where tiles of yellow and brown Nebraska plains stretched endlessly below her.

Earlier in the week she had called Blane at the monastery to tell him about the trip, and he had gone into one of his twenty-four-hour sprees of great resolve. He said he would leave the retreat and fly to Eugene to help her get ready. He told her he loved her, had been thinking of her for months, and he claimed to have had a vision that Jessica would soon be leaving Oregon. He said he'd been uneasy. "I knew something had to be going on with you."

Jessica had heard it all before; his predictability irritated her. It was hard to believe that she had ever wanted him back. She asked Blane if he'd be willing to take Bedlam for a while. He was his dog after all, and she worried that an oafish German shepherd–collie mix would make a poor houseguest when there was so much work to do. At first he agreed, but by the next day Blane's enthusiasm had waned, and he launched into a long complaint about the price of the plane ticket, the press of obligations at the monastery, the impracticality of it all. "They have a no-pets policy here," he said.

She didn't have the energy to fight with him. "Don't worry about it, I'll be fine." She knew she wouldn't hear from him until the next incarnation.

To Jessica's surprise, her mother said she didn't mind her bringing Bedlam along. They'd only had one dog growing up, a terrier named Triscuit who mysteriously vanished one day. Someone in the neighborhood swore she saw him in the zoo, so the rumor went around that he'd wandered into the polar bear's den. Afterward there was much talk about getting a new Triscuit, but Lydia always said no.

A couple of Christmases ago, however, the kids thought enough time had passed that they could try again. They picked out a chow with a leonine head and a black tongue, but when Lydia found out about the plan she was hurt. "A dog for the lonely woman?" she said. "Something to keep me company?" Jessica decided it was just as well. She could almost hear the phone calls: the dog had cut her mother off at the knees, knocked her down, torn after a bigger dog at the park and wandered away—a foil for her self-dramatizations. "I have a better idea," Jessica had said to Davy and Ivan. "Let's get her a stuffed animal or, better yet, let's get ourselves unlisted numbers."

But lately something had changed for Jessica. Cy's bon voyage announcement had been a turning point. Since that moment at the wedding reception it had dawned on her that she'd just lost one parent, and she ought to be good to the other who remained. Later that afternoon outside the museum in Ypsilanti, when she had seen her mother in profile, looking so pensive and alone, she had felt close to her for the first time since before college. She had thought there might be a chance, once and for all, to banish the trouble between them.

When at last the plane descended over Lake St. Clair, where tiny sailboats angled through the wind-rippled water, Jessica looked up the shoreline for the lighthouse where her father had proposed to her mother more than thirty-five years ago. She had seen it before, but today was overcast and she could make out nothing beyond the mouth of the Detroit River and the near shore of Grosse Pointe.

Once, on a family picnic at the lighthouse, her father had explained how the different light filters on his camera worked and why it was so important to show up at the right time of day. It was midsummer, warm and tranquil. Ivan and Davy tossed a Frisbee, while Triscuit ran himself ragged. Their mother, in a straw hat, sat up against the dunes reading a book. Jessica was still young enough then to believe what her father said that day about the nature photographer Eliot Porter, who had quit his teaching career and dedicated his life to close observation. "You just have to commit." Cy had adjusted his aperture. "The rest is easy."

A flight attendant, an older woman with silver hair, came by making final checks. She gave Jessica a maternal smile, then continued down the aisle to her station. Jessica set her watch ahead to East Coast time and looked out the window. Below her was a series of subdivisions, white houses laid out in neat rows. She closed the window blind, shut her eyes, and waited for the plane to touch ground.

PART THREE

My father had not lost his romantic urgency—only the object of his affection had changed. He was in love with cars, had poured all of his restless energy into helping create what many still considered some of the finest unions of beauty and machine: the 1951 Buick LeSabre; the 1953 "Blue Flame" Corvette; the 1955 Bel Air convertible; and the 1957 Chevrolet Nomad, "the Beauty Queen of All Station Wagons."

—From *Dream Machines: My Father, General Motors, and the Golden Age of Car Design* by Lydia Modine

17

LYDIA SAT at the kitchen table amid the paint rollers and drop cloths and waited for her daughter to come back from walking the dog. That afternoon Jessica had looked shocked when they pulled up to the house, in its half-finished state. A crew had painted the back and sides of the exterior bright yellow and touched up the white trim, but the front was still a dingy gray. Jessica couldn't believe that they had left their ladders leaning against the house. "It's an invitation for someone to climb into your bedroom window."

"We have an alarm system," Lydia reminded her. "And Norm only left town yesterday."

Lydia hadn't seen Norm since their disastrous afternoon together. She had planned never to see him again. But just after she'd told Jessica, now almost a month ago, that there was a new man in her life, she realized she would need to find a way to keep Norm in the picture. The day after their date she wrote him an e-mail:

Dear Norm,

I wanted to apologize for what happened yesterday on the People Mover. I don't know what got into me. I must be too defensive about my hometown. I guess it comes from living in a place so many people leave. The truth is, I had a nice time meeting you, and I hope you didn't take my running off too personally. I've been going through a difficult time of late. Perhaps we can try again soon.

Yours,
Lydia

It still surprised her, how the words *He's planning to move in* had tumbled out. Even as she spoke she recognized there was no going back. What could she have said? Just kidding, Jess; there is no man after all. If she did that, her family would think she'd gone insane. They'd never trust her again. No, what Lydia had said was irreversible. What's more, she wasn't so sure if she even wanted to take it back.

After sending Norm's e-mail, she took a long walk through her neighborhood. The sun had slipped through the elms and firs, and the air smelled of cut grass. She passed mothers returning home in minivans with their children and felt a creeping guilt about the plan to which, in her mind, she had already committed.

Perhaps the words hadn't slipped out by accident—in a way she had been scheming something like this all along. That stomachache, all the chances she'd had to tell her children that it had gone away and there was nothing to worry about. But she'd kept mentioning the pain and had even spoken of doctor's appointments. She'd played that card for weeks, and had only let it go when something better came along. Now she'd laid down her new card—Norm—on the table.

The farther Lydia walked, the more it all made sense. She would create a relationship, a whole new life. She'd call a handyman to fix the things around the house that hadn't worked in years—the ceiling fans, dimmers, jammed doorknobs, and loose gutters. Tiles would be replaced, new fixtures and fittings installed, accents added in every room. She'd have the floors stripped and stained, bring in painters to redo the interior rooms. She'd tell the kids that Norm had done most of the work himself, and when the place was ready she'd call Jessica to say that the house was about to go on the market; so if she wanted to sort through her stuff, the time was now.

As she passed through Huntington Woods's tiny town center—police department, fire department, town hall, all quiet— she guessed just how far she'd have to go with her plan. She was sure that at least one of the kids would return to help pack up. Davy certainly, probably Ivan as well. Jessica might need some finessing, but one way or another, she believed she could bring her family home. What they needed to do was spend time together, going through boxes, laying claim to what was theirs, revisiting their family history, in the very house where they had spent the greater part of their lives. There are times, Lydia thought, when a person needed to stop everything and sort through the past. Her children would not have to wait, as she had, until their parents were no longer alive. They could come home now.

Norm was the biggest obstacle, of course. The kids would want to meet him. Lydia could say he was out of town or busy with work in Windsor; she was sure she could hold them at bay for a while. She could even invite Norm on another date, have him show up at the house, wave hello and quickly depart.

Meanwhile she would go to a pharmacy and pick up a dopp kit, shaving cream, razors, an extra toothbrush for her bathroom. At a secondhand store, she would buy men's outfits to hang in her closet, socks and boxer shorts to stuff in one of her bureau drawers. She would get a couple of pairs of shoes in size 11—wingtips and work boots, extra-large work shirts to drape over chairs in the kitchen, in the garage, to hang on the doorknob in her bedroom. She would go to a hardware store and buy work gloves and deftly splatter paint on the clothes and boots.

She would need to drop hints about marriage so the kids wouldn't think she'd simply acquired a roommate. Occasionally she'd mention the word "elope," just as a possibility. She'd have a yard sale, and later she'd put the house on the market. She would buy a FOR SALE BY OWNER sign at a hardware store and when the time came, she'd take it out of the closet and plant it on the lawn. She wouldn't list the house—if she had any takers she'd quote a price well above its value to make sure that it wouldn't sell. She'd maintain complete control.

There was nothing like a long walk to stir the imagination. By the time Lydia reached home, she had mapped out the next few months. Gradually, as the kids settled in, she would scatter seeds of discontent, hint that she and Norm were having difficulties. These would turn to doubts until finally the marriage and the move would have to be put on hold. Lydia would announce that she and Norm were breaking up. She'd take the house off the market, and by then the place would look better than ever. Shiny floors, fresh paint on the walls, renovated rooms, the old American foursquare looking brand-new. The kids would be relieved. All she needed to do was to get them back to see for themselves. *Why leave such a lovely place? All our memories are here.* And by that time, who knew, maybe one or more of them would stay.

"You were gone a while," Lydia said when Jessica returned.

"Bedlam needs *a lot* of exercise." He was one of the most hyperactive creatures Lydia had ever seen. His whole body wagged with his tail, and his long fur stood on end.

"Well, I guess I should unpack." Jessica's bags were still in the front hallway.

Lydia grabbed one and followed her daughter upstairs. "Just a warning," she said. "Your room is a bit of a mess, but we've also made some changes." Bedlam shot ahead of them on the steps and pawed at the door.

"You're not kidding," Jessica said when they walked into the bedroom.

Lydia had organized the drawers and closet, putting the shabby clothes into green bags set aside for the yard sale.

"You could have waited for me, you know. I'll just have to go through all of it again."

"Notice anything different?" Lydia persisted.

Jessica sat down on her bed. "It's hard to tell with these boxes lying around. I see you've gotten a new canopy for the bed." She picked up the yarn-haired dolls from the pillow and handed them to Lydia. "I wouldn't want you to lose these."

Lydia tucked the dolls under her arm. "What about the rug? The duvet? See this art deco lamp? I found it at a great antique shop in Royal Oak. It matches the new slipper shade and wall brackets that Norm installed."

"Where are you finding the money?"

"Don't you like them?"

"Sure, but you're going to end up in debtors' prison."

It was true that Lydia hadn't calculated how much money she had spent. She hated to think of the charges she'd run up in the past month. When the bank statement and credit card bills had arrived the other day, she'd slid them to the bottom of her desk drawer. The cost of the Corolla, even with the great deal she'd gotten on it, was steep enough. She figured she had spent at least ten thousand dollars on the house alone, even more since she'd had to pay premium rates. She hadn't planned to spend this much, but then she hadn't counted on Jessica's reacting the way she did. She had assumed that Jessica would be the last one to come home, and probably not for a couple of months. But Lydia's message about Norm's wanting to elope had clearly turned everything up a few notches.

"It's been much less expensive than you'd think. Norm has done so much work. Cheap labor, you know."

"Not the exterior. Not the floors. Not your station wagon."

"No, but he's done everything else. I'm telling you, he's a cyclone, especially since school ended. He's been going nonstop."

"He must be in quite a hurry to get married and get you out of here." Jessica's eyebrow went up.

Lydia talked right over this, pretending to ignore the implications. "I've told him to take it easy," she said. "He's back in Minnesota for the week."

Which was actually true. He'd gone to Minneapolis to see his daughter. Lydia knew this from Norm's reply to her apology:

Lydia,

That was a first. I've never been ditched on a train before. I had thought that you, of all people, would be a sympathetic audience. Perhaps I misread your books. Or maybe you're the type who only knows how to find fault. I'd expected more, Lydia. At the very least I thought that if we disagreed you wouldn't run away.

Norman

Lydia wrote back, trying to put a balm on Norm's wounded pride, even though his refusal to take any responsibility was infuriating. At least *she* had apologized for her part in the lousy date. It was only when Jessica announced suddenly that she had bought a plane ticket that Lydia realized she would have to scramble to make her way back into Norm's good graces. So, she gritted her teeth and wrote:

Dear Norm,

I discovered yesterday that your web site is back up. Congratulations! I spent much of last night reading through your various articles on Nuplan about sustainable growth, renewable energy, nutrient flows, and yes, green roofs. I hadn't realized when you were talking about Detroit that these roofs would not only cool the city but also provide solar energy, attractive gardens, and even food. I was too quick with my criticisms. These ideas are visionary. Is there somewhere that I might find your collected articles? Are they available on the web site?

Yours,
Lydia

Norm waited until the end of the weekend to write back, and then only offered a single question: "What did *you* have for breakfast this morning?"

It was not exactly an olive branch, but Lydia did think the door was open for a return to civility. With Jessica due to arrive at the end of the week, Lydia had no choice but to keep the flattery coming:

Dear Norm,

Grapefruit.

But if you want to know the truth, I was overwhelmed when we went to lunch. Seeing you in person again after those weeks of (much friendlier!) e-mails, I'd expected something different. I would be embarrassed to tell you exactly what I was hoping for, but suffice it to say that I was in no mood to discuss ecology. So the more you said about your work, the more confused I became. But now everything is different—at least for me. Your ideas make a lot of sense, and the fact is we agree on so much.

Can we pretend that the month of June never happened and make a new start in July? I'd love to have lunch again if you'll consider it. We can discuss renewable energy.

Yours,
Lydia

But despite her throwing herself at him, Norm wasn't budging.

Lydia,

I'm spending the upcoming holiday in Minneapolis. I plan to see my daughter and a number of old colleagues at the Center of Urban Design. I'm not sure when I will be getting back to Windsor. But I do thank you for your message. I'm glad you're enjoying the web site.

Norm

She worried that maybe she had scared Norm off for good. Maybe she had overcompensated and seemed fawning or disingenuous. Was he turning her down? Playing hard to get? How long would he continue to act wounded? She had to think of a way to keep him around.

"He should be here next week," Lydia said now to Jessica, who was sorting through the first of half a dozen yard sale bags. In fact, Lydia was not sure when Norm would return.

With Norm on her mind and workers in the house, Lydia had found it impossible to return to her book. Every time she opened a section of *Dream Machines* she remembered what M.J. had told her. She couldn't give an honest portrayal of her father or any of the GM designers now, knowing what they might have done to Preston Tucker.

The day after her conversation with M.J., Lydia had gone to the car archives. At first she was too upset and embarrassed to tell Walter precisely what she'd heard, so instead they talked about the rented Corsica that was costing her twenty-five dollars a day. Walter said that his daughter was selling her Toyota wagon. "Only fifty thousand miles on it. A fair bet more dependable than that Escort you used to drive."

It seemed a good deal, and Lydia returned to buy the car a couple of days later, sight unseen. This time she asked Walter if he'd show her the rest of the Tucker materials. "I'm telling you, all the highlights were in that stack of papers I gave you," he said. But nevertheless Lydia spent the afternoon looking in the library's files for her father's resignation letter, any proof that he had not been fired. By the end of the day she'd found only a scattering of her father's early drawings and interoffice memos from Tucker suggesting that Gilbert smooth out the racing lines and make the car more family-friendly. All of it only supported the Spiveys' theory.

As Walter walked Lydia to her new Toyota she got up the nerve to tell him some of what M.J. had said. "She gave me the name of the mole, but I swore on my life that I wouldn't tell anyone."

Walter stopped in the middle of the sidewalk. "Whoa. You have a name? You're telling me there *was* a Big Three conspiracy? That's a pretty major claim, Lydia."

"I do have a name, but I can't say who it is, not yet."

"So you're just tantalizing me?"

"I'm sorry. I don't mean to. I got the information from Casper Spivey. You trust him, don't you?"

Walter didn't hesitate. "He's about the *only* ad man in Detroit I'd trust."

"Well, I just have one question for you, then," Lydia said. "It's entirely theoretical, okay? Is it possible that the mole, if there was one, could have been a disgruntled Tucker employee, someone fairly high up who knew all the books, who was fired and then moved to one of the Big Three?"

Walter considered this for what seemed a long minute—too long, Lydia thought. She began to worry that he was putting the puzzle together himself. Only a handful of people had left Tucker in '47. And why else would Lydia be so interested when she was supposed to be writing about GM? Finally, he said, "Yes, it's possible. If there *was* a conspiracy, even likely, I'd say. Maybe you'll tell me his name sometime?"

She forced a smile. "I want to be certain it's true first."

They stopped at the car—a '97 Corolla wagon—and Walter gave her the keys. "I think you're going to be happy with this. You know my daughter's a nurse, so she's taken great care of it, and I checked it over just to make sure. If you have any trouble at all, Lydia, please call me. This car comes with my exclusive Walter Hill warranty. Won't cost you a dime. Guaranteed long life."

Lydia admired the silver wagon, which looked as if it had

been detailed that morning. Even the hubcaps gleamed. Though she'd spent a good part of her career studying theories of car design, she had never paid much attention to what she drove. It hadn't crossed her mind that Cy might long for a luxury car, something sleek and showy.

"Oh, and I have another thing for you, too." Walter reached into his pocket and handed her a gold coin with the number 7 embossed on one side and a horseshoe on the other. He must have picked it up from his weekly trip to the casino. "It's your lucky chip," he said. "Hang on to that, Lydia."

She put the lucky chip in her purse and hugged him. "I will." She went over to the driver's side and opened the car door. "Thanks for everything, Walter. You've been a godsend."

In the days that had followed, Lydia tried to dismiss M.J.'s account, but the more she went back over the pieces, the more she saw how they fit. Gilbert Warren may have been loyal to some, like Harley Earl, but he had turned his back on his father-in-law. Time and again he'd chosen GM over his own family, something she didn't like to remind herself. In fact, her dad was plenty capable of betrayal. M.J.'s theory only confirmed once more that Lydia had never really known her father.

On the afternoon before the Fourth of July, Lydia had her first close call. While Jessica was taking Bedlam for a walk, the handyman showed up at the door unannounced. The sign on his van, parked at the curb, read MIKE "CHICKIE" PATERAKIS, GENERAL CONTRACTOR. Lydia liked him well enough, but she was convinced that he could have gotten a lot more done by now if he weren't such a talker. He had degrees in English and Religion from Wayne State and was back in school again, this time at General Motors Technical College. He had hollow cheekbones, gray streaks in his hair and beard, and the look of someone who rarely ate or slept. HONK IF YOU THINK I'M JESUS, read the bumper sticker on his van. Lydia guessed he'd had more than a few takers.

She worried about Jessica's returning too soon as Chickie walked into the foyer, his utility belt hula-hooping around his bony hips. He'd fashioned an extra compartment on the belt for a paperback and liked to go on at length about whatever he was reading.

"Chickie," Lydia said. "I thought you were all finished. I mailed the check a couple days ago."

"I got it." He grabbed his paperback out of its holster, removed the check from between its pages, and set it on the hallway table. It was for four thousand dollars, materials included. "Have you read this one, by the way?" It was his usual opening line. He held up the paperback—*1957 Chevrolet Parts & Accessories*—the same book that Cy had used when he was fixing up the Nomad. "I want to propose a deal," Chickie said. "I need a restoration project."

A week ago, working near the garage, he had first noticed the Nomad through the window and asked Lydia if she wouldn't mind if he took it for a spin. The car hadn't been driven more than a handful of times since Cy had rebuilt the engine. He had bought new tires for it and taken the car up and down Woodward. Lydia had passed on going along for the ride; "I'll wait until you're finished," she said. But Cy never did get around to the chassis, the trim, the console, the rest of the car. The old body remained.

Chickie had driven his van up the driveway that day to jump-start the Nomad. He asked Lydia how often the car was driven. She told him that her sons sometimes warmed it up when they came home for holidays. "But that's never more than two or three times a year." Chickie looked under the hood and checked the fluids and tires. He was surprised at how well the engine idled.

Lydia watched him steer the Nomad down the street.

"You were certainly gone a long time," she had said when he returned from his test drive.

"I went up Woodward, all the way out to Waterford, gassed it up in Birmingham."

"So how was it?" she asked.

"Like they always tell you," he said with a grin. "Drives like a dream."

Now he put a second check down on the table, this one for six thousand dollars. "I love that car. I want to make it my first big job. What would you say if I took it off your hands for ten thousand dollars? It's a classic, but you know the body needs a lot of work."

Lydia was speechless. She had run up huge bills in the last month, and the money would be a great help. She thought of the people she associated with the car—Cy, who had moved to Phoenix; her father, a different man, possibly, than the one she thought she knew. Lydia couldn't remember the last time she had been in the Nomad. What was she keeping it for, anyway? It was a relic from a world that no longer existed.

Jessica would be back any minute. How could Lydia explain a handyman when all this time she'd told the kids that Norm was doing the fix-it work around the house?

"The car is yours," she said.

Chickie slapped his book against his thigh. "Hot damn. Just like that?"

"The keys are under the seat. I don't mean to be rude, but I'm expecting someone."

He put the *1957 Chevrolet Parts & Accessories* back in its holster and shook Lydia's hand. "So we have a deal." He smiled. "I'll pick up the van later, if that's all right by you. I want to drive my new car off the lot."

Lydia followed him outside to the garage. She didn't want Jessica to see the car. Knowing that her daughter usually walked toward the zoo, Lydia said, "I do have one odd request: if you could take a right-hand turn out of the driveway, I'd be grateful."

"I understand superstition," Chickie said conspiratorially.

Lydia watched as he started the car, pulled onto the driveway, got out and shut the garage door behind him. He gave her a thumbs up, and, just like that, "the beauty queen of all station wagons" was gone.

18

A s soon as Jessica removed Bedlam's leash, he dashed for the water bowl. She put her keys on the front table and picked up a couple of checks that were sitting there: one from someone named Mike "Chickie" Paterakis written out to her mother and another from Lydia to Paterakis General Contracting. Same name as on the van parked in front of the house. "What's all this money for?" Jessica asked.

Her mother came into the foyer looking surprised. "Oh, you just missed the guy who bought the Nomad. He came by to pick it up."

"The Nomad? You sold it?" That was awfully fast, Jessica thought. She bet Norm had found out about Cy's restoration project. He'd probably gotten jealous and wanted nothing more to do with the car. It didn't seem like Lydia to sell one of Grandpa Warren's designs so suddenly. "Did you tell Ivan and Davy?"

"I don't think they'll mind."

Jessica wasn't so sure. "Why is there a check from you to this guy?"

Lydia seemed at a loss for words. "Oh, I told him I'd pay for body paint and any extra parts. That's what the four thousand is for," she said. "Then the six he just gave me is the final payment. He mailed me the first installment already. He did it that way for bookkeeping. Unorthodox, I know—" She grabbed the checks and started hurrying up the stairs. "Anyway, we made a tidy sum."

Two checks for bookkeeping? *We made a tidy sum?* This didn't sound like her mother.

A couple of weeks ago Lydia had been impossible to track down, urgent to finish the house, and had threatened to elope. Now she'd sold the Nomad to a man named Chickie, let Norm run off to Minnesota, didn't seem to mind that the house was only half-painted, the kitchen covered in drop cloths, every room littered with partially packed boxes. And all she'd said about eloping when Jessica had asked was, "Oh, we're still thinking about it. But that's off in the future."

Jessica hadn't known what to expect when she got home—an intervention, perhaps, if it came to that. She had imagined herself facing off against an adversary, or at least finding out what Norm was after. But he was gone for the week. His carrot juice was in the fridge; his power bars and vitamin supplements huddled on a shelf of the cupboard. His work boots sat just outside the back door looking large and tired. His paint-speckled plaid shirts—*I'm a lumberjack and I'm okay*—were everywhere; he must have left one in each room, as if marking his territory.

Jessica hadn't spent so much time alone with her mother since college. She found herself sorting through her old things slowly, often bringing pictures to Lydia's office. "Remember this?" she'd say, holding up a browning photo from the seventies. Jessica liked hearing the stories she'd forgotten: how Lydia sold fire alarms door to door when she was pregnant with Ivan, or the time she met Diana Ross at the downtown Hudson's; what Jessica was like as an infant—choleric, determined, quickest out of the bassinet, first to walk. Here, just the two of them, Jessica and Lydia had quiet dinners, watched Audrey Hepburn movies, and ate Neapolitan ice cream from the box. And her mother hadn't once needled her with *What are you going to do with your life?* or *How long will you stay out west?* Two was a good number, she thought, a simple line. Three, four, and five made a more complex geometry.

But Davy was coming home tomorrow for the Fourth, Ivan was talking about driving in as soon as he could get a few days off, and the yard sale was coming up in a couple of weeks. She had been surprised when Lydia suggested she call the *Free Press* and place the ad—her mother liked to keep everything, and Jessica couldn't help blaming Norm for all of these changes— but she had to admit it would be good to get rid of years of clutter, and to jettison Cy's museum of hobbies at last. She realized that she was locking herself in to stay at least as long as mid-July, but after all, she had come here to keep an eye on Norm, and the way things were going she wondered if she was ever going to meet him.

The next day Jessica went to Royal Oak to get falafel and grape leaves from Mr. Greek's, and she and her mother ate at the patio table, looking through more photographs Jessica had collected.

"Notice the face you're making in this one," Lydia said. "Do you remember why?"

In the picture the whole family sat in a horse-drawn carriage on the main street of Mackinac Island, a Victorian-era resort off the tip of Lake Huron, where cars were forbidden. Ivan, who must have been eight, smiled toothily in a Tigers cap and held Davy the toddler between his knees. Jessica had tucked herself under her mother's arm and wore the most miserable expression. "Was it something I ate?" she asked.

"Actually, yes," Lydia said. The trip had begun in Oak Grove at Lydia's mother's funeral, where Ivan had run out screaming when he'd laid eyes on Grandmother Warren, waxy and rouged in her open casket. "Your father and I thought we owed you a treat after that, so we went straight up to Mackinac, spur of the moment."

Jessica had been five at the time but thought she recalled the cabin where they had stayed. "It had a dank smell and we could walk to the water. And I remember a map over the fireplace."

"That's right; it showed where all the shipwrecks had been, up and down the coast of Lake Huron. Ivan loved that map. We looked all over the island for a duplicate but never found one." Lydia took a bite of the grape leaves.

"So, there was a patch of toadstools out in front of the cabin and later we figured out that you must have helped yourself to a few that morning. As we walked to town I noticed that you weren't looking so good, but your dad thought it would be nice if we took a carriage ride."

Jessica had never heard this story—surprising, since her mother loved nothing more than a good emergency.

"When it finally dawned on your father that you were sick, we went all over in that stupid horse and buggy from pharmacy to hotel looking for ipecac. But no one stocked it and the ferry to the mainland wasn't leaving for another hour. So the carriage driver—I won't forget him—took us to the marina and actually talked some fisherman there into rushing us over to the mainland."

"Why didn't you stick your finger down my throat?"

"You would have bitten it off."

Jessica laughed. Bedlam came over and lay under the table looking cute so he could get some scraps. Jessica scratched his head with her toes.

"There was a lot of chop out there, and your father kept joking with Ivan that we would be next on the map of maritime disasters. I was furious, completely beside myself. Cy was supposed to have been watching you that morning, but now here he was making light of a crisis. Anyway, the rough ride and the smell on that boat alone should have been enough to make all of us sick. But you held on and we found a pharmacy in Mackinaw City."

"The only real memory I have from up north is when you panicked and couldn't drive across the Mackinac Bridge. God, I was so mortified," Jessica said. "I almost took the wheel, remember? I would rather have driven right off that bridge than sit by the side of the road waiting for a cop. I can still picture the heads turning and staring at us. Why, oh why, do girls have to be thirteen?"

Just then Bedlam shot out from under the table and started barking at the backyard fence.

It was Davy, walking in the back gate. Lydia jumped up from her chair and went to give him a hug.

"Hey, I thought you weren't getting here until tonight," Jessica said. Her brother put down his shoulder bag and rubbed his bloodshot eyes. He was a wreck. Jessica could only imagine what he'd been through in the weeks since he'd left Oregon. She hadn't really spoken to him since then—his cell phone was always off or he didn't pick up—but she knew that he and Teresa were still battling out their relationship. It looked like Davy hadn't packed much, as if he'd left in a hurry.

"I'm a fugitive." He knelt to scratch the dog.

"From what, honey?" Lydia asked.

Or rather *from whom*, Jessica thought.

"You don't want to know the details," he said.

Later that night they went to see the fireworks show at the Huntington Woods municipal golf course. Having slept all afternoon, Davy now seemed willing to talk about Teresa. She'd told him she wasn't angry that Lowball had failed; it wasn't about the money. She just wanted Davy to stop and figure things out, once and for all. "But you know, all we ever do is talk, or at least that's what it feels like to me," Davy said as they sat down on a blanket in front of the clubhouse. "It's like she wants something else from me, but she won't tell me what."

A real commitment, Jessica was about to say, when an older man in a Havana shirt walked up to their mother. "Hello there," he called out. A young girl, no older than three or four, held his hand.

"Walter!" Lydia exclaimed. She got up to greet him, and Jessica remembered her mother mentioning him before; he was her friend from the library. Walter shook hands with Jessica and Davy, said he'd heard a lot about them. "And this is my granddaughter, Camille." She hid behind his leg as Jessica waved hello.

"So, what brings you to the neighborhood?" Lydia asked. She seemed almost self-conscious as she touched the back of her hair.

"I heard there's a great fireworks display here."

"It's my favorite," Lydia said. In fact, the local show had always been something of a joke when the kids were growing up.

"How's the Corolla working out?" Walter asked, then turned to Jessica and Davy. "I gave your mother my lifetime warranty. She's the star of the archives. We've got to take good care of her." Jessica liked the way he kept one hand behind his back as he spoke; he seemed shy, yet dignified.

"The car is excellent," Lydia began, but Walter's granddaughter tugged at his shirt.

"I guess I better get back to her folks," he said. "They're just down the fairway. See you later. Very nice meeting you."

When Walter had walked away Jessica said, "Nice man," then, "Is he single?"

Davy laughed. "He's a bit old for you."

Jessica gave him a little push. "He seems like a gentle soul. What do you say, Mom? Were you ever interested?"

"His wife only died a couple of years ago, and did I mention that I'm rather seriously involved?"

"Did you hear the way he emphasized *lifetime warranty*?"

But Lydia wasn't having it. "I'm happier than I've ever been," she said. She smiled as if to say *end of story*, then turned to Davy. "So, let's get back to Teresa." But the first fireworks shot into the air, bright shatters of red and gold, and Davy shook his head. He'd shared as much as he was going to, for now. Jessica wondered how her brother could be so great at easing others through their problems, but hopeless when it came to his own.

That night they returned home to find that Bedlam had knocked over a can of paint in the kitchen, covering the new floors in white paw prints. Davy grabbed the dog by the collar and yanked him outside.

"Be careful!" Jessica yelled. "He doesn't know any better." She soaped a cloth and started cleaning up the wet paint. Her mother laughed and blamed herself for not putting the cans away.

"It would be nice if Norm could finish what he started," Jessica said.

"I know what you mean." It was the first time her mother hadn't defended him.

Davy came back inside. "You've really got to do something about that dog, Jess. You can't just let him roam. His tail is a wrecking ball."

The next morning, after Jessica took Bedlam for a long run, she and Davy went down to the basement to clear out their father's hobby museum. Jessica had already begun sorting through some of his things, surprised that Norm hadn't left his mark here. She figured it would have been his first order of business.

"So, what's the plan?" Davy asked.

"Let's put all the yard sale stuff in the garage. I'm going to turn this basement into a dog pen."

"Have you asked Mom?"

"She's fine with it. She's fine with everything lately. Have you ever seen her this loose on the reins? Does she seem like a woman in love to you?"

Davy set up a record player on Cy's old workbench and began untangling the cords. "She says she's happy." He shrugged. "Who knows what a person in love looks like?" Jessica eyed him sharply and Davy, as if anticipating what she was about to say, added, "This is not about me and Teresa."

Jessica said nothing more, and together they brought the exercise equipment, fishing rods, telescope, and woodworking tools into the garage, which looked like an open cave without the Nomad.

Davy took off his glasses and glanced around. "I can't believe she just sold it without telling anybody. I guess it's good that she's moving on and everything." He seemed wistful for a moment. "I kind of wanted that car. I mean, it was an *inspiration*. Where would the world of rockabilly be without the 57 Nomads?"

Jessica was about to tell him about Lydia's odd behavior on the day she sold the car, and that business about the two checks, but Davy looked so forlorn she decided to save this information for later.

She hauled more of her father's things—including a pile of books like *Do What You Love and the Money Will Follow* and *Fire in the Belly: On Being a Man*—to the garage, while Davy organized Cy's record collection. Some of Cy's clothes dated back to the seventies, to the days before Lydia had taken over his shopping. There were lean pants and wing-collared shirts with bizarre prints that made Jessica dizzy. One was a wearable canvas of people on a fox hunt; some carried bugles, others carried guns; all were trailing a pack of dogs. The hunters wound around in a repeating line from collar to pocket to shirttail. Jessica searched the entire shirt. Only the fox was missing from the scene.

As she continued sifting through boxes for the yard sale, Jessica found her mother's wedding gown, balled up and wrinkled, stuffed among Cy's old workout tapes. On top of the dress lay the black-and-white photo of the bouquet. She could almost see her mother ripping the dress out of its airtight bag and snatching the picture off the wall, and she felt bad all over again that she'd gotten angry at her on Cy's second wedding day. She folded the gown and carefully set it aside, along with the picture, for safekeeping.

After the holiday weekend the painters returned to work—a dozen men up on ladders, blasting Van Halen into the neighborhood, taking breaks in the shade of the front porch. Jessica and Davy had finished clearing out the basement and their bedrooms, filling up the garage with items for the yard sale.

That morning Jessica climbed into the attic. It was the first thing she had thought of when Lydia suggested the yard sale, but her mother had told her they'd get to it later. "Norm and I have been working on it," she'd said. But when Jessica switched on the overhead light she gasped. There were boxes, old furniture, and crates, stacked high and reaching as far as she could see.

"Mom!" she called. "Davy!"

Her brother appeared first. "Wow," he said. "I didn't remember there being so much junk up here."

"Yes, honey?" Lydia's voice floated up. Jessica rolled her eyes.

"I thought you said you and Norm had taken care of the attic."

Lydia came partway up the stairs. "I didn't want to bother you."

"Well, that's helpful. You expect us to sort through all of this in a few days? The yard sale is this weekend."

"Goodness, no. I thought you could pick out a few things, then go through the rest later."

"It's okay, Jess." Davy put a hand on her shoulder. "We don't have to deal with it all at once."

But Jessica was annoyed. If she'd known there was this much more work to do, she wouldn't have taken such time with old photographs and notebooks, going carefully through each item. It didn't make sense that Lydia would lie about the attic. In fact, much of her behavior wasn't making any sense. Her mother had been curiously absent lately, not at all the hovering figure Jessica had always known. Normally Lydia hated to be left out. But since coming home, Jessica had found *herself* in the role of seeker, looking for answers and stories, while her mother spent long hours closed off in her office. Working, she said. Or on e-mail with Norm? Jessica wondered.

"Where is Norm?" she asked, the question that had become her refrain. "Shouldn't he be back by now?"

"It would be nice if we could get a hand," Davy agreed. "This place is a disaster. And it must be a hundred degrees up here."

Lydia explained that Norm's daughter had been "having

some problems"—"depressed," Lydia whispered—and that he'd decided to stay on longer in Minneapolis than planned. "He coddles Tracy like you wouldn't believe. The slightest trouble and he rushes off to save her. She never dealt well with her father's leaving, and now that she knows about me, she's pulling out all the stops."

"So she's *pretending* to be depressed?" Jessica asked.

"Maybe. People do that kind of thing, you know. Either she's pretending or she *is* depressed, which is why she's clinging to him."

Davy wiped the sweat from his forehead. "Well, can you get him *un*clung?"

The phone rang and Lydia dashed downstairs to get it.

"That psycho could become our stepsister," Jessica said to Davy.

"Just what we need." He sighed. "What do you say we get out of this sauna?"

Jessica expected to find her mother in her office, talking to Norm. Lydia had been on the phone a lot lately, off whispering in a corner, like a schoolgirl with a secret crush. "So you're not sure how serious it is," she was saying into the receiver. "Here, why don't I put Jessica on." Her mother motioned to her from the office.

It was Cy.

"Hiya, Jess. I'm trying to figure out what happened to the Spiveys," he began. "M.J. left a cryptic message on our voice mail, and I can't get in touch with her. Apparently something happened to Casper. All she said was, 'Ellen, call back, it's about your dad.'"

"That's it? That could mean anything."

"She had a tone of gloom and doom. I've been trying their number all day, but no one answers. I'm wondering if you wouldn't mind checking on them."

"Of course," Jessica said. "I'll let you know what I find out. I'm sure they're fine." But when she hung up she was irritated at her mother for passing the duty on to her. Wasn't *she* the

Spiveys' new best friend? "Dad wants me to drive to their house. What do you think happened?"

Lydia leaned in the office doorway. "I don't know."

"We've got a lot to figure out, Mom."

"What do you want to do?" She could hear the impatience creeping back into Lydia's voice.

"For starters, we'll have to change the date of the yard sale. I don't see as we have a choice. That attic is a junker's paradise. The house is a complete mess." *And,* Jessica wanted to say, *I haven't even met this elusive boyfriend of yours to make sure he's not some highway killer.*

"Are you sure? I can go check on the Spiveys." Lydia folded her arms in front of her and rubbed them as if she were cold.

"No, that's all right," Jessica said. "I told Dad I'd do it."

She called the *Free Press* and pushed the yard sale date back another week, to Saturday, July 21. Jessica figured that had to be enough time to organize the attic and deal with the Spiveys, though there was no telling how long it would be before Norm's daughter would let him go.

After Lydia went downstairs, Jessica shut the office door and dialed Steve at Oasis. "I think you might have been right about my mom," she said. "It's looking more and more like early onset Alzheimer's." For some reason she couldn't bring herself to tell the truth now. A lie seemed so much easier.

"I knew it. All the symptoms were there. Look, you take care of her. We'll hold your job."

"I'll be back as soon as I can," Jessica said.

No one was home at the Spiveys' condo, but several newspapers, in varying shades of discoloration, were scattered near the door. This looked worse than she'd thought. Had Casper died? Were they both in the hospital? Was M.J. inconsolable and shut away in the apartment? Jessica rang the doorbell and waited. She tried to look through the windows, but the shades were drawn. She checked the reserved space for the black Town Car—empty—and combed the parking lot, to no avail.

When she got home and reported the news, Lydia called the police. None of the precincts had a report on Casper. Jessica phoned local hospitals, with a growing sense of dread, but turned up nothing.

That night Lydia seemed unusually pensive as she brought out a large bowl of tomato and basil pasta to the patio for a late dinner. Davy tried to assure them that if something were terribly wrong, M.J. would have said so. Then again, Jessica pointed out, Casper was in his mid-seventies; he looked good but could have had a heart attack or a stroke.

Their mother spoke up. "All those years working for Ford might have finally caught up to him." The patio floodlight cast an odd half-moon on Lydia's face. "My father died of overwork, you know. He was only a year older than I am now."

An awkward silence hung over the table.

"Well," Davy said, and began to serve the dinner. "I think there's nothing to worry about."

19

ON THE SAME AFTERNOON that the painters finished the kitchen, the central air conditioning gave out. It was a Friday, one of the hottest days of the year, and past business hours, so Lydia knew she would have to call in emergency service. She should have expected something else to go wrong on top of the complications with Norm and her worries about the Spiveys. A day and a half had gone by since M.J.'s ominous message, and still no one had heard from them.

At first Lydia hadn't taken the news seriously. It occurred to her that M.J. might be trying to make her daughter nervous, much in the way that Lydia had done with Jessica a few weeks ago. She wondered how much she and M.J. had influenced each other without realizing it. M.J. had impelled Lydia to set up a date with Norm, and perhaps Lydia had given her an idea for how to get Ellen's attention. And the truth was, Lydia was still upset at M.J. for dropping that news about Gilbert Warren. She had been so casual yet deliberate, as if it had been a play for control.

But as the hours went by Lydia grew concerned. She had

liked the Spiveys, after all, and in their company at the DIA the day had seemed full of possibility. What if something *had* happened to Casper? What would it mean if M.J. became a widow? Lydia couldn't imagine M.J. alone, even for one minute, without her counterpoise.

Lydia thought about Ellen, that serious face in all those photographs, the only daughter who had left her parents behind. She had lived nearby for thirty-five years. If her father died or fell ill, she'd almost certainly return home. It felt like a long time ago since Cy had been here, saying goodbye, and to Lydia's surprise, she did not miss him. Somewhere along the line she must have accepted that he was gone for good.

Lydia found an old fan in her closet and decided to bring it to Jessica's room. Already the house was uncomfortable and humid, and as she walked down the hall she could hear Davy sighing. But it was Teresa on his mind, not the heat; he spent a lot of time on his cell phone, pacing on the back patio. As Lydia slowed her steps she heard him say, "She thinks that Lowball was all I ever cared about. She said I acted like I had one shot and one shot only. I told her I didn't want to be like Dad, never sticking with anything for more than five minutes. She said that was an excuse."

"Maybe she feels like you shut her out." Jessica's voice carried a note of exasperation.

"Yeah, she'd told me that one before. I just wanted the business to make it, that's all. I figured if I could get Lowball off the ground and pay Teresa back, maybe even put some money away, then we'd be happy."

"Well you're never going to be happy if everything's about tomorrow. I know this story too well, Davy."

Lydia took this as her cue. She walked into Jessica's room with the fan and said, "Here, this is for you. I left a message with the air-conditioning repair people, but I don't know when I'm going to hear from them. I'll see if I can find a fan for your room, Davy."

"Thanks, Mom." He was leaning against the desk that Lydia

had turned into a vanity table, fiddling with a bottle of scented moisturizer.

"So, what are we all talking about?"

Jessica sat cross-legged on the floor, going through one of the attic boxes, while Bedlam lay on his side, his muzzle at her knee. She gave Lydia a look as if to say, *You know perfectly well.* "We're talking about fear of failure, emotional unavailability," she said flatly.

"Afternoon-talk-show stuff," Davy added. He put down the moisturizer and moved to the bed, picking up a photo album.

Lydia plugged in the fan and turned it to medium speed. She noticed that Jessica's hair was tied up in the silk scarf that M.J. had picked out for Lydia's date. "It's supposed to be ninety degrees today," Jessica said. "For all Norm's supposedly done, he could have gotten the air conditioning checked."

"You're right, it's pretty bad. We should go have an early dinner," Lydia suggested. "We can sit in a nice cool restaurant, then maybe see a movie."

"Sounds good to me." Davy turned the pages of the photo album. Lydia wanted to say something about Teresa, get the kids talking again; she wished she'd heard more of their conversation.

Jessica pushed a box against the wall. "I called Ivan today, told him your boyfriend is still AWOL. Are we ever going to see him? When's he coming back?" Lydia started to respond with her usual deflection but Jessica overrode her. "It's been two weeks now, and you don't seem to care. I thought this guy was all googly-eyed about you, Mom. I don't get it. Doesn't he want to meet us? Or is he going to hang out with his psycho daughter all summer long?"

For a moment, Lydia felt like confessing—all of it, right here. If she admitted that she'd made everything up, she wouldn't have to play out the charade any further. She had brought Jessica and Davy home; they'd spent some good time together. She didn't need to put them through this. It would be so much easier just to stop with the lie.

But as much as she wanted to tell the truth she couldn't, not when her daughter was angry, not without all of her kids here. The time had to be perfect, and Ivan was still in D.C.

"Norm's coming back this weekend," Lydia announced instead. "I'm supposed to meet him tomorrow, as a matter of fact."

Just that morning she had logged on to nuplan.org, and had seen that Norm would be speaking in Dearborn tomorrow. *Come Hear Me Talk About Tucker,* the message line read. Lydia followed the link to a web site called greencar.org. On the program for the Fifth Annual Green Car Convention, celebrating new technology in clean emissions, she found Norm's talk: "Preston Tucker and the Greatest Car Never Made: Learning from the Past to Make a Better Future," by Norman Crawford, Ph.D.

At first Lydia thought she'd show up, go to the lecture and prove to Norm that her apology had been sincere. But her being there didn't guarantee that he would be friendly with her again. Realizing how much she needed him, if only to put in an occasional appearance, she had to come up with something better. So, she typed a note:

Dear Norm,

I hope you had a nice time with Tracy and a happy Independence Day. I got a delightful surprise myself. Two of my kids have arrived for an extended vacation.

So I see from your web site that you're speaking on Saturday about Preston Tucker. Well, I learned something recently about Tucker that I thought might interest you and even add to your talk. It's a lot to go into here, but perhaps we could meet before the Green Car Convention. I think you'll find the information fascinating. It has to do with the Big Three contributing to Tucker's demise.

Looking forward to hearing from you.

Yours,
Lydia

Jessica was startled. "Just like that, he's coming back. Why didn't you tell us earlier? I wish I'd known when I talked to Ivan this morning. He's driving the old Taurus here."

"Really?" Lydia hid her delight.

"He mentioned he might be coming."

"I told him not to bother, but he wouldn't listen. You know how he gets when there's trouble at the corral. Saddle up and ride. Our own John Wayne."

"I wouldn't say there's trouble at the corral."

"What do you think, Davy?" Jessica turned to her brother.

"Don't bring me into this. I've got some work to do in the garage," he said, and left the room.

"The fact is, Mom, I've been here two weeks and *only now* are we meeting Norm. There's an endless amount to do in that attic. No way in hell we'll finish by the yard sale, and I don't know how much longer I can stay. I had to lie to my boss, you know."

"What did you tell him?"

Jessica looked surprised by the question. "It doesn't matter," she said, after a moment. "But I don't want to keep making up excuses."

Lydia was beginning to know what she meant a little too well.

When Jessica headed off to take a shower, Lydia signed on to her e-mail. Norm had replied:

Dear Lydia,

Of course I'd be glad to meet with you and hear about your Tucker news. The convention kicks off at 11:00 and I'm scheduled to speak at 12:30. We could head over early, if you'd like. I'll bring my red pen.

All best,
Norm

P.S. That's nice about your kids.

We could head over, Lydia repeated to herself. Thrilled that the lure had worked, she wrote back right away. Explaining that Jessica and Davy would need the car in the morning, she asked Norm to pick her up at the house. She sent directions to 309 Franklin and named the time: ten forty-five. "It's the one getting painted. No need to come to the door. I'll be waiting on the porch." Toward the end she wrote, "I'm glad we're getting along," then signed off, "Warmly, Lydia."

She shut down her computer and went back to Jessica's room, where her daughter was drying her hair with a towel. "Well, Norm should be by tomorrow just after ten-thirty," she said casually. "I told him he better be ready to work, but he has things to do at his apartment. So we're going to go over there for the afternoon."

"I see. Been missing him, huh?"

"It's nothing like that."

"I've looked through *Redbook*, Mom. I know all about sex over sixty."

Lydia smiled. "I'm not sure you do."

While Jessica and Davy were getting dressed, Lydia went down to the kitchen and called Cy again. When he answered he seemed to have forgotten why she might be calling. "So, I hear you're tying the knot. I think that's wonderful, just terrific," he rushed on. "But I'd hoped you might tell me yourself."

Lydia hesitated. "We're playing it by ear."

"Remind me of this fellow's name."

"Actually, I'm calling about Casper," Lydia interrupted. "Have you heard anything?"

"Oh, he's fine. Fractured shoulder and whiplash, but he just got out of the hospital. A little accident, that's all." He went on to tell how the Spiveys were driving on slick pavement outside of Saugatuck and slammed into a divider. "They did quite a number on the Lincoln," he said. "I think they're going to have to ditch it."

Cy never ceased to amaze her. "We've been worried sick. Why didn't you call sooner?"

"I tried a few times. The line was busy."

Cy said that M.J. had banged up her wrist pretty badly and was wearing a cast. Casper had a neck brace and sling, and he was facing a steep fine for driving illegally. "But there's a silver lining to everything. At least his driving days are over."

"So how are they getting back to Detroit?" Lydia asked.

"That's exactly what Ellen and I were just arguing about. She's not handling this well at all. She's thinking about flying to Michigan, renting a car, and driving back with them. I told her M.J. can rent a car, but she said they'd be too traumatized to make the trip. So let them stay in Saugatuck for a couple of weeks, I told her. That's no hardship. There's the lake, it's artsy, there's plenty going on this time of year. M.J. can drive back when she's good and ready. I think I've finally talked Ellen down."

"You know what we could do," Lydia said, thinking out loud. "Ivan's coming in tomorrow so we'll have an extra car here. We could send Jess or Davy to get the Spiveys this weekend." As much as she wanted all her kids here, the house was beginning to feel crowded, and Lydia was surprised to find herself actually thinking that she might soon want a respite. And the last thing she needed was Cy and Ellen coming back.

"Wow. That would be very generous," Cy said. "Should I talk to Jess and Davy?"

"That's okay. I'll do it. Tell Ellen not to worry. We'll take care of everything."

Lydia wrote down the name and number of the hotel where the Spiveys were staying, hung up, and went out to the porch.

When Jessica came outside, Lydia told her about the accident and didn't hesitate to get to the heart of the matter. "M.J.'s too skittish to drive home. Someone needs to pick them up in Saugatuck, so I told your father one of us would do it."

"Is that our job?"

"I said we'd take care of it. They got lucky, you know; they could have died." Lydia paused. "Well? What do you think?"

"You mean you want *me* to get them?"

"Maybe you and Davy could go tomorrow. Ivan won't get in

until later. I'd do it myself, honey—but I'm meeting Norm, re-member? But let's not worry about this now. Why don't you pick the movie—the paper's in the kitchen."

Jessica looked dismayed. "You and Davy should go," she said. "It's been a long day. I think I might just go to bed."

The next morning Lydia made coffee and opened the kitchen windows. An overnight rain had lowered the temperature and the air smelled of rust. Already running late, she put boxes of cereal, bowls, and spoons out on the table, then ran upstairs, where Jessica's and Davy's bedroom doors remained closed.

Lydia showered and dressed, put on lipstick, and for a change wore her hair down. The three-hundred-dollar Pari-sian outfit caught her eye right away as she peered into the closet. Her legs looked surprisingly pretty in the slit skirt and slingbacks; and though she'd worried that minus the scarf the boat-neck shirt would be too revealing, she liked the way it hung on her shoulders. She couldn't understand why she'd made such a fuss.

When she went back to the kitchen Davy was eating a bowl of cereal. "Wow, Mom. You look great. I guess it's the Norm ef-fect."

"Well, now you can see him in the flesh."

"Actually, I don't think I can meet him. I have to catch the eleven-oh-five train. Teresa called late last night, and she gave me an ultimatum. I have to get back to Chicago right away."

"Just like that? But what about the Spiveys?"

"I'm sure Jess can take care of it."

"Can't you take a later train, honey?"

"The next one's not until six. I'm sorry, Mom. I promised Teresa."

At ten o'clock Lydia went upstairs to wake her daughter, who, for the first time since she'd come home, was sleeping in. Bedlam had climbed onto the bed and was splayed out, pushing her to the edge. "I wanted to make sure you said goodbye to your brother. He's taking off soon. And Norm should be here in a half hour."

Jessica nudged the dog off the bed. "Davy's leaving already?" She was still half asleep. "Are you taking him to the station right now?"

Lydia had realized that if she took Davy herself Norm might arrive, leaving Jessica to meet him on her own. And Lydia wasn't about to let that happen. "His cab is on its way."

"You called a cab? That's ridiculous. Nobody calls cabs around here. I'll drive him. I know he wants to meet your Norman conqueror."

"It's just lousy timing," Lydia said. "So we'll see you downstairs soon?" She shut the door, and quickly ducked into her office to call a cab for a ten-thirty pickup. She wished that Davy could see Norm, too. But all she needed was for one of her kids to glimpse him from a distance—one witness would have to do.

She went downstairs and told Davy she'd already arranged a cab for him. Jessica was exhausted, she explained, and they may as well let her sleep in.

"Can't get rid of me soon enough, eh?"

"The sooner you get back to Chicago," Lydia said, "the sooner you'll work things out with Teresa."

But when the cab pulled up to the curb ten minutes late, Davy still hadn't finished packing, and Jessica sat on the porch with a cup of coffee. She wore sweatpants and an old red pullover, making no effort to look presentable. Lydia went down to hold the taxi.

She was leaning into the passenger's side window when, out of the corner of her eye, she saw Norm's convertible coming up the street. She looked toward the porch, where Davy had joined his sister. Lydia stepped away from the cab, and as Norm pulled up behind it, she turned to wave to the kids. "Here he is now," she yelled. "My goodness, we're running late."

She saw Jessica and Davy squinting at the man behind the wheel. Norm parked and began to get out of the car, when Lydia rushed over to him and nearly shut his leg in the door trying to stop him from going any further. "Look over there. It's my kids. Go on," she said. "Wave hello."

Norm seemed confused, so she grabbed his elbow and held

up his arm. He gave a partial wave while pulling away from her saying, "What? What are you doing?" Lydia ducked under his arm and gave him a big I-haven't-seen-my-lover-in-two-weeks hug. Then she pushed him back into the driver's seat and slammed the door shut.

Hurrying around to the passenger's side she called up to the kids, who were now making their way down the steps. "Bye, Davy. Have a safe trip. Bye, Jess." She waved. "I left the Spiveys' info on the kitchen table. Love you," she yelled and climbed into the car. She leaned over to Norm. "Let's go!"

They pulled out even as Jessica and Davy were walking toward them. "Bye!" Lydia said to fill the air. "Bye!" She turned toward Norm as if to kiss him. Only when they were safely out of range did she draw back and ask, as if everything were perfectly normal, "So, are you ready for your talk?"

"What the hell was that all about?" Norm asked.

"Oh, I'm sorry. I always get emotional when my kids leave. Davy had to go back to Chicago early."

"You were certainly in a hurry to get out of there."

They turned onto Woodward and headed toward the highway. "I'm terrible with departures," Lydia said, leaning away. "Why linger and prolong the letdown?"

Norm adjusted his side mirrors. "Well, it sure took me by surprise," he said. He smoothed his ponytail and touched the rims of his glasses, as if to busy his hands while recovering from an affront.

Lydia felt the urge to change the topic. Without thinking, she launched into the story that M.J. had revealed, filling in the spaces with her own deductions, about what really happened to Tucker. She said that she couldn't believe it at first, but Norm's conspiracy theory had turned out to be true.

"There were a lot of people out to get Tucker," she explained as Norm turned off I-96 and headed for Dearborn. "But one man had all the inside scoop. I can't tell you his name because I promised not to betray my source. But a single individual had access to all of Tucker's records, and he alone leaked them to GM.

"So, just like you said, Norm, there *was* a Big Three conspiracy. GM passed all the mole's information onto the press and prosecutors at the SEC. Not long after that, Tucker was too busy with court dates to make cars."

"That's quite a story, Lydia." Norm didn't seem as shocked as she'd expected, but he wasn't smug about the news either. For that, at least, she was grateful.

As they drove past Fairlane, Henry Ford's sprawling estate, and turned at the Ford Museum, Lydia wondered again if she would ever fully process what her father's likely betrayal had meant to her, to her work, to countless lives both during and after Tucker's swift rise and fall. Tens of millions of dollars and thousands of jobs had been lost. The impact on the future of postwar transportation was immeasurable, all because of her father's wounded pride.

Norm pulled into a park within view of the famous Ford Rouge plant. "A lot of Ford people will be here, actually. I think they're starting to think in the right direction, if we can wean them off SUVs." He told the parking lot attendant that he was with the convention, then pulled onto the grass, parking under a sign that read FUEL CELL CONVERTIBLES.

Norm grabbed his briefcase from the back of the car, took out some typewritten pages, and started writing in the margins.

Lydia began to have misgivings about what she'd said. She worried that he'd try to track down her "source," that he'd go to the car archives and find out that her father worked for Tucker. Why did she keep putting herself in a position, with her children, with Norm, with everyone lately, where she had to say *something*, and the words kept coming out? "I hope you won't use my name." Lydia looked him in the eye.

"Oh, don't worry about that." Norm hastily scribbled on the back of a page. "I'm talking about the fate of maverick designers. It's a cautionary tale."

"I still haven't even confirmed what I just told you."

Norm stopped writing for a moment. "The whole point of my talk is to get the big corporations to listen to the visionaries. I don't want the Tucker tragedy to happen again." He gestured all around him. The park was dotted with cars like Norm's—ordinary-looking compacts that ran on natural gas, hydrogen, or electricity.

"Okay," Lydia said, while Norm continued to write. "I just want to be sure."

"So, what do you think?" He looked at his watch. "We've got more than an hour to kill before my talk. If you don't mind, I'd like to make some changes to this. Why don't you look around, check out the exhibits."

It was calming to tour the booths on emergent technologies, watching engineers demonstrate their inventions, and after a while Lydia felt sorry for not saying a real goodbye to Davy. She had left without her purse or keys and here she was, stuck, playing up to Norm in order to keep her secret. She had almost handed over her father's name to him.

She took flyers from the Sustainable Energy Association, Electricore of Illinois, the Sons and Daughters of Mother Earth. Many had driven long distances just to park their hybrid cars and stand next to poster boards that read *MPG Unlimited* and *Take a Pass on Greenhouse Gas*. She checked out the display for the Electric Drag Racing Club and the Great American Solar Challenge, where later today ten solar cars would begin a race across the plains, over the Rockies, to finish in, of all places, Oregon.

When Lydia returned to the spot where she'd left Norm, she couldn't find him. She waited for ten minutes next to his green convertible and, when he still did not appear, she went into the main tent to find a seat for his talk.

A colleague of Norm's was introducing him as a "pragmatic utopian" and a "modern-day green knight." Norm took the dais and surveyed the crowd of no more than fifty people. His eyes stopped briefly on Lydia, and she could have sworn that she saw him press his lips together, as if to say, *I'm not responsible for these words.*

20

AFTER DAVY LEFT, Jessica sat on the front porch, stunned by her mother's swift departure. She had assumed after all the build-up that Norm would stop in for breakfast or at least come up and introduce himself. He'd been gone for over two weeks, had never met the family, and still had barely bothered to get out of his car.

For all the time Jessica had put in worrying about him, though, he didn't look so threatening. From a distance, anyway, he seemed nothing like the hulking figure that she had imagined. If this was a "man of appetites," he had an impressive metabolism. He looked like a lot of people in Eugene—a little stooped and washed out. This should have given her comfort, but it only addled her more that Norm wasn't the man she'd expected.

Inside the house, the air felt trapped and heavy. Jessica wanted to call her mother's cell phone and demand to know what was going on, but there were Lydia's purse and phone on the front hall table. It made no sense, how she'd taken off like a shot, waving her arms. She hadn't even said what time she'd be back or when Ivan would arrive. The more Jessica thought about this rescue mission for the Spiveys, the angrier she got. Someone had to put her foot down. If Lydia wouldn't do it, then it was up to her.

Jessica went into the kitchen and grabbed her mother's note. It had Cy's number in Arizona and Casper and M.J.'s hotel information in Saugatuck. Enough was enough. Her father would have to solve this problem on his own.

"You sound very tense," he said, after Jessica had told him she had far too much work to do. "I know change can be hard. We've been in transition ourselves. Ellen and I are getting into Pilates. You should try it. We got the instructional video and the ball. It's doing wonders for our stress—"

"Dad," she interrupted him. "I don't think you understand. I'm *not* picking up the Spiveys. Period. That's it."

"I think your mother will be disappointed."

"You're in no position to speak for her. If you want the Spiveys to have a ride home you should fly here and do it yourself."

Nothing seemed to register with her father. "I'm reminded of a Hopi saying: Do not allow anger to poison you."

"This is not about my anger, Dad. It's about you dumping your troubles on other people. You know what I've been doing? Going through the basement, which is filled entirely with your crap. What do you want me to do with it?"

"This kind of conversation is not constructive, Jess. But when you feel better, I want you to know that I'm always available." He spoke at an oddly rapid pace, his voice rising. She recognized this as his obscuring mechanism, like a squid clouding the water with ink.

"I'm not doing it," she repeated, but quietly now. "You'll have to find some other way."

After hanging up, Jessica went to her room and found Bedlam pawing through old sheets, making a nest for himself on the floor. She finished going through the boxes of towels, sheets, duvets, blankets, none of them worth keeping. Then she went up in the attic and tunneled in deeper, working in the inferno without bothering to bring the boxes down. It felt good to sweat, the dust turning to dirt, sweat sliding down her arms. She pushed aside the furniture, tore through boxes barely looking at their contents before deciding *this is to keep, this is to throw away.*

She set Ivan's toys by the stairs. There were matchbox cars, hot wheels and metal soldiers, a poster he used to keep over his desk of Evel Knievel up on one wheel, his red, white, and blue cape flowing behind him: "There's a little Evel in all of us."

She hunted down everything she could find that she knew with certainty was her father's. She couldn't believe how much stuff he had left. Not just video equipment, adding machines, radios, golf clubs, and the laminator that Davy had used to make fake IDs for his band. Cy had left his baseball card collection with the complete 1961 Tigers, high school report cards, projects and diplomas, even his birth certificate. He had left a box of his father's poker chips and the vintage card table where Kurt Modine hosted his UAW friends on Saturday nights; next to it were half a dozen more boxes of his mother's pictures, letters, jewelry, and clothes. Jessica set all this aside to mail to Cy in boxes stamped FRAGILE, HANDLE WITH CARE. The rest of it she hauled down to the garage. When she had moved everything of her father's she could find, his stuff for the yard sale spilled onto the driveway.

Jessica was lying on her back on the warm slate patio when her mother appeared around the side of the house. "What are you still doing here?" she called out.

"Don't look at me. How about you? What exactly were you up to this morning? You took off so fast you forgot your purse and keys."

"Wait a minute. That's not what I'm talking about," Lydia said. "You were supposed to pick up the Spiveys. Why aren't you on your way to Saugatuck?"

Jessica looked at her watch. Four o'clock. It wasn't like her mother to ask her to leave the house to drive clear across the state on an errand. Lydia was the type to overcompensate, always going out of her way to take care of every small detail. She never would have asked her kids to do something like this before. "Sorry, Mom," Jessica said. "But there's been a change of plan. I called Dad and told him to come get the Spiveys himself."

"You didn't."

"Sure I did."

"He's in Arizona, for God's sake." A worried look crossed her mother's face. "Dammit," she said, and went inside.

Clouds had bunched to the south over the zoo, the scent of a coming thundershower in the air. Jessica got up and stretched her back, then went into the house to grab trash bags for her father's junk.

Her mother slammed down the kitchen phone. "They already bought tickets. Can you believe that? They're actually coming." She sat down heavily at the table. "I wish you'd told me you didn't want to go."

"We have too much to do." Jessica couldn't help but smile a little. She felt almost happy at the thought that she had finally gotten through to her father.

"He said you were very negative."

"I have every damn right to be."

Lydia looked out the kitchen window, where the sky had grown dark. "I know it's not your fault, but I thought we'd agreed you were going to do this."

"Well, it doesn't matter now, does it? Why do you care so much about the Spiveys, anyway?"

The question hung in the air. Her mother sighed and looked out toward the garage. "What's that stuff?"

"It's Dad's. It won't even all fit in there." Jessica grabbed a handful of trash bags, but as she started to tear them into sheets, the rain poured down.

She and her mother shot out the back door and tried to cover Cy's boxes, but with nothing to secure them, the bags kept blowing away. Lydia was trying to cover an old globe, and Jessica was doing the same with some winter coats, when the two of them stopped and looked at each other, both drenched, and began to laugh. Jessica threw the coats into the air. The globe, made of paper and cardboard, seemed to melt in her mother's hands.

Back inside, Jessica showered and put on a pair of shorts and a T-shirt from the organic grocery with the words *Shiitake Happens* on the front. She took Bedlam down to the kitchen and saw that the rain had let up, and her mother and Ivan were laying Cy's things around the patio to dry. Jessica went out to say hello to her brother.

"Shiitake happens?" He gave her a hug. His shirt was damp and sweat beaded at his temples.

"You look like you could use a cold drink." Jessica held on to Bedlam's collar.

"And a shower. The AC in the Taurus is shot."

She let go of Bedlam, and as Ivan kneeled down to pick up a box, the dog licked his face. "Yuck. Is this your beast?"

"Bedlam, Ivan. Ivan, Bedlam. You asked for a shower," she said.

"He's a scraggly son of a bitch, isn't he? There, there." He patted the dog. "I think I'm going to call you Dirty Harry. So what can I do?" he asked. "I want to make myself useful."

In the attic Jessica showed him the stuff that she'd set aside, but he wasn't much interested in lingering over his old toys. He had clearly come here for one reason—to finish the job where Norm had failed. He skipped the shower and went straight to work.

Too tired to do any more today, Jessica joined her mother for a glass of wine on the front porch. "So Norm didn't look at all as I'd pictured him," Jessica began. She went out to the end of the front walk to see how far the painters had gotten with the house. They'd finished half of the front now and had taken most of their ladders away.

Lydia sat on the top step and sipped her wine. "The house should be done by Friday," she said, ignoring Jessica's comment.

"I had hoped to meet him, you know. And Davy did too. When are we going to have a chance?"

"It shouldn't be long. He just got back, so we had lots of appointments today."

"But he should be *here*, Mom, helping us out. I mean, what exactly happened this morning?"

"Do you really want to know?" Her mother stood up. "Wait here." She set down her glass of wine and went back inside. A minute later she returned with a marker and a red and white sign: FOR SALE BY OWNER.

Jessica's heart sank.

"We saw a real estate lawyer today and we've had this sitting around just in case." Lydia wrote her phone number in the white rectangle and held out the sign. "Would you like to do the honors?"

Jessica sat down on the steps and crossed her arms. No, she wasn't going to do the honors. So they had been thinking about this all along. "And where are you moving to?" she asked.

"We're working on that," Lydia said. "I'm not worried. We'll find something."

"You're sure you want to go through with this? It's a huge step, you know. I hope Norm's not pushing you into it."

"*We* want to do this. Can't stay here forever."

"Well, it's your house." Jessica turned away.

Lydia planted the sign under a dogwood tree on the corner of the front lawn. As she returned to the porch a van pulled up to the house. The side read, in large letters, MIKE "CHICKIE" PATERAKIS. Wasn't this the same van that had been here a couple of weeks ago?

A cheerful, gaunt man came up the walk. He had a "Chickie" patch on his beige workshirt and the pallor and shape of an El Greco martyr. "Hallo," he stopped in front of Jessica and bowed. "I've seen *your* picture around the house. You must be the daughter. What brings you around?"

Before Jessica could answer, Lydia rushed toward him. "Chickie," she said. "How's the Nomad working out?" She turned to Jessica. "He's the guy who bought it."

"True enough. That's one reason for my visit. And here's another." He reached into his workbelt and pulled out a book. "Have you read this one, by the way?" It was a copy of *Together on the Line*. "I found it at The Browsery. Wanted to get your Jane Hancock."

"I'd be glad to," Lydia said, taking the book.

"Hey, the yellow looks great. I told you those painters were fast. I bet they've finished up the kitchen, too. I'd love to take a look."

Jessica wondered why Chickie seemed to know so much about the house.

"We'll only be a minute," Lydia said, already opening the front door. "You can wait outside."

"Why?" Jessica asked, but her mother didn't answer. She went down to the curb and inspected Chickie's van. The sign on the side said he was a general contractor. The back was covered with bumper stickers, and when she looked in the windows she saw a mess of books, newspapers, wood scraps, fixtures, electric wire, piping, and tools.

As Jessica walked slowly back to the house, her mother and Chickie reappeared. "How's the garage looking, Jess? Chickie needs some missing parts to the Nomad. What are they, again?" she asked him.

"A couple of fender skirts." He wiggled his finger in his ear. "I know I saw them when I was looking the car over. But I realized I drove off without them."

Jessica told him that the garage was packed at the moment and she'd have a difficult time finding anything there. "If you'd like, you could come by our yard sale on Saturday. By then we'll have everything cleared out of the garage."

But before Chickie could answer, Lydia said, "Oh, no. I'll just bring you the fender skirts when they turn up. I have your address."

"I don't mind coming by. I'm a junker from the old school." Chickie started down the steps. He stopped and did a double take at the FOR SALE BY OWNER sign. "Wait a minute. You didn't tell me you were selling," he said. "I wouldn't have done such a thorough job if I'd known you were planning to move. We could have cut corners, you know."

"What are you talking about?" Jessica asked.

Lydia answered for him. "Oh, nothing. He just did some touchup, a little here and there."

Chickie stopped at the bottom of the steps. "Touchup? You're joking, right?"

"Just joking," Lydia said and gave Jessica a wink.

"You almost had me there." He saluted. "Well, Godspeed, Lydia. And good luck with your new life." He climbed into his van, tapped the horn, and drove away.

21

S O WHAT WAS that about?" came Jessica's inevitable question.

Lydia continued to surprise herself with how easily she had spun false stories—and how quickly the stories turned on her. She wondered if she'd ever get a moment of peace. Each time she left the house she worried that her whole scheme would fall apart in her absence. But it was almost worse to stay here. She couldn't sit on the porch and enjoy a summer evening without stepping into another trap that she'd set herself. And now, with the Spivey-Modines on their way and a yard sale with a bunch of strangers nosing around—probably Cy himself would be there—she began to feel the walls closing in.

"Chickie is nuts," she said. "Did you see those bumper stickers on his van? 'Honk If You Think I'm Jesus.' He probably does think he's Jesus. So it's better just to go along."

Jessica was looking at her skeptically. "What work did he do in the house, Mom?"

"Like I said. A little here, a little there. He was the first to answer the ad, and he test-drove the car the same day Norm left. We agreed on a price but he couldn't afford it, so I let him put in a few fixtures and do some touchup where Norm hadn't finished. A couple days' work, that was all."

Jessica leaned against a pillar and crossed her arms.

"He'd like to think he did a lot more. You could see he's delusional."

"He didn't seem delusional to me."

"Well, you live in a town of eccentrics."

"How would you know?"

To put an end to the interrogation, Lydia said, "I can't wait to be free of the rowing machine, all those fishing rods, and specialty tools. What use do I have for a home brewery kit, I'd like to know? Do you think I've been listening to your dad's Grand Funk Railroad albums?" Jessica did not crack a smile so Lydia continued. "Why stop with your father's things? We're having a yard sale—might as well make it a big one. I know I have some old clothes I'd love to get rid of, too."

The air-conditioning repairman arrived at the beginning of the week, and the cool house seemed to give everyone a shot of energy. While Jessica put prices on her father's things and Ivan went through his own closets and boxes, Lydia trimmed her wardrobe. Boiled wool cardigans followed scuffed and worn loafers into yard sale boxes. She picked through books in the living room, pulling out Cy's thrillers and self-help titles and dry history texts that she'd shelved without finishing. She asked Ivan to haul down old furniture from the attic that she'd never thought of parting with: her first dining room table, wobbly and loose-hinged, seatless chairs with broken arms, her mother's formica dinette and folding tables that had long depressed Lydia; even now she could almost see Ginny eating a Swanson dinner while watching Walter Cronkite. She'd even kept the old Zenith, her father's RCA Victor, and 78s of Big Band music.

She hadn't realized that she owned some of the ugliest wicker furniture in the world, pink and white patio sets from her mother's porch in Farmington Hills. She had a metal sign from the Detroit Zoo—PLEASE DON'T FEED THE ANIMALS

—maybe stolen by Jessica's scavenger boyfriend and hidden in the attic for safekeeping. There was an old chandelier, chests and boxes of rusted car parts that might have belonged to Cy, Cy's father, or even Gilbert Warren.

Lydia kept Jessica and Ivan so busy there was hardly time for them to catch up, or so she hoped. But after glimpsing her kids working together in the attic or pausing for sandwiches, she realized that Ivan could be a good influence. Like Davy, he didn't seem too bothered by the idea of Lydia selling the house; maybe he was telling Jess to look on the bright side. Her sons, Lydia realized, trusted her without question. She had to push away the feeling of guilt, for it was too late to do anything but carry on.

Now was the time to hint at trouble spots in her relationship with Norm, and when Lydia told her kids that Tracy had had another crisis and that Norm had already flown back to Minneapolis, she lowered her eyes and said, "It's causing some stress between us." She felt Jessica staring at her, not saying a word.

By the middle of the week, the living room and dining room overflowed with furniture, books, and records for Jessica to sort and price. Ivan set aside his grandfather's tackle box. Jessica saved her grandmother's art deco lamps, prairie-style stained glass windows, and painted plates from Spain.

Ivan had transformed into a man on a mission, lugging all the heavy boxes to the curb. So much unsaleable junk had piled up that they had to call a truck to take it away. "Does Chickie Paterakis do hauling?" Jessica asked sarcastically. But Lydia just laughed this off.

On Thursday evening, two days before the yard sale, Lydia was sweeping the front porch and Jessica was getting ready to take Bedlam for a walk when a small U-Haul pulled up to the curb and out stepped Davy, unannounced. He waved and went around to the back of the truck as Jessica tied Bedlam to one of the porch columns.

"Are you sure that's a good idea?" Lydia asked.

"Don't worry. He's not going to tear the house down."

But Lydia wondered if the house actually could fall down. She headed to greet Davy, excited and nervous at the same time, wishing she felt better to finally have all of her kids home.

To her surprise, Teresa appeared from the other side of the truck. She wore a dark suit and stacked heels, her hair pulled back into a ponytail. With her little glasses, she looked like the star of the debating club all dressed up. "Hello," she said, setting her bag down by the curb and giving Lydia and Jessica stiff hugs.

Davy slid open the gate of the truck to reveal office chairs, desks, filing cabinets, even cubicle partitions. "It's the Lowball closeout," he announced, mock cheerfully. "Everything must go."

"This is going to be a pretty big yard sale," Jessica said in what Lydia was beginning to think might be the understatement of her life. She reached over to help Teresa with her bag.

"No. I've got it," Teresa said and bent down, her ponytail twisting like a tight little fuse.

The next morning, the kids posted yard sale signs around the neighborhood, in coffee shops and grocery stores, while Lydia hid in her office with the door closed. Walter called to ask how the Corolla was working out and Lydia told him just fine, though in fact she'd barely driven it since Jessica had arrived.

"I haven't seen you at the library lately," he said. "Everything okay?" Something in Lydia's voice must have prompted such a question.

"Of course," she said, and, perhaps to prove that all was well, told him about the yard sale.

"I'd love to stop by," he said. But after hanging up she wasn't sure why she had invited him.

At some point during the week she had lost any resistance she might have had to selling off her things. She had only herself to blame for the way this "move" had accelerated. Only a day before the sale, and she couldn't remember what she'd kept, what she'd thrown away or let go of. Every item that came down from the attic might as well have been a memory. She felt lightheaded, almost amnesiac. A great weight had been lifted, but she had no way of calculating the loss.

Later, Lydia looked outside where Jessica, Davy, and Teresa were gathered on the front lawn. She overheard Davy wondering out loud whether Norm would ever grace them with his presence. She pulled away from the window and asked herself how much longer she could go on pretending—she didn't think she could bear seeing him again.

In his speech at the Green Car Convention Norm broke every promise he'd made. He said that a single coward had cut down one of the great industrial visionaries of the twentieth century. General Motors had a clear hand in Tucker's undoing—information that had been verified by a notable automobile historian. "I can't divulge her name," Norm told the crowd. "But I can say that she's written some very well-received books and lives right here in the area." Lydia had sat there humiliated, looking around to be sure that she didn't see anyone she knew. This time she was too bewildered to summon the energy to fight. When Norm's presentation was over, she walked off while he went around the convention squeezing the hands of corporate reps and bathing in the light of his friends' admiration.

She had watched the launch of the solar car race and late in the afternoon met up again with Norm, who drove her back to 309 Franklin. She was furious but knew she couldn't alienate him further. After miles of silence, just as he was turning onto her street, she said, "Interesting talk. I'd hoped you wouldn't say who I was or that I'd confirmed the conspiracy." He began to explain, but she shrugged and stepped out of the convertible. "It's water under the bridge now. So I guess we'll be in touch."

She hadn't heard from him since and wished more than anything that she could announce to the family tonight that she and Norm were breaking up. "You were right," she could say to Jessica. "It all happened too fast." Lydia could say that they'd had a terrible fight, perhaps in the aftermath of Norm's flying off again to Minneapolis. She'd seen a side of him, she could say, that made her seriously doubt their future. Looking out the window, she saw how much work her kids had done preparing for the yard sale. "I just decided things weren't right," she could say and leave it at that. But then Lydia caught a glimpse of the FOR SALE BY OWNER sign, and knew she had gone too far.

Ivan called from the stairway, interrupting her train of thought. She opened her office door.

"This you've got to see, Mom." He was holding an old crate. "I think it's one of Grandpa Warren's designs." He set the crate on the floor and opened the top, scattering dust and flecks of old newspaper.

"Where did you find this?" Lydia exclaimed.

"In a corner of the attic, partly covered with insulation." Carefully Ivan pulled out a clay model car, built to one-eighth scale, unpainted but sealed with shellac to keep it from cracking.

Back in the fifties, Lydia's father had shown her the whole process of car design. He began with sketches and renderings, then created small-scale models, shaping and reworking the clay. Eventually, with Harley Earl's approval, the best of these smaller models would be made into full-scale clay prototypes. Then a whole team of designers, with Earl at the helm, would mold and perfect the life-size car, painting and adorning it so that even up close it looked like a production model.

The clay car Ivan held up was a two-door, more streamlined than those her father would have designed at GM. Lydia had never known him to keep any models. She would have been surprised if Mr. Earl had allowed one to leave the GM studio. Ivan turned the car and before Lydia even saw it she knew it would be there—right in the middle—the third headlight, the "cyclops" eye, trademark of the Tucker car.

"Isn't this cool? I've never seen an actual clay model," Ivan said. "There are tons of boxes from Grandpa and Grandma Warren's house up there." Lydia had moved all of her parents' boxes to her own attic after her mother died, but had managed to look through only a fraction of their belongings. The car had been up there all these years.

"There was an old portfolio sitting under this box, too. Want me to bring it down?"

Lydia traced her finger over the hood of the car.

"Mom?" he asked again.

"Of course," she said, only vaguely aware of Ivan stepping away.

Here was the Tucker Torpedo, engine in the rear, all-hydraulic drive, "more like a Buck Rogers special than the automobiles we know today." Lydia could hardly believe that she was holding in her hands the very source of her father's dispute with Tucker. She took the model into her office to compare it to the advertisement on her wall:

Now! FLOWING POWER!
Sure as a mighty stream, moves from engine to wheels
for a ride as free as a seagull's glide.

The year after this advertisement had run, drumming up support for "The Car You've Been Waiting For," Tucker's emphasis had changed from power to safety, from the Torpedo to the Tucker "48," and Gilbert Warren was out the door. Lydia hadn't yet looked through all his papers. After talking to Walter outside the library, she'd lost heart.

Ivan returned from the attic with an old carrying case under his arm. The zipper was rusted, so he pulled it open slowly. The smell of dust and old cloth kicked up in the air, and Lydia felt vertiginous, wanting at once to rip the portfolio open and close it forever, not seeing what was there. Inside were sketches of the Torpedo from a dozen different angles. With its sharp nose, tapered back, and art nouveau shape, the car was the very picture of *built for speed.*

"Looks like the Batmobile," Ivan said.

"I think these are his early drawings." Lydia laid them out gently around the office. "The car got more practical later." She had read in a design book once that her father had originally wanted the steering wheel in the middle, in line with the "cyclops" eye. Passengers would sit in movable seats on either side, and the car would have T doors like the later DeLoreans.

"We should get these framed." Ivan studied each picture closely. "Can you set them aside?"

Lydia was lost in thought. She barely even noticed when Ivan left, taking the clay model downstairs to show Jessica and Davy.

She gathered the sketches into a pile and opened the portfolio. As she was about to slide them back in, almost relieved not to have found anything there, she changed her mind and put her hand in the pocket of the portfolio. She pulled out a manila envelope. Clasped and sealed, it had no name or address on the outside.

She cut the envelope open and spilled its contents onto her desk: the same ad that hung on her office wall, some of the same articles in the *Chicago Tribune* and *New York Times* that Walter had copied for her. An actual transcript of the radio broadcast by Drew Pearson, another copy of Tucker's "Open Letter," and the newspaper photograph of Tucker emerging from the courthouse in 1950, cleared of all charges.

Underneath all the clippings she found a letter, folded into an unsealed number-10 envelope and addressed, in her father's crabbed hand, to Preston Tucker, Ypsilanti, Michigan. The return address was the Warrens' house in Indian Village, Detroit. But the letter had no stamp or postmark, no indication that it had ever been sent. Lydia's pulse quickened as she opened the envelope and began to read the typed words:

January 25, 1950

Dear Pres,

I am writing to congratulate you on your victory. It's been a Pyrrhic one, we all know. But justice, at least in court, has prevailed. And I'm happy for you.

I feel I need to clear the air on a few matters now that this thing is over. First I want you to understand that I had nothing to do with the leak to Drew Pearson that started this whole mess. He was fed that trumped-up story by someone at the SEC and not, as I've heard in certain quarters, by me or others formerly in your employ who might have had an ax to grind.

I have read in the papers that you believe certain "spies" or "traitors" conspired with the government to cook your goose. I wish to make it known to you that I am neither spy nor traitor, and to my knowledge nobody at General Motors has so much as lifted a phone to hasten your undoing. I have spoken to no one here or in the press about your methods and have said not a single word against you. At the same time, when you might have needed a friend in court, I have not spoken up for you either. Mine has been the silence of the one cast out, something I have chosen to live with.

The truth is, I had expected more of you. When I left Ford to work with you, people told me I was foolish hitching my wagon to the bumper of a used car salesman. The press has called you brash, careless, a charlatan. But I believed that we could make the first truly new automobile in a generation and I maintain today that my design could have been that car. You disagreed. We call that a difference of opinion. But you didn't have to give Alex all the credit after I left. You didn't have to say that I represented the old design. You actually pointed your cane at the door. I'll never forget it. There was no conversation. Everyone in the shop heard your voice that day.

Now I thought I should let you hear mine.

Sincerely,
Gilbert

22

B Y THE MORNING of the yard sale, Jessica was amazed at
how much everyone had accomplished in the past week.
The painters had finished yesterday, and with the boxes
and furniture all out of the house, she saw how beautiful
the place looked, with the new paint, fixtures and crown mold-
ing repaired, the ceiling fans in the bedrooms gently spinning
for the first time in years.

When Davy and Teresa had climbed out of the U-Haul the
other night she'd figured, Here comes trouble. But instead
they'd gone straight to work, unloading the truck, running to
the store for cleaning supplies, making themselves so busy that
they didn't have time to argue. Teresa dusted the entire house
and polished the brass lamps in the living room, while Davy
washed windows and set up tables on the lawn. On Friday
morning, Teresa got up early and made brunch for everyone,
roasted potatoes and egg frittatas so oversalted that Jessica's
heart went out to her.

Jessica realized that in the past three years of Davy and
Teresa's relationship, she had never gotten to know this

thoughtful, determined woman Davy had fallen in love with. In a way, she had never considered Teresa beyond the label of Davy's girlfriend, and now Jessica had to admit that both she and her mother had been guilty of enforcing that sense of distance. For the first time, Jessica saw that Davy and Teresa were more than just a bickering couple, and she found herself genuinely saddened when he drove her to the train station later in the afternoon. Jessica pictured Teresa looking out the window of the Amtrak train as she headed to Cleveland to stay with her family for a while; Teresa's father and brothers would pick her up at the station, asking "So, how's Davy?"

Ivan had marched in here like a mad general, and in the past few days he'd been on a charge. He'd cleared out the attic almost by himself, put yard sale posters all over the neighborhood, and moved the FOR SALE BY OWNER sign closer to the curb, so people could see it more easily from the street. He'd persuaded Jessica, still uncomfortable with selling the house, to pretty the place up for potential buyers. Jessica had cut black-eyed Susans and zinnias from the back yard, arranging them in vases in the living room. Part of her was curious to see what her mother would do if she received an offer.

Ever since Ivan's arrival, this closing out and moving had taken on a real momentum, and Jessica, like everyone, had been caught up in it. She'd been here three weeks and had gone through a century of keepsakes and heirlooms. It would be, by the end of the day, a retrenchment of the Empire of Lydia. As much as Jessica wanted to hold on to her childhood home, she knew that her mother probably ought to move forward, step beyond the borders she had drawn around herself.

Norm, apparently, was much to thank for this progress, though they had done all the work without his help. Lydia had said he'd gone back to be with his daughter again, and had hinted that it was causing a rift.

"Aren't you bothered that you haven't met Norm?" Jessica had said to Ivan. "*I* haven't even met him. No one has."

"Sure, it's odd," he agreed. "But Mom knows what she's doing. I swear, you worry about her almost as much as she worries about you."

Jessica ignored this. "It seems that suddenly all is not well on Fantasy Island."

"Relationships are hard. Just ask Davy."

"Well," Jessica said. "I guess we'll wait and see."

Among the early arrivals at the yard sale were the Spiveys, with the Spivey-Modines in tow. M.J. came up the steps first in a black linen tunic, black beads, and what looked to be a very large comb that she wore to one side of her hair. Even the cast on her wrist was black, all of which made her stand out on this bright summer morning.

She gave Jessica a hug. "Lovely to see you," she said. "Now show me to the china."

Just that morning, Jessica and her mother had argued about whether to sell Lydia and Cy's wedding china. Lydia said that as a gift from her mother it had sentimental value and besides, wouldn't Jessica want it for herself some day? "No thanks," Jessica said, and in the end Lydia decided to sell her own and keep her mother's china. Cy and Lydia's wedding gifts—silver and crystal, gravy boats, and soup tureens—sat out on a table next to the dogwood. Jessica pointed M.J. in their direction.

"So where is your mother, dear?" M.J. asked.

Lydia had opted to station herself out back and let Jessica and Davy work the front of the house. "She's running our furniture department," Jessica explained. "You'll find her on the back patio."

She greeted her father and Ellen, who both looked fit and tanned. Cy, in a melon-colored shirt, wore wraparound mirrored sunglasses. Ellen had added light auburn highlights to her hair. Her cropped pants matched her pink sleeveless polo; her eyes had the cerulean look of colored contact lenses.

"So how was the trip back from Saugatuck?" Jessica asked.

"Slow," Ellen said. "We had to keep the folks in the back of the van. They're not much into motion right now."

Casper limped up the steps, refusing any help. He wore a foam neck brace, his arm in a sling, and white gauze over one eye. Even limping and looking battered, he was still a charmer. He kissed Jessica's hand and whispered in her ear, "I understand you ordered our drivers. What do we owe you?"

She smiled. "Nothing at all. But if you'd like a butter dish—"

M.J. was admiring the china and showed some of the pieces to Cy. "It's similar to the pattern we gave you. That same blue floral. Are you using it?" she asked.

If Cy noticed that this was the china from his first wedding, he didn't say so. "We had a dinner party just last week. The plates were a big hit." It was impossible to read his eyes with his sunglasses on. "Hey, while I'm standing here, Jess." He held up a shopping bag. "There's something I wanted to give you."

Moving some of the china aside, he pulled out several photographs in eleven-by-seventeen frames and rested them on the corner of the table. "This one's from Sedona." He put his arm around Jessica. He was acting as if their argument had never happened. "You probably don't remember John Wayne's *Angel and the Badman.*" He pointed to the mountain backdrop in the photograph. "That movie was shot here. The scenery is spectacular."

It looked like a slightly out-of-focus postcard. "I love the reds and oranges," Jessica said.

"I took it at sunset." He lifted up the next photograph. "Recognize any of these people?" It was Davy, Jessica, and Ivan lined up on the steps on their father's wedding day. Jessica had not remembered smiling—she'd felt rushed and annoyed with her mother for wanting to take pictures—but somehow she and her brothers all looked happy, almost serene. "I found it on an old roll," he said. "I think it's definitely the best ever taken of you guys."

Which was true. Since the photograph was black and white, even the Lady Bird Johnson suit had a certain flair. Jessica couldn't get over how content everyone looked on a day that they knew was going to be miserable.

"I love how this picture is from our special day," Ellen put in. "Drat. Did we leave our wedding album at Mom and Dad's?"

"The kids will get a chance to see it later. But do you like the matting and frame? I did them myself."

Jessica worried that her father was going to claim that he'd taken the picture, too; then Cy said, "Your mom has a great eye for her subject. There's one for each of you."

Jessica was caught off guard. "Thanks." She hugged her father. "Your pictures are good, too."

"They're okay," he said. "So where do I deliver these?"

She led everyone to the right side of the yard, where Davy was making a transaction in Lowball's going-out-of-business sale. Whatever he sold today would end up covering a big check that he planned to write Teresa. Jessica knew that the money didn't matter to her, but it certainly meant something to Davy.

Along with the office furniture and supplies, he had added his first drum set, the four-track recorder that Cy had given him for his sixteenth birthday, old copies of *Rolling Stone* and *Billboard*. Jessica thumbed through the milk crates full of tapes and albums: Pearl Jam, Nirvana, Eddie Cochran, the Stray Cats, and obscure Motown groups like the Velvelettes and the Fascinations.

When Davy finished selling off a fax machine, Cy gave him a copy of the photograph. Davy seemed touched and looked a little guilty, perhaps for selling gifts that he'd gotten from his father. But Cy didn't seem to mind. As he headed toward the back yard, Davy popped a tape into a boom box he was selling. "Remember this one?" he asked. "Are you ready for some 'Hot Rod Boogie'?"

He'd dug up an old 57 Nomads tape that his father had recorded. Cy laughed and told Ellen about his fleeting career as his son's band manager. "You never should have quit that group. You guys were going places."

Davy took a pair of drumsticks from the table and did a quick riff on the drum set. "I still play sometimes," he said.

A barrel-chested man called out, "Hey, champ, how old's this desk?" Davy turned the music down, and Jessica led her father and Ellen around to the back of the house.

Lydia's parents' old furniture cluttered the patio, and already a good number of people were browsing, but Jessica couldn't find her mother anywhere. She must have gone inside.

Ivan had temporarily removed part of the side fence so the patio flowed into the driveway and garage. Cy's museum of discarded projects was now an open bazaar.

Ivan, who stood outside the garage door, waved them over. "Ellen, so glad you could make it," he said politely. He gave them quick hugs. "I wonder if you'd do me a favor, Dad, and spell me for a while."

"You're putting me to work?" Cy seemed surprised but game.

"I think you'll recognize a few things in here."

Cy leaned Ivan's copy of the photograph against the garage wall and almost immediately was drawn in by his old stuff. He looked through his books and picked up the radio-controlled biplane. "I remember this," he said. "It used to drive your mother crazy. I flew it into the aviary once, had to call the zookeeper to get it. Remember that time I lost it on the roof and climbed out the attic window? I almost pitched over." After a few minutes of looking around, he said, "Hey, something's missing in here. Where's the Nomad?" He turned to Ellen. "Remember when I told you about that old engine I restored?"

"Mom sold it," Ivan said.

Cy seemed momentarily stunned. "Boy, your mother is moving awfully fast."

Jessica thought about Chickie Paterakis and glanced around the garage for the Nomad's fender skirts. She'd become almost certain that Lydia had exaggerated the amount of work that Norm had done. On this score her mother had not changed: she was still going out of her way to protect the man she was with.

"Where is your mother's intended, by the way?" M.J. asked. She and Casper had made their way slowly to the garage.

Ivan said hello to the Spiveys, then excused himself. "Someone needs to man the front tables," he said. "I better let my mother answer for her intended."

Casper pointed with his good arm toward the kitchen door. "There she is now." Lydia was walking out of the house followed by a man with a beard, a woman in a poppy-print sundress, and their two young children.

"You want us to hold down the shop?" Cy asked Jessica.

"That would be great, Dad. Thanks." She went to the patio as the family of four moved toward the other side of the yard. "Who were those people?"

"They were looking at the house. I took them on a tour."

"Twenty-four hours and you're already getting bites. How about that?" She heard the tension in her voice. Her mother smiled uncertainly, and Jessica wondered if she weren't feeling the same doubts. "The Spiveys are here with Dad and Ellen."

Lydia brightened. "They are? Terrific. Let's go see them."

As they walked back to the garage Jessica thought it odd that her mother would be so excited when just yesterday morning she seemed to dread this reunion.

Lydia greeted the Spiveys and began to shake Ellen's hand just as Ellen hugged her. They ended up in an awkward half embrace, Lydia patting her shoulder, saying in one long stream, "Lovely to meet you. Congratulations. Did you have a nice flight? How's Phoenix?"

Ellen was remarkably poised, almost annoyingly so. She gave long, considered answers to Lydia's questions, as if she had rehearsed them. Jessica still couldn't believe that this was her stepmother. Thirty-five years old, and the bright outfit made her look like a woman in charge of a carpool. The possibility that Ellen and Cy would have kids—half-siblings—never seemed more real than it did at this moment. But somehow Jessica didn't mind the thought.

"So we're all wondering about Norm," Cy said. "What *can't* this guy do. The house looks spectacular."

"He didn't paint the house." Jessica stepped in. "Mom hired someone for that. She's hired a few people, in fact."

"Casper, M.J." Lydia interrupted, and grabbed their hands. "I'm so sorry about your accident. You probably want to sit down."

"I guess we'll go man the tables," Cy said with a little wave. "But we do want to hear more about Norm. You're not off the hook yet."

Lydia led the Spiveys to the patio, while Jessica helped Casper and M.J. into their chairs.

"Well, it was the damnedest thing," Casper began once they were settled, and he proceeded to tell the whole story of their accident. Jessica had already heard the details from her father. M.J. must have sensed this because she cut her husband off as he was talking about the nurses, and turned to Lydia. "So what are your plans, dear?"

"My plans?"

"You know, the future?"

Just then Davy appeared, waving to Jessica; he and Ivan probably needed help. As Jessica excused herself she heard her mother say, "Actually, I have something I need to tell you."

She paused to listen, but Davy grabbed her hand and led her to the family who'd been looking at the house.

"So what do you love best about it?" the woman in the sundress asked.

"Well, if you're outside you can always hear the zoo," Jessica said.

"We're taking the kids over there today." Her two towheads were bouncing on Davy's office chairs.

"It's a great zoo," Jessica said. "No cages. But don't worry. The animals almost never get out."

The woman laughed but Davy shot Jessica a look. She glanced around for Ivan and saw through the small crowd that he was on the sidewalk talking to a man with a short ponytail. Parked just beyond was the green convertible that Jessica recognized from a week ago. *Norm!* she thought, and hurried toward them.

23

A COUPLE OF DAYS AGO, Lydia had not been looking forward to seeing the Spiveys at the yard sale, but now she couldn't have been happier to have them here. As soon as M.J. asked about her plans, she wanted to rush upstairs and bring her father's letter down. But she had to tell them the whole story first, from beginning to end: how she'd come to believe what M.J. had said, how Walter had confirmed that a spiteful former employee could have ruined Tucker, how Ivan had discovered the wooden box in a faraway corner of the attic, exactly what the clay model looked like and the way it felt— warm to the touch, as if someone had just finished working with it.

Lydia described the sketches—the centered driver's seat and T doors, the art nouveau styling. "It would have been a beautiful car," she said. Then she told them how, on an impulse, she had checked the pocket of the portfolio. She explained how much of the Tucker's history was contained in that small package of clippings, from the ads to the bad press right up through the trial. "Finally, under the whole stack, I found a letter—" She paused, and in that suspended moment, something occurred to Lydia that took shape as she spoke. "It was a letter from my father to Preston Tucker," she said. "He wrote it just after the acquittal, and it completely refutes what Mickey Gibson told you."

She summarized it now for Casper and M.J. "My father said he had nothing to do with Tucker's undoing and neither did anyone at GM, so far as he knew."

M.J. seemed about to say something, but Lydia held up her hand and spoke first. "You were right about one thing, though: my dad *was* fired. And he was bitter about it, too. He said that Tucker had even pointed his cane at the door and humiliated him in front of the other workers."

"Well, I'll be damned." Casper sat back in his chair. "I wonder how Mickey got it so wrong."

Lydia had already been thinking about this. "My father was fired in a terrible way, soon he was working for GM, and not long after that someone was leaking secrets to the press. Maybe Mickey or someone else on the inside just did simple deduction. Who had a bigger vendetta than the designer whose plans were scrapped and was then so rudely shown the door?"

"I'm still confused about something," M.J. said. "It seems odd that your father would have that letter. Where did he get it? How did he get it back?"

"He didn't get it back," Lydia explained. "He never sent it. That's what makes the story so interesting." She had barely slept last night thinking about this, and now she told the Spiveys why she believed that her father had never mailed the letter. She knew him well enough to surmise that he thought it wasn't *his* job to "clear the air." *He* had been the injured party, and Tucker had never bothered to contact him and apologize. Gilbert had written the letter for himself more than anyone, and once he had finished it and read it over, he must have addressed the envelope, then decided, This is not *my* responsibility.

In the back of her mind Lydia knew now that she would finish her book. All along she had wanted a subject she'd have to struggle to understand. Her father had lived the social history of the dream machines, when the rallying cry of the great designers had been out with the old, in with the new. He'd worked with Ford, Tucker, General Motors, had made cars "for every purse and purpose," all of which would cause the growth of the Interstate, the dislocation of families, and ultimately, for Lydia Modine, of 309 Franklin Street, Huntington Woods, Michigan—a good deal of sadness as well.

Her family history had been marked by unsent letters. Her mother had never written her parents to resolve their bad feelings over Gilbert's and her departure from Grand Rapids. Her father, reading Tucker's obituary in 1956, had almost certainly regretted never sending the letter he'd written six years before. After all, his one-time mentor had likely gone to the grave believing that Gilbert had betrayed *him*, not the other way around.

Lydia told the Spiveys to wait a moment while she went upstairs to grab the portfolio. "I want you to see the letter for yourselves."

Getting up from the table, she considered the secret she was keeping—her own letter as yet unsent—and knew she could not keep it for much longer.

Lydia went into the house through the kitchen and stopped at the front door to check on the yard sale.

As she stepped onto the porch and scanned the crowd, she spotted Jessica and Ivan on the front sidewalk. Framed against the Spiveys' van, in the same vest that he'd worn at the museum, was Norm.

And he was talking to her kids.

Lydia stared, as if by doing so she might make Norm disappear. But instead he only seemed to grow larger. "Shit!" she said, but she felt like screaming. She wanted to run down the steps and gag him.

Was it already too late? Had he said too much?

In her panic—she could think of nothing else to do—she stepped back into the hallway and set off the alarm.

The noise in the house was piercing. She grabbed her purse

from the table, then rushed outside, shutting the door behind her. People in the yard held their hands over their ears.

Ivan, Jessica, and Davy were already on the porch.

"I don't know what happened," Lydia yelled over the alarm. "Oh, no—I think I just locked myself out." She fumbled through her purse. "I can't find my keys!"

"Calm down, Mom," Jessica said.

Ivan tried the front door, but it had locked automatically behind Lydia. She couldn't look at her kids. Instead she kept yelling, "Go around to the kitchen! You need to get inside and turn this thing off!"

Jessica and Davy jumped off the porch and headed for the back.

Without another word Lydia flew down the stairs to where Norm stood frozen, watching the spectacle. "What are you doing here?" she hissed.

"I saw the yard sale in the paper."

"Well, you have to leave!" She grabbed his arm and led him to his convertible.

"Why? What's wrong with you?"

"It doesn't matter. But you have to go *right now!*"

She must have looked like a fury, because he did not so much as pause. He walked around to the driver's side, started his car and, shaking his head, drove away.

Lydia had to get out of here. She dug into the pocket of her purse where she kept her keys, jumped into her own car and sped off in Norm's wake, not even looking back toward the house. When he turned right on Woodward, Lydia stayed straight, driving toward the town of Royal Oak.

Couples sat in the sunshine having brunch on the café patios, sipping their coffee and reading newspapers on benches outside the shops. Mothers strolled down the sidewalks peering into windows, their children tugging at their arms.

Gripping the wheel, Lydia turned onto the first residential street she could find, went up half a block, and pulled over to try to calm down.

Stupid, she chided herself, and got out of the car.

She had parked on a tree-lined street. A mix of bungalows and small Queen Annes lined the uneven brick sidewalks. Behind her, Lydia could hear the soft murmur of midtown Royal Oak.

She walked up the block past an open house on the corner and continued on, just to keep her feet moving. She passed another yard sale in the next block, a small collection of antiques, toys, posters, a bicycle with training wheels.

She wondered if, by some stroke of luck, Norm had said nothing to the kids. Perhaps she had arrived on the scene just in time. Last week Jessica had only caught a glimpse of Norm. Perhaps she and Ivan didn't know who the man in the vest really was. They could have been greeting him as just another customer. She thought of Norm's face when she first saw him framed against the van, but she couldn't remember his expression; it was all a blur.

And what was Norm doing there, anyway? He hadn't come to apologize; he'd seen the ad in the paper, he said. Lydia remembered what he'd told her on the People Mover: one person's trash is another's treasure; he loved a good yard sale. Why hadn't she anticipated that this might happen?

She stopped in front of a cream-colored house with an OPEN HOUSE sign strung with a clutch of balloons. In four blocks she'd passed three open houses and just as many yard sales. Before long, she would have to go home and face her own clearance—and her children as well.

Lydia watched as a young couple headed into the cream-colored house. It was a craftsman, with a front porch and a pair of Japanese maples in the garden bed. The porch reminded her of her own house, only this was much smaller, with a slate roof and dark red trim. Glad for any excuse to kill more time, she went up to take a look.

The inside was bright and open, with a kitchen that blended into the living area. It was a one-story house with two small bedrooms, but somehow the place felt airy and spacious. Lydia was looking outside at the tidy back yard when the realtor stepped away from the young couple and asked if Lydia had seen the garage.

"It's my favorite part of the house," the realtor said. She had white-gray hair and wore a dark floral dress with a large brooch in the shape of a sunburst.

The garage had been converted into a studio office. A built-in desk ran the entire length of one side; on the opposite wall, a long rectangular window filtered light into the room.

"The owner's an artist," the realtor whispered, stepping inside. "Minimalist. I shouldn't be saying this, but not my cup of tea. She'll do a single horizontal stripe on an eight-foot canvas. This is where she paints."

It felt nothing like a garage. It was quiet, with a pair of large skylights, wood floors layered with patterns and colors. Lydia liked the idea of working where a car used to be, and wondered what it would take to convert her own garage into something like this.

"So how many of you would be living here?" the realtor asked.

The question might have bothered Lydia had it not come from someone her own age.

She thought about it for a moment, then said "Two."

The realtor smiled. "This house is perfect for two."

24

I F THE ALARM wasn't enough to chase the yard-salers away, the two cops pulling up, their siren still yap-yapping as they got out of the car, very nearly was. A crowd had formed on the sidewalk, and Jessica, who had only a few minutes ago cut off the alarm, stood in the doorway. She could hear Bedlam howling in his basement cell.

Ivan was in the yard explaining to the cops that it was only a false alarm. He turned to the crowd and said, "It's okay, everybody. Just an accident. Please go back to what you were doing."

"Not so fast," one of the cops said. "Who's the owner of this house? How did you trigger the alarm? Do you have a permit for this yard sale?" Ivan answered with the deferential patience of the model citizen he had always been.

As the cops complained about the tables encroaching on the sidewalk, Jessica went over to talk to Davy, who sat on a metal filing cabinet in front of his going-out-of-business sale. "And to think I was doing so well." He checked his watch. "Ten-thirty already. We've still got a lot of stuff left."

"There's always eBay," Jessica said.

"So what the hell happened?"

She explained that the second she'd spotted Norm, she

made a beeline for him. He'd seemed surprised by the way she ran up to him and said, "We've been waiting for you." In fact, he'd taken a step back. "I'm honored, I guess, but may I ask what for?"

"You've been gone for three weeks and we've done all the work without you. We've been waiting to meet you but you're never here."

"Meet me?" he'd asked.

At that point Ivan had joined them. Jessica let him know that this was Norm.

"Nice to finally see you face to face," Ivan had said, shaking his hand. "You're not what I expected."

Norm seemed to shrink under Ivan's grip and could only get out a few more words, which Jessica, now recalling the story for Davy, could not exactly remember. "I think he said, 'Can we start this over again?'"

"And that's when the alarm went off," Jessica said. "Next thing I knew I was running through the house, punching the code on the alarm box. When I got outside—and I swear it was only a minute later—Ivan told me that Mom and Norm had rushed off as if they'd just robbed a bank."

Davy hopped off the filing cabinet and looked over to see how Ivan was doing. He had a hand on one of the cop's shoulders. Soon the officers shook his hand, climbed back into their patrol car, and were on their way.

As the crowd thinned, the Spiveys and Spivey-Modines, who like everyone else had come out front, barraged Jessica with questions that she couldn't answer.

"So where did your mother go?" Cy asked.

"I didn't even see her leave."

"They took off like Bonnie and Clyde," Davy said.

M.J. scratched under her cast. "Maybe we should send out a posse." She started to laugh.

"This is serious." Jessica was annoyed that M.J. found the situation funny.

"I know, dear." M.J. patted her arm.

◆ ◆ ◆

Eventually everyone went back to where they'd been—Jessica and Ivan to the front, Davy to the side of the house, Cy and Ellen to the garage, and Casper and M.J. to the patio, where they stood in for Lydia. By the end of the morning they'd sold a good half of the items. Davy and their father had particular success; little remained of the office supplies and exercise equipment—all of it priced to go.

In the early afternoon the Spiveys loaded into the back of their rented van. Jessica thanked them for their work.

"I'm sorry about your mom," Cy said to no one in particular. "I'm sure she'll show up soon."

"We know," Jessica said. "She always shows up."

Ellen climbed into the passenger seat. "Give your mother our best," she said.

"And could you make sure she gets her copy of the photograph? It's in the garage." Cy smiled, his teeth bright against his tanned face. "There's one for you, too, Ivan." He put on his mirrored sunglasses. Jessica glimpsed her own reflection in them as she hugged her father.

As Cy was about to close the door of the van, M.J. leaned forward. "I wouldn't worry about your mother, my dears. As we like to say, *'Le coeur a ses raisons que la raison ne connaît point.'*" She sat back, as if she'd summed up in a phrase all there was to know.

"Perhaps you'll tell us what that means?" Casper asked, and M.J. said, "The heart has its reasons that reason knows nothing of."

Jessica was putting some of the boxes back in the garage when Walter Hill, her mother's friend from the library, drove up to the house. He was embarrassed at having arrived so late and apologized for getting the time of the yard sale wrong. "So is your mother here?" He was in slacks and a faded black polo shirt. His cheeks seemed flushed as if he'd been in a hurry.

Jessica refrained from telling him what had happened. "She stepped out for a while."

Walter asked about the FOR SALE sign and seemed surprised that he hadn't heard about the house going on the market. "She's not leaving the area, is she? You know, your mother . . ." he began, and a worried look crossed his face. "We've known each other for a long time. I'd hate it if she moved."

As frustrated as Jessica was with Lydia right now, she was touched by how her mother's friendship mattered to this man. "She wouldn't leave Detroit," Jessica reassured him, though it occurred to her that at this point anything was possible.

"Well, that's good news." Walter seemed relieved. "Your mother's one of a kind. We need to keep her around." He cast his eyes over the remains of the yard sale. "I get more calls about her books than anyone's by far. She's the best car historian going, and you know why? She's a storyteller."

When Ivan came up and introduced himself to Walter, Jessica took the opportunity to free Bedlam from the basement. She walked the dog past the zoo to the park, thinking about her mother as a storyteller. Trouble was, at the moment too many parts were missing from the story. Norm had looked so confused when Jessica had accosted him, and her mom had seemed nothing short of panicked. Hours had gone by, and still no one had heard from her. Davy had called her cell phone and got her voice mail instead. In the past when she ran off she always called soon after to say where she had gone—a final gesture in her play for attention. But lately it seemed that she would rather no one know.

When Jessica and Bedlam returned to the house, Walter was helping her brothers move tables from the front yard down to the basement. Walter looked a few years older than her mother, but he seemed in pretty good shape. Still, he didn't need to be lifting tables, and she said so.

A band of sweat had gathered on his brow. "It's my penance for missing a great yard sale." Jessica was oddly charmed by his stubbornness.

For the next hour or so they cleaned up the yard. Everything that was left fit into the garage. Ivan walked the last wobbly chair through the door, slid it closed, and announced that he was starving. When he and Davy went in the house to make sandwiches, Jessica sat on the porch with Walter, who was finishing a glass of water.

"Well, I should be getting home," he said, a touch of melancholy in his voice. "But please tell your mom that I stopped by." His nice pants were streaked with dirt, his collar askew, and it occurred to Jessica that he had stayed all this time waiting for Lydia to return.

Jessica went into the kitchen, where her brothers were eating corn chips and sandwiches at the counter. A bit of turkey fell from Ivan's sandwich onto the floor, and Bedlam snatched it up. Ivan pushed him with his foot as the dog made his getaway.

"Don't do that," Jessica scolded.

"Dirty Harry can handle it. He's a tough dog."

Bedlam hid behind her. She made a sandwich and brought it to the table. "Why don't you guys come eat here," she said after a long silence. "Let's talk about this Mom situation."

Davy sat down with his back to the yard. Ivan got a beer from the fridge and settled in kitty-corner to him by the wall where family pictures used to be. Lydia hadn't rehung them since the painters had finished the kitchen.

"First she hires a guy, Chickie Paterakis, and claims he did no work," Jessica began. "But he obviously did a lot of the work around here. I'm beginning to think that Norm did nothing. I mean, his shirts are all over the house, his boots are by the back door. Did you see all those power bars and vitamin supplements? There's evidence everywhere. But where is *he*, I'd like to know?"

"That scene last week when I was headed back to Chicago. That was weird," Davy added.

"Remember I told you how she wouldn't give Davy a ride to the train station, made him take a cab," Jessica said to Ivan. "When Norm drove up to the house, Mom flew into a frenzy, just like today. It's getting ridiculous. She seems bound and determined never to let us meet him."

"Maybe he's a vampire," Ivan said. "She's trying to keep him out of the daylight."

"She's supposed to be in love with this guy. She talked about eloping with him, living with him. Is this what they call crazy in love—setting off the alarm just for kicks?"

"Who said she did that? It's not her fault the alarm went off."

"Are you sure? Then how did it happen? Mom claimed she didn't have her keys, but then she drove off."

Ivan hesitated. "I think you're overreacting. She was flustered."

"When was the last time Mom called you, Ivan? You used to talk at least every week."

"We still talk. She's been a little distracted, but a lot's going on."

Jessica leaned forward. "And Davy—you've had the worst month of your life. But when's the last time Mom called you or sat you down and asked how you're dealing with work and Teresa? A few months ago she was all in your business. Not anymore."

Davy considered this. "She *has* been busy," he said uncertainly.

"But Mom's always been busy. That's never stopped her from picking up the phone or, more likely, getting in a car and driving to Chicago to make sure you were okay. If she were herself she'd have knocked on your door the same day Sanjay announced that Lowball was folding."

The phone rang and Jessica jumped up. "All I'm saying is, it's time to stop defending her and start to take inventory—and I'm not talking about books and furniture."

"If it's her, be nice," Davy said.

"Where do you think she's calling from this time? Canada? Prison?" Jessica picked up the phone.

But it wasn't her mother; it was the woman with the kids from the yard sale. She and her husband liked the house a great deal, she said, and wanted to come back in the next day or so with other members of their family. She asked if an offer was already on the table and Jessica said she couldn't answer that question; her mother was away at the moment.

"The price is too high, but if you're willing to negotiate . . ." the woman's voice trailed off.

Jessica took her name and number and told her that Lydia would call her back.

"See, I told you," she said to Ivan, her voice rising. "Now we've definitely let things go too far. That was somebody putting an offer on the house." Jessica gripped the edge of the counter. "Already. Can you believe it?"

Ivan took a swig of beer.

"What? It doesn't bother you?"

"No, not really," he said.

"Davy?"

"Well, I kind of knew it was going to happen, didn't you? When you put up a FOR SALE sign, eventually you get a buyer."

"So you're just going to sit there?" Jessica couldn't believe how casually they were taking this. "It's a big deal, you know. This is where we grew up! Don't you care?"

"We don't live here anymore, you know." Ivan seemed nonchalant. "It's Mom's life, and she's trying to get on with it. Who are we to stop her?"

"That's what you always say. Whatever she does is fine with you. Maybe she *is* off robbing banks. You'd be all for that, if she said it made her happy. You never think for yourself, Ivan. You just do her bidding."

"Hey, I'm not the one who flew back here in a tizzy."

"She made me fly back here."

"Nobody made you do anything," Ivan snapped.

"She said she was *eloping*, remember? And the way she described Norm sounded like an FBI profile. She kept disappearing. I couldn't reach her. Disappearing, like she has now. And the two of you sat back and watched. You kept apologizing for the guy. And look at you now, still chewing your cud."

This got Davy's attention. "Come on, Jess—this isn't about Norm. It's about selling the house. That's what's getting to you.

But you're the one who put the ad in the paper for the yard sale. And you've been pretty much helping Mom pack up for three weeks. So don't blame us."

"But I didn't do all that to sell the house. I came here to make sure that Mom was all right and to prevent her from tossing everything away. I thought it would be good to thin out the closets, and I wanted to help her get rid of Dad's stuff in the basement. I was even having a good time until last week when suddenly this yard sale turned into a huge bazaar. As soon as you got here, Ivan, this whole moving thing kicked into high gear."

"So, you're upset that Mom's selling the house, and now it's all my fault," he said, rolling his eyes.

"Do you realize that she doesn't even have a new house to move into? She's under the spell of this troll we still know nothing about. She's spent thousands of dollars that she doesn't even have, essentially forcing herself to downsize—and now suddenly she's selling *everything*. She even pawned off the Nomad without telling anyone. Look at us." A helpless feeling came over Jessica. "Here we are again, all gathered in the kitchen exactly as we were a couple of months ago, trying to figure out what's happened to one of our parents."

Davy raised his eyebrows. Ivan pushed his plate aside, looking exasperated, though all he said was, "Dad's wedding was different. That was like a sendoff to the netherworld. With Mom it's a new beginning, and she knows how to take care of herself."

Jessica threw up her hands. "I forgot—Dad is the root of all evil. Are you going to be fifty years old and still saying, 'I hate my daddy'? He's not a monster; he's just weak, that's all. And if you've got a problem, you ought to let him know about it."

"Oh, this is rich." He laughed. "You've been spinning your wheels since college. Running off with a New Age idiot, shacking up in Oregon because why the fuck not, taking a job at a grocery, throwing your life into a *void*, basically blowing your entire education. And you're giving me advice."

Davy slammed his hands on the table. "Enough already! I'm

so goddamned sick of fighting!" He got up suddenly, and Jessica followed him as he took off for the stairs. "We're not finished here," she called out. "You wouldn't be so miserable if you didn't run away all the time."

Davy stopped at the landing and turned around. "Oh, is that so?"

She was going to tell him how sad she felt the other day thinking of Teresa on the train to Cleveland. She remembered that moment she decided to go to Oregon with Blane; she had felt reckless, free, yet as she threw her duffel into the back of his van, she already knew when she would call her mother—hours later, after they'd crossed the Mississippi into Iowa. Jessica had intended to stay in Oregon for a week or two, but after a while she found that it was easier just to remain there, and so she did. "I guess all of us are runaways," she said to Davy. "Seems to be a family trait."

After a while Davy came back downstairs.

"Sorry." Jessica was scratching Bedlam, who cowered at her feet.

"So do you feel better?" Ivan asked.

"I'm fine," Davy said. "You should ask Jess."

She thought of telling her brothers that she was applying to graduate school, that in fact she had been thinking about it for some time. She didn't know where she'd be next year, but it felt good to have the beginning of a plan. As much as she wanted them to know about it now, she didn't want to make any promises until she was sure. Stay tuned, she wanted to say. "Yeah. How about you, Ivan?"

"I'm all right, a little beat."

Davy cleared the table and put the dishes in the dishwasher. "When Mom comes home, let's let her do the talking. No need to drag an explanation out of her."

Jessica agreed, and they all went into the living room to talk the rest through.

25

LYDIA WAS SITTING on the sidewalk patio of the Acorn Café in Royal Oak when rain clouds moved overhead, sending everyone inside. After the open house she had returned to her car, sat in the driver's seat for a few minutes, then decided to walk into town to let more time pass. She ordered a seltzer at the café and sat in the shade, trying not to think about the alarm incident. She was sure that she could come up with something to say, and the more she lingered in Royal Oak, the less she worried about it. Instead, she found herself thinking about *Dream Machines*.

She took out a notepad from her purse and began to fill it with memories about her father. It had been a long time since she had sat down and actually worked. Now it was all she wanted to do, no longer just an idea or a way to escape her disappointments.

The rain caught everyone by surprise, and she waited it out huddled with a group of strangers under the café awning. Looking toward the sidewalk, she watched a young girl in a sky blue dress rush to the door of a parked car; a large woman, probably her grandmother, trundled behind her with a newspaper over her head. The woman opened the door, and the child yelled at her as she went around to the driver's side.

It occurred to Lydia now that her whole idea—luring her kids home in the hope that they might stay—had been crazy, almost as crazy as the lies she had told and the trouble the lies had gotten her into. But now with all her children home again, gathered together for her sake, she realized that it was far too much to ask. She didn't know if she even wanted it anymore.

When the summer shower abruptly ended, Lydia walked back to her car in the damp heat and drove home.

Besides the FOR SALE sign now closer to the curb and the tamped-down front lawn, there was little evidence that the yard sale had ever happened. The garage door was closed, the fence back up, and the Spiveys' rented van nowhere in sight.

Lydia ran her hands over her hair before going into the house.

"Over here," Jessica called from the living room, more pleasantly than Lydia had expected.

She went in and sat down on the rocking chair. "I found my keys," she said weakly.

"Quite a day." Jessica seemed contemplative, as if she'd been on the living room couch all afternoon. She sat between her brothers, the three of them in a row, like a jury. Lydia waited for *Where have you been?* or *What was that all about?* But her daughter remained quiet. Lydia wondered if her kids already knew everything and were ticking like bombs, waiting for another white lie to set them off.

"Did you have a chance to meet Norm?" she asked, and almost hoped that Jessica would blow up right now, just let her have it and put an end to the charade, once and for all. But Jessica said, "Not really. We'd only just begun to say hello when I heard the alarm."

"So you didn't talk to him?" she asked again.

Davy shook his head.

"I wasn't even sure who he was," Ivan said.

Lydia couldn't stop herself, knew that she was going to

make something up again. "Sorry I flew off like that. Norm found an open house in Royal Oak. We had just that small window of time."

Nobody asked a follow-up question: *What about the alarm? Why did you take so long? Where's Norm now? What about the problems you said you two were having?* Jessica looked at her like a therapist, stoic and unblinking. Ivan and Davy would not quite meet her eyes. To fill the space Lydia went into a long description of the open house: "The place is just perfect for two. Bright and open. It has a lovely writing studio in the back."

"Sounds nice," Davy said. None of the kids seemed angry, just quiet and depleted.

Lydia changed the subject. "So, how did the yard sale go? It almost looks as if it never happened."

Davy and Ivan had calculated how much they'd made: sixteen hundred and thirty dollars. "Dad's not a bad salesman, either," Ivan said, in what seemed a genuine compliment.

"People will buy anything," Davy added. They'd sold the one-eyed camel, the pink wicker furniture, the Evel Knievel Stunt Action Play Set, even the office partitions. "Your friend Walter stopped by after everyone had gone home. We told him not to worry about it, but he insisted on helping clean up. He really wanted to see you."

Jessica leaned forward and broke in. "You got a phone call, Mom," she said, then casually, as if it were just another message she was passing on, "Someone wants to buy the house."

"Who?" Lydia sat up.

"That family you showed it to."

"What did they say?" Lydia asked.

"They want to come by tomorrow."

"Gosh. I hadn't realized this would happen so soon." Here was a good opportunity to remove herself from the jury's gaze. "I think I'll go upstairs and take care of some things before I call them."

No one said anything as she hurried up the stairs. Lydia closed her office door and sat down.

She was startled to find that the idea of selling her house—

something she had never seriously considered—did not seem so far-fetched after all. Not just because she'd overspent fixing it up and had gone so far as to put a sign in the front yard. Not for practical reasons. Even before she saw the bungalow in Royal Oak today, she had somehow imagined herself in such a place. It was as though just picturing another possibility, with or without the apocryphal mate, had eased her away from here. In the past six weeks, she had begun to let go of this house.

It would be easy, she realized, to continue with her invented story. She saw now that her children would let her. All Lydia had to say was that she and Norm had broken up and that she was moving on with her own life.

But the thought of this seemed, finally, unbearable. She knew there had to be an end to her inventions. How could she expect her book to be true if she couldn't tell the truth herself?

She sat at her computer picturing her father typing out his letter, thinking of what to say. "Dear Norm," she began. She wrote a few lines, deleted them, wrote a few more, until finally:

I started this message apologizing for my behavior this morning, but it occurred to me that I've spent much of our correspondence apologizing to you. I have no idea why I should be saying I'm sorry when, ever since we met for lunch you've been rude, selfish, and petulant. Ultimately I have nothing to apologize for, though perhaps I ought to say that you've been caught in the crossfire of some family issues.

As for the Tucker situation, I wish you hadn't betrayed my confidence the other day, especially since I have now discovered that what I told you was untrue.

If you want a more detailed explanation, you can read my next book.

Lydia

◆ ◆ ◆

After sending the e-mail, she flipped through the pages of the notepad she'd been writing in, and found the realtor's business card. As she set it down she saw, amid some loose change on her desk, the gold coin with the number 7, her lucky chip from Walter. She turned it over and rubbed her thumb on the horseshoe embossed on the other side. She thought about how generous Walter had been, helping with her research, getting her such a deal on the Corolla, stopping by to help out with the yard sale. She would go by the library, tomorrow if she could, and take him out to lunch, thank him for all he'd done for her. She slipped the lucky coin into her purse, picked up the phone, and dialed.

It was five o'clock when she went back downstairs. The kids were in the kitchen reading the newspaper. The room seemed still, as if no one had spoken for hours. "So do you want to see the new house?" she asked.

They looked at each other as if caught unprepared. Jessica folded the paper and laid it down on the table.

"The new house?" Davy said. "Okay."

Soon they were all piled into the station wagon, driving across Woodward through the main drag of Royal Oak. The car was silent as a temple, which made Lydia partly grateful but anxious all the same. She turned left at Plymouth, the first residential street, and four blocks later pulled up to the curb by the OPEN HOUSE sign: number 313.

Davy finally broke the tension. "It's nice," he said, getting out of the car.

Ivan followed him up the steps.

"And I like those trees in the front," Davy added. "What do you think, Jess?"

She stood on the sidewalk looking as if the short flight of steps were a mountain she wasn't about to climb. "Looks small."

Lydia stepped onto the porch. "It goes a ways back."

Ivan pulled on the door handle. The house was locked. He and Davy peered into the windows. "Good floors. High ceilings."

They stepped aside as Jessica made her way up to look. "I thought you said the house got a lot of light."

"It does, honey, the studio in particular."

"Are you sure you're *both* going to fit in there?" Jessica asked, almost contemptuously. She had her back turned. Still the emphasis on the word *both* was undeniable.

"So. There's something I've been meaning to tell you all." Lydia spoke quickly; any delay might make her lose her nerve. "Maybe we can sit down and talk before the realtor arrives."

Jessica turned around and took a deep breath, almost as if she were the one about to make a confession. She glanced at Lydia, a look that seemed to tell her that she already knew— then joined her brothers on the steps. Ivan and Davy, like patients in a waiting room, looked guarded.

Lydia sat down next to them. "I'm buying this house," she announced. "*I'm* buying this house," she repeated. "Just me."

The kids didn't say a word. Again she knew she could save the story, tell them that she'd had a terrible fight with Norm and hadn't had the courage to admit that the relationship was not working out. She could say she'd been furious when he'd shown up at the yard sale, that she'd set off the alarm in a frustrated rage.

"Jessica, when I told you that I'd met a man—you seemed so incredulous that I could meet someone new. I wanted to prove you wrong." Lydia noticed that Davy had dark circles under his eyes. Ivan's mouth was turned down. "I know that I told you I'd made an instant connection with Norm, that we planned to move in together, and then that we were thinking of getting married. I said he'd done a great amount of work to make the house look better than it ever has."

She fixed her eyes on Jessica, and recalled something M.J. had said about children being mirrors for their parents. When Lydia had looked at her kids growing up, she saw her own reflection and when they left she had felt diminished. But now when she looked at her daughter she didn't see herself anymore, only someone who shared a certain resemblance.

"Norm did none of that work," Lydia continued. "He's

never even been inside the house. I hired a handyman—Chickie Paterakis, the guy who bought the Nomad—he did all the fix-up." Jessica nodded and looked at her brothers, and Lydia was suddenly sure that they'd all figured it out. "So you know already?" she asked. "How long have you known?"

But they wouldn't answer her question. This time not even Ivan would help her. His face had turned sharp and expectant. "Go on," Jessica said.

"I met him at the museum the day of your father's wedding," Lydia continued, and went into the whole story, from the message board to the e-mails to the disastrous date. "I left him in the Renaissance Center. That was the day I called you, Jess."

"But why?" Her daughter looked caught between anger and bewilderment. "Why did you do it?"

She thought of telling them what M.J. had said about her father's betrayal of Tucker, and the letter she had found. But now was not the time—she would tell them that story later—because there was no point in blaming M.J. or Norm or Cy or anyone else for something she herself had done. "My excuse was loneliness, I guess. I've missed you all more than you can understand. And when I saw that my lie might bring you back home, well, it was hard to stop." She realized then that she had gotten her life back, only a different one than she'd imagined.

"What about *us?*" Jessica asked.

"Remember at the orphaned-car museum when you put your hands over my eyes and said, 'Emergency rescue'? That was the best I'd felt in a long time, just knowing that you all came to get me. I know I told you I was desolate here, and I'm sure I made you feel awful about it," she said. "I went too far. I don't know what else I can say."

"You went way too far." Ivan shook his head. "I've never known you to lie before, Mom. Can you imagine if we pulled a stunt like this with you?"

Lydia wondered how, after today, she would ever regain their trust. How could they see her the same way when she had staged this elaborate drama and made them unwitting players? "I would never do anything like this again."

Ivan looked defeated.

Davy stood up and walked down the steps. "I don't know what we did wrong, but it must have been something."

"No, it wasn't your fault."

Jessica grabbed Davy's hand, led him back to the steps, where they both sat down. "What I want to know is what you were afraid of," she said. "Did you think that after Dad left we were just going to write off the whole family?"

"I worried that the next time you all came home to pack up the house and go through our stuff, I might not be here. I saw you so seldom, and I'm not trying to be dramatic this time, but I didn't want what happened to my mother to happen to any of you. I thought we could go through the boxes together and settle estates. I know I've been difficult. Particularly with you, Jess."

Nobody said a word for several minutes. Then a breeze blew in, scattering leaves and blossoms across the yard.

Ivan tilted forward to see the trees rustling above them.

"Look at the balloons," Jessica said, nodding toward the OPEN HOUSE sign. The balloons leaned to the right, then snapped up and back as the wind shifted.

"That's July in Michigan," Davy said.

Lydia was grateful that the talk had turned to something so simple as the weather. It seemed a good place to start.

The kids stood up, and as Lydia rose to join them the realtor came up the steps.

"What a picture," she exclaimed, adjusting her sunburst brooch. "The whole family out on the porch."

She shook everyone's hands and took out a huge ring of keys from her purse. Jessica, Ivan, and Davy huddled behind their mother as the realtor tried different keys in the lock. At last the deadbolt clicked, the door opened, and Lydia stepped into her new, empty house.